CHRISTOPHER BUSH
THE CASE OF THE HAPPY WARRIOR

CHRISTOPHER BUSH was born Charlie Christmas Bush in Norfolk in 1885. His father was a farm labourer and his mother a milliner. In the early years of his childhood he lived with his aunt and uncle in London before returning to Norfolk aged seven, later winning a scholarship to Thetford Grammar School.

As an adult, Bush worked as a schoolmaster for 27 years, pausing only to fight in World War One, until retiring aged 46 in 1931 to be a full-time novelist. His first novel featuring the eccentric Ludovic Travers was published in 1926, and was followed by 62 additional Travers mysteries. These are all to be republished by Dean Street Press.

Christopher Bush fought again in World War Two, and was elected a member of the prestigious Detection Club. He died in 1973.

CHRISTOPHER BUSH

THE CASE OF THE HAPPY WARRIOR

With an introduction
by Curtis Evans

DEAN STREET PRESS

Published by Dean Street Press 2019

Copyright © 1950 Christopher Bush

Introduction copyright © 2019 Curtis Evans

First published in 1950 by MacDonald & Co.

Cover by DSP

ISBN 978 1 913054 09 0

www.deanstreetpress.co.uk

INTRODUCTION

Labouring under Suspicion
Christopher Bush's Crime Fiction in the Postwar Years, 1946-1952

Seven years after the end of the Second World War, Christopher Bush published, under his "Michael Home" pseudonym, *The Brackenford Story* (1952), a mainstream novel in which a onetime country house boots boy, having risen for some time now to the lofty position of butler, laments the passing of traditional English rural life in the new postwar order, as signified by the years in which the left-wing Labour party held sway in the United Kingdom (1945-51). The jacket description of the American edition of *The Brackenford Story* reads, in part:

> *The Brackenford Story* is the story of a changing England. William saw the political enemies of the Hall gradually successful, whittling away the privilege it stood for. He saw squire begin to sell his land, the taxes increase, the great Hall sold, the beautiful trees along the drive cut down. And then with a Second World War, nationalization, rationing, pre-fabricated houses and queuing. William recalled with gratitude the kindness of his masters and their sense of responsibility for others. He saw that the bad old days of Toryism were not so bad after all. And he never lost his sense of outrage at the loss of something he felt was worthy of preservation.

A few years earlier, in July 1949, Anthony Boucher, the postwar dean of American crime fiction reviewers and a highly socially conscious liberal (small "l"), wrote with genial bemusement of the conservatism of British crime writers like Christopher Bush, in his review of Bush's latest crime opus, *The Case of the Housekeeper's Hair* (1948), making topical mention of a certain anti-Utopian novel penned by a distinguished dying tubercular English writer, which had just been published in June. "However much George Orwell, in *Nineteen Eighty-Four*, may foresee the forcible suppression of 'crimethink' under 'Ingsoc,' English socialism in 1949 takes pleasure in exporting mystery novels which disapprove of the Government and everything about it," Boucher observed with wry irony. "Like most of his colleagues, Christopher Bush is tartly critical of the regime; and an understanding of his unreconstructed Tory attitude is necessary if you're to hope to understand the motivations of this novel."

In both the detective novels and mainstream fiction which Christopher Bush published between 1946 and 1952, Bush, like many other distinguished mystery writers of the Golden Age generation (including Agatha Christie, Dorothy L. Sayers, Georgette Heyer, John Dickson Carr, Edmund Crispin, E.R. Punshon, Henry Wade and John Street), indeed was critical of the Labor government and increasingly nostalgic about a past that grew ever more golden in blissful, if perhaps partially chimerical, remembrance. Yet keeping Bush's distinct anti-left bias in mind, fans of classic crime fiction will find between the covers of the author's crime novels from these years--*The Case of the Second Chance* (1946), *The Case of the Curious Client* (1947), *The Case of the Haven Hotel* (1948), *The Case of the Housekeeper's Hair* (1948), *The Case of the Seven Bells* (1949), *The Case of the Purloined Picture* (1949), *The Case of the Happy Warrior* (1950), *The Case of the Corner Cottage* (1951), *The Case of the Fourth Detective* (1951) and *The Case of the Happy Medium* (1952)--fascinating observation of postwar social malaise in the age of British imperial decay and domestic austerity, as well as details about the rise of rationing, restriction and regulation, the burgeoning black market and, withal, that ubiquitous flashily-dressed criminal figure from Forties and Fifties Britain: the spiv (dealer in illicit goods).

Puzzle-minded mystery readers also will find some corking good no-nonsense "fair play" mysteries. "Few writers can equal Christopher Bush in handling a complicated plot while giving the reader a fair chance to solve the riddle himself," avowed the American blurb to *The Case of the Corner Cottage*, while Anthony Boucher applauded Bush's belated return to the American fiction lists after the Second World War, declaring: "It's good to have Mr. Bush back after too long an absence . . . he presents the simon-pure jigsaw-puzzle detective story with unobtrusive competence."

Concurrently in the United Kingdom, author Rupert Croft-Cooke, who himself wrote fine detective fiction as "Leo Bruce," pointedly praised Bush's "urbane and intelligent way of dealing with mystery which makes his work much more attractive than the stampeding sensationalism of some of his rivals."

In the pages which follow this introduction by all means attempt, dear readers, to match your keen wits against those of that ever-percipient gentleman sleuth, Ludovic Travers. Frequently in tandem with his old friend Superintendent George Wharton and with occasional input from his smart and sophisticated wife Bernice Haire, the former classical dancer, Ludo continues to hunt, in his capacity as a sort of special consultant to Scotland Yard (or "unofficial expert," as he puts it), more not-quite-canny-enough crooks. Additionally Ludo, a confirmed fan of American crime films like *The Blue Dahlia* (1946) and *Call Northside 777* (1948), comes to find himself in ownership of the Broad Street Detective Agency, perhaps the finest firm of private inquiry agents in London. In these old and new capacities in the postwar world Ludo confronts his greatest cornucopia of daring and dastardly crimes yet.

Curtis Evans

To

ALLAN BENNETT

(and wee Christopher)

with happy recollections

Part I
THE PROBLEM

Chapter 1
AUNT ALICE

AT FIRST SIGHT it may seem an astounding coincidence that two members of a family group, and each unaware of the other's action, should have considered it necessary to ask for the services of a detective agency, and the same agency at that. I think I can prove otherwise, and, even if I can't, the facts still remain. Alice Stonhill and Peter Wesslake did precisely what I have said, and what's more—

But that's getting too far ahead and it's worth more than a preliminary couple of minutes to get certain things clear. What detective agency, for instance, and how I got mixed up in the matter myself. Just two preparatory minutes, then, and we'll be back with Alice Stonhill and her nephew, Peter Wesslake. Don't think of that Peter, by the way, as an English name. His mother was Danish, and she intended it for the Danish name that it is. She called him Pater, which is the Danish pronunciation, and it was he who gradually brought it round to the English form. But that doesn't alter the facts—that his mother was Danish and his name originally pronounced in the Danish way.

But to get back to the question of the detective agency. It was the Broad Street Detective Agency, owned and run by Bill Ellice. It's a solid business, and George Wharton—Superintendent Wharton of Scotland Yard—and I once had the chance of acquiring it when Bill had the itch to retire. But George was urgently asked to stay on at the Yard and the deal fell through. I didn't worry. Bill's been a friend of mine for years, and I got the habit of dropping in most days and lending a hand at this and that. More than once when Bill was away I took over and ran things until he got back.

Normally my only job used to be acting as assistant—stooge isn't too hilarious a synonym—to George Wharton, as what the Yard is pleased to call "an unofficial expert". It was in the intervals of murder enquiries, then, that I used to fill in my time with lending a hand to Bill. Bill seemed to like it. Perhaps he thought I made a little comic relief. For one thing I don't look like a detective—or do I? Maybe there are detectives who are six-foot three in height, lean as rakes, hatchet faced—-a Sunday paper of the baser sort once called mine patrician—and with eyes that demand the use of horn-rims. Then too, I haven't any text-book methods. I steer, as they say, by guess and by God. My brain is agile enough and of the hither-and-thither crossword kind, and I never lack for ideas; in fact, I'm generally harassed by them. I hate loose ends and unsolved problems and I love the study of my fellow men. I'm also in the happy position, thanks largely to inheritance, of not caring a damn. I love work and I try to be helpful even if it has to be in my own peculiar way. Not that I'm obstinate or cantankerous; at least George Wharton and I always stagger along somehow. As for Bill and me, we get on so well that Broad Street is almost a snuggery away from home.

Bill's is a good business, as I said. One of the biggest insurance companies has him on their books, and he does quite a lot of work for the London and provincial stores. Mind you, his isn't a Pinkerton's. His staff varies between ten and a dozen, and there's also that stout old trouper, Bertha Munney, who does the secretarial work with the aid of a recently acquired assistant. Bill can afford to pick and choose his jobs. His is the only agency that consistently advertises in the best papers, and he gets his private clients from that and from recommendations. Now do you see what I mean when I hinted that it wasn't so much of a coincidence after all that Alice Stonhill and Peter Wesslake should have asked for interviews? When people find themselves with a tough problem, and there's only one detective agency advertised in the kind of papers they read, the whole thing seems no coincidence at all. In any case there's no time to argue the point. The two minutes are up and we're in Bill Ellice's office and it's about ten minutes to eleven on the morning of Friday the 7th of May, and the year is 1948.

"Well, Bill, I think I'll be moving along," I said. "Not that I've anything particular to do."

Bill's stoutish and well into the sixties, quiet-spoken and with a bedside manner that's perfection itself and principally because it isn't unnatural or forced. He glanced up at the clock as I rose from my seat. We'd just had an hour's session discussing the moves in a case of suspected arson.

"I think there's someone rather interesting due in a minute or two. Why not go inside"—it was the inner room he meant—"and have a peep at her?"

"Young, is she?" and I raised flippant eyebrows.

"Quite elderly," Bill told me, and not reprovingly. "Sounded very interesting. Quite the lady, too. Most indignant when I suggested we should call on her instead of her coming here. Told me she wasn't all that old."

"Where's she coming from?"

"Winstode. Know it at all?"

I said I knew it had a really good golf-course and it was about forty minutes' run in a car. I also remembered that just on the outskirts of the town there was a really first-class residential hotel, the Malfroi Arms.

"That's where she's living," Bill said. My eyebrows lifted again.

"Must be pretty moneyed then. The Malfroi Arms is the sort of place that starts off at ten guineas a week."

Bill shrugged his shoulders. Soak the rich wasn't the agency motto. The buzzer went. Bertha was saying that Mrs. Stonhill had arrived.

"One minute exactly and then show her in," Bill said. He looked up at the clock and then at me.

"Five minutes early—if that means anything. Going inside?"

I slipped into that inner room. Its one window overlooked the cobbled yard of a wholesale warehouse and there was also a private door. The other door, through which I'd come, had panels of three-ply and every word came clearly from Bill's office. I left that door just ajar and took a quick look at Alice Stonhill as she came in. There was no risk. A new client's first eyes are always for Bill first and then for the room.

I don't think I'll ever forget my first sight of her. She was quietly and, what, as a man, I might call perfectly dressed. Her hair was silver and her eyes seemed to me to have a humorous twinkle. She was tiny—five-feet two at the most, and slim—but she had the poise of a six-foot duchess, lorgnette and all.

"Mr. Ellice?"

There was a charm in those two words. Let me go further and say that never did I make a better guess. Hers, I thought, was the voice of a woman of the world, old in experience and amusedly disillusioned.

Bill must have smiled and nodded.

"I'm afraid I'm dreadfully early," she was going on. "Punctuality, Mr. Ellice, is one of my few remaining virtues."

"And an admirable one, Mrs. Stonhill, if I may say so. Do sit down . . . A cigarette? You do smoke?"

"But of course," she said, and gave a delicious little chuckle. "I'm not so old that I've discarded all the vices."

Somehow I had to risk another moment or two of the door ajar. I saw Bill hold the lighter and I heard her thank-you.

"But you're not old, Mrs. Stonhill," Bill told her in his fatherly way. "My mother, now: she's well over eighty."

"In three weeks' time I shall be eighty," she told him just as quietly, and there seemed to be some amusement in the riposte. "But we mustn't waste your time talking about me. You want to know my business. Why I'm here."

"But of course," Bill said. "And why are you here, Mrs. Stonhill?"

"Just a moment," she said. "Permit me to use the frankness of age. Everything that is said between us is strictly confidential?"

Bill leaned forward in the swivel chair.

"You were recommended to us, Mrs. Stonhill, or you simply saw our advertisement?"

"The advertisement," she said, and again gave a little chuckle. "Not that I didn't make enquiries."

"We're open to every enquiry," Bill told her, "but I'd prefer you to take my word. Everything that's said in this room has the privacy of a confessional box or a doctor's consulting room. If I agree to work for you, Mrs. Stonhill, you and your interests will be those of a doctor's patient. If you ask something that we're unable to undertake, you'll be told so frankly, and then we'll forget you were ever in this room at all."

It was as if that last word had the force of a suggestion. I saw her head move and in a moment I knew her eyes might be on my door. Very gently I moved it forward and the lock slid silently into place. But before it did, I heard something else, and it was a something that made the fingers of my free hand go to my glasses. That's a nervous trick of mine when something unexpected happens or I feel myself on the edge of some dramatic discovery.

"Business, then, Mrs. Stonhill," Bill said. "You want us to help you in some way?"

"Not me," she said quickly, and all that playful irony had suddenly gone from her voice. "It's my niece I want you to help. I want to stop her from being murdered."

You can have the story either way. I have what some people regard as an uncanny memory, and I can remember practically every word that was said in that room. So you can have Alice Stonhill's story as she disjointedly told it, and with no chronological sequence: in other words, a catechism and the facts that ultimately emerged and could be sorted and adjusted to sequence and order. You might call that the shorter way, but there's another. I can do the sorting for you and give you both background and facts. You leave it to me? Then I'll take the longer way, and it's the one that may be the shorter after all. So let's lead off with a tiny genealogical tree.

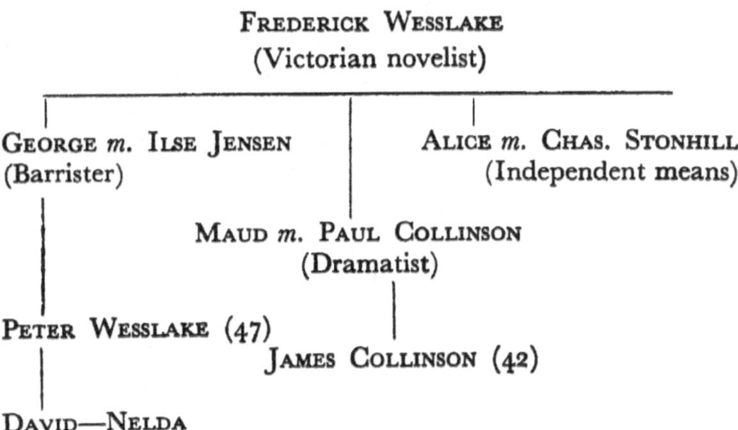

There you have the Wesslake family, with the cousins, Peter and James, and their Aunt, Alice, the only survivors; except too, for Peter's children. Peter's name I vaguely remembered, and only because someone had once told me that Peter Arden of the adventure-thrillers was really a Peter Wesslake. James Collinson's name I knew well enough. He was an author of the historico-literary type, and an authority on the Elizabethan age, and he'd also written at least two fairly successful historical plays. What I didn't know was something Alice Stonhill told Bill Ellice—that the cousins were the joint authors of that fabulously popular series of detective novels that had appeared for some years under the name of Colin Lake.

Alice Stonhill had no children. Her husband had been a wealthy man and the two had travelled extensively. He had been dead some ten years and his finances had been knocked askew by the depression. But Alice Stonhill still apparently had considerable means, even if in these days of no domestic help she lived in what she described as a cottage—The Briars, Ashenby, Buckinghamshire. But she wasn't there all the time. For quite long periods, whenever, in fact, she felt like it, she would shut up the cottage and depart for the Malfroi Arms. The Major Laddon who kept it was a distant relation on her late husband's side, and a room was always kept for her there. For that gratification of a whim, she always insisted on paying. James Collinson, the younger nephew, was a bachelor. Peter, the elder, had married a Drina Farman, and there were two children: David, aged twenty-two, and Nelda, aged twenty. In nineteen-forty-five Drina had divorced him, and he had at once married a Camille Grace. She had been a mannequin, and he had first seen her at one of the fashionable stores where he had attended a dress-show with his wife. It was this niece-in-law that was the cause of Alice Stonhill's visit to the Broad Street Detective Agency. So much for the general background.

"Before we go into the facts about these supposed attempts to murder," Bill was asking, "just why should he want to murder her?"

"I can't give you the facts," she said. "An old woman like myself has no means of finding the facts. I can only tell you what I surmise. Not, again, that I haven't made some enquiries."

According to her the position was this, and to me those surmises, as she preferred to call them, added up to motives that were only too strong. James Collinson had independent means. For years those partnership detective novels had been less and less fun, and now he was definitely refusing to collaborate further. And he, according to Alice Stonhill, was the one who supplied an enormously attractive sophistication and a charm of style. Peter had furnished plots and ideas, and had written such parts of books as had demanded no more than action and movement. Those partnership books and the films based on three of them had brought in big money—the bulk, in fact, of Wesslake's income, and now the total loss from that source would put him in queer street. Sales of the Peter Arden books, after the fantastic sales of the war years, had heavily slumped, and the stock formulae which was their basis had been worked to death. Peter Wesslake had made big money, but he had been a big spender. Alice Stonhill doubted if he had in the bank the equivalent of a year's necessary income. There was the value of his lease of the town flat, and the ownership of his small country house near Sevenoaks, but beyond those it was doubtful if he had more than a few hundreds in reserve.

And so to Drina Farman, the wife who'd divorced him and resumed her maiden name.

"She's a poor, besotted fool," Alice Stonhill said. "She'd take him back tomorrow. And she's the one with the money. I happen to know, and for the simple reason that Camille told me so, that Drina approached her only six months ago—and possibly at Peter's instigation—and offered her quite a considerable sum of money if she'd get a divorce."

I think Bill's look must have been an unspoken question. It was a question I was asking myself.

"I think I can guess what you're wondering," she said. "It's why I should be on the side of an ex-mannequin and not on the side of his first wife."

"We have to look at things from all angles," Bill told her tactfully.

"Then I'll tell you," she said. "In the first place he should never have let Drina divorce him. There were times in my own married life, Mr. Ellice, when I could have found grounds for divorce. But we're none of us without fault, and, after all, we do marry with our eyes open. But the girl, Camille, was genuinely in love with him. I don't quite know if she still is—but I do know that she's frightened. And I like her. I won't have her victimised—or worse."

"Yes," Bill said, and I could imagine him giving that frowning look while his fingers slowly caressed his chin. "And it's about that worse, as you call it, that you're here. You'd like to tell me about it?"

There were two happenings that looked like attempts at murder though, as she was careful to point out, each might be charitably regarded as a curious kind of accident were it not for what she'd evidenced as motive. The first happening had been at Wesslake's house—Millside, in the village of Burnbury, which is just beyond Sevenoaks. A married couple ran the house and garden, and at the time of the occurrence in question, James Collinson was staying for a weekend with the Wesslakes. David Wesslake was there too.

"That's the son by the first marriage?"

"That's right," she said. "David's twenty-two and wants to be an artist. He's studying in Paris. It's all very peculiar to me, because he seems to spend far too much time at home."

The garden of Millside, like most southern gardens surrounded by chestnut woods, was infested with jays that had multiplied unchecked during the war. The previous year they had stripped every row of Millside peas and Peter Wesslake was determined it shouldn't happen again. So he and Collinson armed themselves with .22 rifles and put in a whole February Saturday in an attempt to thin them out. Each had his own area and each had a cold lunch and a thermos and from the house Camille heard quite a number of shots. She had said she would come to the woods herself in the afternoon—it was a beautiful day and the first primroses were showing on the sunnier banks—and there was one path which she would be almost certain to take. She took it, and when she was well into the wood there was the crack of a shot and she literally felt the wind of the bullet by her head. She was hatless, and she afterwards found it had actually clipped her hair. Both her husband and Collinson denied having fired at that particular time or in that direction. Wesslake said subsequently that he had heard someone else shooting in the wood with a .22 rifle, though he hadn't caught sight of the man. Naturally that couldn't be proved. Collinson had heard the shots which he thought were from Wesslake's rifle. He also hadn't seen the supposed third man, but he couldn't disprove Wesslake's statement.

"And where was David?" Bill asked her.

"He was somewhere in the woods too—painting." Then she must have caught another look. "But he didn't have a rifle. Besides, you can't imagine David shooting at anything."

Bill grunted.

"And the second occasion?"

That had been also at Millside during another weekend about a month later. Collinson was again there and so was David. Frank Deen, Wesslake's secretary, was there too. Short drinks were being served in the lounge before dinner. Wesslake preferred whisky, the other men had sherry and Camille had a gin and lime. Very soon after dinner Camille had a dreadful attack of what the doctor termed gastritis, the symptoms being wrenching pains in the stomach followed by acute diarrhoea. The doctor was very promptly called but it was almost a week before Camille recovered.

"You said the drinks were being *served*," Bill said. "Just what does that mean?"

"Well, it was Upman who brought the tray in," she said rather impatiently. "He's the man of the married couple. Does every sort of job from butlering to gardening."

"Who handed the drinks round?"

"Mr. Collinson actually did."

Bill grunted again.

"And this attack couldn't have been caused by anything she ate at dinner?"

"How could it?" There was a certainty and almost a triumph. "Everyone ate the same at dinner. It was only her drink that was different."

"And what did the doctor diagnose as the cause?"

"He said it was just something that had violently disagreed with her. He told her that later, of course, when she was almost better. I think that Peter had squared it with him in some way; told him she was subject to gastritis or something like that."

"As soon as the doctor arrived, did he give an emetic?"

I think she saw the implication in Bill's question for there was a certain hesitation about her answer.

"Well, no . . . he didn't."

"And what are the relationships at present between husband and wife?"

"He's rarely at Millside now, and when he does come down he's what I might call unnaturally and endearingly solicitous. A kind of secret irony or sadism, if you know what I mean. It's more frightening than if he were openly cruel to her."

"Can you give instances?"

"Well, he goes out of his way to correct, far too charmingly, little social slips or gaucheries of speech. Just reminding her very cleverly of her origins."

"And she's still at Millside?"

"Now—no. She was heading for a nervous breakdown, and I insisted she should come to the Malfroi Arms. She's there with me now."

"And the husband?"

"He spends most of his time at the flat in town. Flat 8, Bridge Mansions, Westminster. He works there with his secretary."

"The secretary doesn't enter into this in any way?"

"Deen?" She gave a little laugh. "Not in the least. He's a colourless sort of person who's been with Peter a good many years."

There was a minute or so of silence while Bill took some notes. It was his voice that broke it.

"And there've been no other suspicious happenings?"

"None . . . Unless it was the fire."

"The fire?"

"Yes," she said. "The fire in the summer-house at Millside. Peter suddenly announced in February that he was going to use the summer-house for working in. He had a larger window put in and electricity run on from the house and a desk and things installed, and an electric fire."

"Why choose February?"

"Exactly! I admit we had a few lovely days in spring, but it did seem rather absurd, especially as Peter was always one for comfort and self-indulgence. And then before he'd been using the place for more than a week or two, there was a fire. The whole thing was gutted."

"It was insured?"

"Oh, yes. I believe there's still quite a lot of arguing going on about compensation, or whatever they call it. That's what seemed to me to be suspicious. That, and one other thing."

The other thing was the typewriter, and when Alice Stonhill mentioned it, it was again with a certain triumph. That woman was certainly very far from a fool, and she'd done a useful bit of thinking out. Wesslake had been much attached to that oldish Remington portable, but it hadn't been left in the summer-house the night of that fire. Camille had seen it in his bedroom. And yet it should have been left there, for he was intending to work there the next morning.

"Was Deen with him?" Bill asked her.

"He was always there when Peter was working," she said, and added a rather important something else. "What I can't see is how that fire could be a part of the campaign against Camille. Unless it had been intended that she should have been burnt in some way, or suffocated."

That was all. A new silence indicated that Bill was taking notes or making a decision.

"And what do you suggest we should do about all this, Mrs. Stonhill?" was what he said.

"That's for you to say, Mr. Ellice," she told him quickly. "As my husband would often put it, I'm prepared to buy a dog. I don't propose to do any barking myself."

"That's frank enough," Bill said. "I'll be frank too, Mrs. Stonhill. I don't see at the moment what we can do. Mrs. Wesslake is safe enough with you, I take it?"

"I think so," she said, but with none too much certainty. "And today week Peter's going away for three weeks. It's the P.E.N. congress at Copenhagen, you know, but he wants to go a week earlier and look up any family connections."

"The P.E.N. congress?"

"Yes," she said. "It's an international association of authors and writers. Each year there's a congress in a different country. Last year it was Sweden."

"Is Collinson going too?"

"He's not a member," she said. "Besides, I want him for my birthday party. It's on the 29th. Everyone's coming to it—except Peter."

Bill told me afterwards that a roguish look in her eye made him ask the question.

"And not the first Mrs. Wesslake?"

"Oh, yes," she said, and it was definitely amusedly. "Drina's coming."

"Then there oughtn't to be a dull moment," Bill said dryly, and then, quickly, "Perhaps I shouldn't have said that."

"But why not? I'm quite looking forward to it."

Bill grunted yet once more.

"Well, Mrs. Stonhill, you've come to me for advice. I'll give it to you. But you won't like it. It's that you should tell everything you've told me to the police."

"No!" Never was a word more emphatic. "I'm responsible in a way for the family and I won't have its name dragged in the mud."

"But suppose something does happen. Then you won't be able to stop this dragging in the mud. The police and the Press can't be silenced."

"Isn't that why I've come to you? Nothing *must* happen. That's what I'm prepared to pay to have stopped."

"Listen, Mrs. Stonhill," Bill's voice was quiet and enormously persuasive. "I've got myself and this agency to consider. If anything did happen and a man of mine was, say, acting as bodyguard at the Malfroi Arms, then that man and this agency would be brought in. I don't believe that anything so serious as murder is likely to happen, but I daren't take the risk. If it did happen, then we'd be accused, and rightly, of keeping back vital information from the police."

"Why do you suggest that nothing so serious as murder may happen?"

"I'll tell you," Bill said. "I mayn't have all the facts and I've met none of the parties, but this is how I work things out. Six months ago the first Mrs. Wesslake tried to bribe the second one to get a divorce. The attempts didn't come off. Very well then. Wesslake tried another method: what you might call the warning or the frightening one. Do you know anything about small calibre rifles?"

"Not a thing."

"A .22 could kill a man at shortish range, say ten to fifteen yards. He was hidden in the undergrowth and he shot at that range, and at so big a target, that he couldn't have missed. What he did was to shoot to scare. The same with that cocktail business. He slipped a big dose of calomel or something like it into her drink. The attack came and she thought there'd been an attempt to poison her—

which was just what he wanted her to think. Remember that he was perfectly safe because the doctor would have given evidence that there was no poison. In other words, and to sum up, I don't see that Mrs. Wesslake is in any serious danger. In spite of that, I still think you should go to the police. If you prefer not to, then all I can do is suggest that if any more queer incidents take place, you should get into touch with this office at once. It's available for calls day and night."

A long silence, and again it was Bill who broke it.

"Think it over carefully, Mrs. Stonhill. Ask yourself if Wesslake really means business. If he does, why should he have advertised his intentions by those two abortive attacks?"

"I believe him to be a desperate man."

"But why? Desperate enough to commit a murder, I mean."

"Because he's always had and demanded a luxurious standard of living, and now there's the prospect of his having to live on a pittance." The little laugh was definitely contemptuous. "You don't know Peter Wesslake."

"Well, there it is," Bill said resignedly. "Are you prepared to agree that things should be left as I suggest?"

"Well, perhaps yes," she said. "But I shall take my own steps to protect both myself and Camille."

And that was where I tiptoed towards the outer door. The door was closed gently behind me and I slipped out to the yard and round into Broad Street. I nipped into Bertha's room and asked her to signal me when the client was on the point of coming out. I asked her to do something else, and because I'd had a brainwave. All I wanted at the moment was for Mrs. Stonhill to be aware of me, and no more.

CHAPTER 2
PETER WESSLAKE

From the front door a passage-way leads past Bertha's room to the little waiting-room. I was in that passage when Mrs. Stonhill left

Bill's office and I was artistically disposed at Bertha's door in such a way as to have the passage partly blocked.

"But I really can't wait," I was saying to Bertha. "The appointment was for twelve o'clock and it's now half-past."

"Mr. Ellice will be free in a moment," Bertha told me. "Mr. Travers, wasn't it?"

"Mr. Ludovic Travers," I repeated with dignity, and then was stepping inside Bertha's room. "I'm awfully sorry," I said to Mrs. Stonhill, "I'm afraid I didn't see you."

"Mr. Ellice is free now, Mr. Travers," Bertha said sweetly. "I'll take you through in a moment."

She followed Mrs. Stonhill through to the outer door. A dark car drew up—apparently it had been waiting during that long interview—and when it moved off, I moved off too—into Bill's office.

"What was the idea?" Bill said.

"I wanted her to have a good look at me," I told him. "Once-seen-never-forgotten, if you know what I mean. And I think she did. She gave me a charming smile."

Bill's look was still an enquiring one.

"You wanted to know what the idea was," I said. "Well, we might have to undertake her case. You might think I'm the sort of person who could handle a part of it. At the Malfroi Arms, shall we say. And if so, what better method of getting acquainted than for us both to discover we've been clients of the Broad Street Detective Agency." Bill merely grunted. What he wanted was for me to sit down for a minute and discuss that interview. Did I think he'd handled things the right way?

I said he'd been discretion itself. I went further and said that intimidation theory of his was in my judgment dead right.

"Talking of that," Bill said, and absent-mindedly passed me his lighter though I hadn't a cigarette in my mouth, "what are your ideas about the old lady herself?"

"She's a character," I said. "I like her. I rather wish she was my grandmother."

"She had me about her age," Bill said. "I didn't put her at a day over seventy."

He rubbed his chin for a moment, then wanted to know what I thought about her story.

"You could see her and I couldn't," I said. "All I can judge is that she likes to consider herself the decidedly active head of the Wesslake family. And why not? I think James Collinson's her white-headed boy but she doesn't like or trust Peter Wesslake. That's why she was only too ready to take sides with the Camille woman. She may even have put ideas into her head. And it may have been Alice Stonhill who lent a hand in breaking up the partnership between Collinson and Wesslake in the matter of the Colin Lake books."

Bill looked as if that didn't help too much, and it didn't. He'd been thinking more about her story and what truth there was in those murder or intimidation attempts.

"If you want conjectures," I said, "there're any amount of them. Wesslake's attempts might have been serious. The shot might have been intended to kill, but missed. The dose that was put in the gin and lime might have been thought lethal, but it wasn't. After all, it did shake his wife up pretty badly if it took her a week to get over it. And then there's quite another side which we haven't considered at all. Either Peter Wesslake or James Collinson, for all we know, might have fired that shot. Either of them—we don't know the circumstances—might possibly have dropped that dope in her glass."

"Let's leave the whole thing," Bill said, and got to his feet.

"And yet you don't like leaving it."

"Why shouldn't I?" he said, and gave me a quick look. "As far as we're concerned, it's either a dud or else it's dynamite. We don't want duds, and dynamite's risky stuff."

"But suppose she does ring again and reports that something else has happened? There'll be the same problem—to do something about the case or wash your hands of it."

"Nothing *is* going to happen," he told me doggedly. "I still think the whole thing was intimidation. Wesslake's trying to scare his wife into giving him a divorce and the old lady's going to fight like hell to stop her doing it."

That was how we left it but I knew that even that confident reiteration had its background of doubt and regret. Bill had had to turn away a case well out of the rut, and, what was more, refuse a client who was as curiously fascinating as he'd ever had. For that was how I was feeling, too. Alice Stonhill was a woman I wanted to see again. I was itching to study her: to know what was really behind those twinkling old eyes of hers, and if in that defence of Camille there was more than a matriarchal urge. I wanted to see those two women of Wesslake's, and Wesslake himself, and Collinson. And since, as I have said, an unsolved mystery gnaws at me like an aching tooth, I knew in my unspoken mind that by hook or by crook I would somehow contrive to see them all.

My flat is in St. Martin's Chambers which is as handy a place as any in town. I had just finished dinner there with my wife that night when the telephone went. It was Bill Ellice.

"Something queer has happened," he said.

"The old lady's rung again already?"

"Queerer than that," he said. "A client's coming at ten tomorrow morning and you'd never guess whom."

"Camille?"

"Wesslake," he said. "It's about that fire at his summer-house. That's all I know. He spoke very guardedly."

"What'd he sound like?"

"Nothing out of the ordinary. Just a touch of the hearty."

"And he's due at ten," I said. "Thanks for the news, Bill. I'll be right there."

But that news was making me restless again; you know the sort of restlessness that makes you want somehow to anticipate events. It was information about Peter Wesslake that I needed, or so I thought, and in the flat there wasn't a reference book to help me. My *Who's Who* did give me James Collinson and I hoped for some cross reference to Wesslake, but there wasn't one. All it told me was what I very largely knew—that he was unmarried, was an authority on the Elizabethan age, had written *The Italianate Englishman*, *The Other Donne* and another half-dozen books, and was the author of three plays, one of which, as I remembered, dealt with Amy Robsart.

I slipped along to my club and there looked up an authors' reference book. Peter Wesslake, under the name of Peter Arden— "Arden for Adventure" was his publishers' slogan—had written to date some twenty-five novels, and of the titles given I remembered only three—*Madman's Farm*, *Danger in Eden* and *The Man Who Knew*, and maybe because each had been filmed. I also learned that his publishers were Morris and Hunt, and that he was forty-seven years old.

There was no cross reference to Colin Lake, and so it seemed that the pseudonym of the cousins was something of a secret. There were twenty of the Colin Lake detective novels, and their publisher was Harold Land. I remembered several of the titles, and especially *The Bishop's Niece* and *Pigs' Market*, each of which had been filmed. And that was all I learned. There was no mention of a club or clubs or I'd have rung up some acquaintance or other who happened also to belong, and so have learned perhaps a considerable deal.

The next morning was a repetition of the one that had preceded it, and there I was in that inner room with the door ajar. And once more the one who entered was vastly different from what I had thought. Maybe it was Bill's mention of heartiness that had made a false anticipation, for I'd expected someone big and beefy. But Wesslake was only of medium height, and rather spare, and the first thing about him that literally flashed into view was his head of blond hair brushed back from the forehead. It was the kind of hair that has boosted the price of peroxide, a kind of ash-yellow and it seemed the more dazzling because it rose from a face that was more red and purple than I'd have liked my own to be. But that face was well cut; I'd have called him almost handsome in a florid kind of way.

But the heartiness was there right enough, and from the first moment of ushering in. Out went his hand as he stepped forward. There was a smile.

"Glad to meet you, Mr. Ellice."

I quietly closed the door and, why I don't know, I was still thinking about that hair. There had been something vaguely familiar, or was it symbolic, about it, and then I suddenly remembered that he had had a Danish mother. In Denmark, and in all of what I might call the blond north, one sees heads of hair like that. And often with eyes of a clear blue. But what colour Wesslake's eyes were I didn't know.

I put my ear to the panel and for the moment the talk was about books. Wesslake, I guessed, had imparted the news that he was an author. Perhaps he had been trying to impress Bill with that, and at any rate Bill was talking manfully about books. And he too must have done some over-night research for he actually knew an Arden title or two. Wesslake's voice, by the way, was quite a pleasant, if slightly plummy, baritone.

"I gave you a hint of what I'd like you to do for me," he said, "but now I'm here I don't feel so happy about it. It's such a small job."

"Little fish, they say, are sweet," Bill told him with a rare jocularity.

"I hope this one will be."

"Just before we get down to it, Mr. Wesslake, were you recommended to us or did you see the advertisement? We always like to know."

"Just the advertisement."

"Well, I'm glad it's bringing in dividends," Bill said dryly. "And now to business. You'd like us to do what?" Once more we heard about the summer-house at Millside. Wesslake thought the fire had been caused by a short circuit but the insurance people were making all sorts of difficulties about payment.

"That's rather exasperating," he said, "considering the fire took place in March. And there's something more serious. I'm getting of the opinion that there's some personal reflection on myself. I'll be blunt. I think they have an idea the fire was a fake."

"But surely that's preposterous! A man of your standing, Mr. Wesslake. You're not hard up?"

"Even if I were, I don't think three hundred pounds would make that difference. If I ever turned crook it would be for a considerable deal more than that."

Bill gave a little laugh, so the statement must have been intended as a joke. I thought it subtle the way Wesslake had switched that little matter of needing the money.

"What is the Company?"

"The London Providential. They handle all my insurances—except life."

"And what do you want us to do in the matter?"

"Make your own enquiry on my behalf. I rang them up yesterday and said I was having an investigation made for my own satisfaction. That's what I want. And I'm not afraid of what you'll find. I'll give you my word here and now that I'll stand by your findings. But, and it's a big but, if you do find evidence of faking, then I want you to find the faker. That clear?"

"I wish all clients were as clear," Bill said. "But let's look on the bad side. Suppose it was a fake. Could you give me a list of possible fakers?"

Wesslake gave them, and he seemed to be quite serious about it all. John and Edith Upman came first. They were the married couple who ran Millside. Then there was Frank Deen, Wesslake's secretary, and, finally Mrs. Wesslake and Wesslake himself and his son David. They were the only people in the house on the night of the fire, and never a one of them had the barest suspicion of a motive.

"There's my wife, of course," Wesslake said off-handedly, and something told me we were getting places at last. "She was just a bit awkward about my working in that summer-house and having it messed about, as she called it. But you can't call that a motive for burning the place down." Bill dismissed the idea as ridiculous, though he, like me, must have felt the faint hovering of something in the dim background.

"She's down there now?"

"As a matter of fact she isn't," Wesslake said. "She's staying with an elderly aunt of mine at Winstode—the Malfroi Arms. She was a bit run down and is having a holiday." And so to sheer business. The summer-house was completely gutted but Bill would have a free hand at Millside. Wesslake had with him a claim's inventory, and Bill pronounced it reasonable enough. There were matters of retainer and final payment and the rendering of reports.

"If anything turns up quickly, let me know," Wesslake said, "but only till Thursday next. On the Friday I'm going to Copenhagen. The P.E.N. congress, you know. It doesn't open till the 31st but I want to put in a week's holiday beforehand. So hold everything till I get back. That mayn't be till the 12th of June. My mother was Danish and I'd rather like to take advantage of the congress to look up any family connections. So you'd better hold everything as I said, till I get back."

"I get you," Bill said. "But two other things. You've warned this married couple that a man or men of mine will be coming down?"

"I haven't," he said, "but I'll do so straightaway."

"The other thing's this. I hate reiteration, Mr. Wesslake, but I'd like to have it perfectly clear and in the agreement. Everything's strictly confidential as between you and me, but if we should happen to uncover any dirt—well, we uncover it. Everything will still be confidential, but I'd like to know, just between ourselves, how that's going to affect yourself and the insurance company?"

"Whatever you uncover, they'll be told," Wesslake said, and I thought, rather stiffly.

"That's fine," Bill said. "We shall always be behind the scenes and no more. Your interests are ours. That's the only reason I asked the question."

"Well?" Bill said as I came through to the office.

"Well yourself," I said. "You saw his face. I didn't." Bill fingered his chin.

"I think he's getting a bit scared. I wouldn't be surprised if the London Providential have something on him. I think he's sort of hoping against hope we can do the miraculous for him."

"Was his manner nervous?"

"It was rather hard to see under the veneer," Bill said; "you know—that man-of-the-world heartiness. He has a funny little nervous trick, by the way. When he's debating something he pinches his nose, like this. He did it once or twice when I put a ticklish question."

"But why the devil should a man like him do such a fool trick as faking a fire?"

Bill shrugged his shoulders.

"Some sort of superiority complex. We've been up against it before. Sort of, 'I'm Wesslake, the famous author. No one'd doubt my word. I could pack a court with witnesses,' and so on."

"Do you think he's possibly feeling the pinch already? I mean, is he really hard up for three hundred pounds?"

"It isn't three hundred pounds clear profit," Bill reminded me. "Besides, how could he be feeling a pinch already? His publishers must have stuff on hand and there ought to be back royalties still to come in. That's what puzzles me. If he faked it, then why the devil did he fake it?"

"My guess is that he did," I said. "He knows the insurance people are wise to it and we're his last hope to keep him out of a scandal, or jail. But if that's so, and the summer house was absolutely gutted and the insurance people already have been there and collared possible evidence, why should he expect us to get him in the clear? Doesn't it strike you that he may have some faked evidence ready for us?"

"I'll call Palton off that other job and get him down there," Bill said. "He won't pull any wool over Palton's eyes. And I think I'll have a private word with the London Providential. I can get an introduction all right."

"I'll keep my eyes and ears open too," I told him. "If anything should happen to turn up, I'll get in touch at once."

I jotted down a note or two from the notes he'd taken and then I used the telephone in Bertha's room. It was eleven o'clock and Wesslake had said he was lunching with a publisher at the Café Royal at one. That was reasonably distant from his Westminster flat. All the same, I fixed it to call on Margale first.

At half-past eleven I was at Hampstead and Margale was waiting for me. He's a bit more than an acquaintance and not quite an old friend. How he regards me I don't quite know, but he did try to pull my leg.

"What's it all about? Scotland Yard on the scent?"

"Nothing so lucrative," I told him. "Just a little private matter."

"Well, have a sherry first."

"A bit early," I said, "but if it's good sherry I will."

"The thing's this," I said, and you'll acknowledge at once that I'm very high up in the Ananias class. There was a time when I lied timorously and with a blush, even in the sacred cause of Justice. Years of association with George Wharton soon got me out of that.

"You going to Copenhagen for the P.E.N. congress?"

"I'm not," he said. "Can't afford the time. I've a book due at the publisher's in three weeks from now."

"Just something I wanted you to do for me," I said casually. "Not that it matters. There's another way of doing it."

He offered to put me in touch with a man who, he thought, was going. I said it wasn't all that important, and it was all very friendly and polite, like two Frenchmen approaching the same door. We left it that I'd do my business on my own. Then over the sherry I put an innocent question or two and he was telling me all about the congress and the work of P.E.N.

"We should have gone to America," he said. "It was their turn for the congress but the monetary restrictions kyboshed it all. Then the Danes kindly stepped into the breach at short notice. As late as February, I think. Wait a minute. I think I have it here."

He found one of the P.E.N. news leaflets issued to members and said he'd been right. Then he passed it to me. I oughtn't to have called it a leaflet for it was more of a six-page brochure. I looked through it quickly—and then something caught my eye. It was something extraordinary, or at least it seemed so at the time. I know that I dropped the brochure and my fingers went to my glasses. But he noticed nothing.

"Do you want this badly, or may I keep it?" I said. "I'm rather interested."

"You ought to become a member," he told me. "You're qualified. You've written books."

I said that *Kensington Gore* and my other two items of murder chit-chat were hopelessly in the past. He said they still made me qualified.

"I'll think about it," I said. "But if I'd known about this Copenhagen congress as early as January I might have tried to join then."

"We did have a preliminary hint very early in February," he said. "I'll look it up and make sure."

He was that methodical sort of chap whom it's hard to put off, but I persuaded him that it didn't matter. Then I refused a second sherry, uttered a deal of thanks and went off. It was then well after midday and it seemed to me that Flat 8 at Bridge Mansions, Westminster ought to be safe.

I took a bus instead of the Tube to make doubly sure and most of the time I was thinking of that queer discovery I'd made. Then I imagined I was in Bill's office and I was telling him about it and propounding a theory and he was knocking holes. It was quite an enjoyable argument, except that soon that theory didn't look half so promising as when it had flashed into my mind in Margale's room.

It was ten minutes to one when I entered the block of flats. They were expensive ones—the kind that start at three-fifty and end up about five-fifty pounds for the pick. I couldn't judge what Flat 8 was like since I didn't know the number of rooms. All I wanted at the moment was to run my eye over an at present unknown quantity—the secretary, Frank Deen.

I was lucky, for it was he who came to the door. Alice Stonhill had described him as a colourless sort of individual and she wasn't far out, even if once more I was seeing a man who was far different from what I'd imagined him. He was of medium height and looked about fifty, and his hair seemed to have aged prematurely to a snowy white. I had a curious uneasiness when I saw him.

"Hallo," I said. "Aren't you new?"

"New, sir?" His look was a probing one.

"I haven't seen you here before," I said with a naive surprise.

"I've been here for a good many years," he told me, and there was partly reproof and partly what I took for a definite uneasiness.

"Curious," I said. "Is Mrs. Wellington in?"

"Wellington?" he said. "There's no Mrs. Wellington here, sir."

I let my eyes shift to the door.

"Good Lord!" I said, and hoped I looked a bit of a fool. "I'm so sorry, I thought this was flat eighteen."

At once we were all smiles and affability. I said I'd been wool-gathering and I was always a bit hazy about numbers, and he did some deprecation, and that was that. I smiled and he smiled and off I moved up the stairs to the next floor. Ten minutes later I was out on the pavement again. Everything seemed to have been perfectly managed. In the main hall had been a list of tenants, and I doubted if Deen or Wesslake was acquainted with the Mrs. Wellington who had Flat 18. It wasn't that, then, that accounted for the faint cloud that still lay across my mind. Just what that cloud was it took me quite a few minutes to discover—that there had been about Frank Deen a something that was dimly familiar.

I rang up my wife and went home to a service lunch. Bernice—you may or may not remember her as Bernice Haire, the classical dancer—was due out with friends that afternoon and, as soon as she'd gone, I rang Bill Ellice. He was out but half an hour later he gave me a ring.

"Busy?" he said. "If not I'd like a quiet word. Can't talk about it over the telephone."

I said my own news would keep. Outside the flat I hopped a lucky bus and in twenty minutes was in Bill's office. He'd moved quickly. Sir George Aulney of Mutual Empire Insurance for which Bill worked, had rung London Providential, and Bill had had his interview.

"We were right," he told me. "It's dynamite about that fire. The way it was told to me, the whole thing stinks."

"Then what about our enquiry?"

Bill made a wry face.

"They'd like us to go ahead with it. Why shouldn't they? They know their assessor's report. What we find won't alter that, unless we turn up some new faked evidence." He shrugged his shoulders. "That doesn't concern us. We've agreed to enquire into that fire and we start, for all Wesslake knows, with a clear sheet."

"Know what was fishy?"

Again Bill made a wry face. His voice lowered.

"Traces of candle grease."

My eyebrows lifted.

"The old trick. Inflammable material handy and up she goes when the candle burns down. And Wesslake's a detective story writer! What did he hope? The heat would remove traces? A sort of destructibility of matter?"

"They all make slips, you and I know that. But there's something trickier. The typewriter."

"They know about it?"

"Not that he took it to the house that night. Something worse than that. He was fool enough to claim for a Remington portable and he must have dumped an old scrap machine there. He forgot you could still check its number and everything even after the fire."

"My hat!" I said. "Whatever made him do a damfool thing like that? Cupidity, or what?"

"Don't know," he said. "All I know is the position's this. They know he doesn't want a scandal and they're hoping he'll accept very much lower than his claim. Scandal won't do them much good either. And you and I know that arson cases are tricky. He's a man of good character and standing and that might weigh pretty heavily if it came to a case."

"But Palton's going down there?"

"First thing in the morning. It's a waste of time in my view but you never know."

That was all from his side. I gave him that brochure open at a certain page and pointed something out. He had a look at the cover before he read what I'd wanted him to see.

"List of new members," he read. "Peter Wesslake. And the date of this is February."

He frowned.

"What's the value of it to us? They had thirty or forty new members."

It was on the tip of my tongue to tell him, and then something changed my mind. Contract bridge isn't the only thing in which it's the unforgivable sin to deceive one's partner. But I had my reasons for holding something back.

"Just confirmatory evidence of his being a P.E.N. club member," I said. "And about the Copenhagen congress. I thought you might be interested."

He nodded sort of automatically and gave me the brochure. I put it back in my wallet, and do you know what I was cocksuredly saying to myself? I'll bet you'd never guess, but it was this.

"If Wesslake *should* decide to murder his wife," I told myself as I folded that brochure carefully in, "then this is a little something that's going to help to hang him."

CHAPTER 3
GOODBYE TO A THEORY

I'D ASKED Bill to do a thing or two for me, or rather to get Palton to do them while he was on that fire enquiry at Millside. Nobody had told us anything of the present whereabouts of the first Mrs. Wesslake, for one thing, and we had no idea at the moment where David Wesslake might be. We'd inferred from what his father had told us that he wasn't now at Millside. Possibly he'd gone back to Paris, but I thought we ought to know. As for James Collinson, I knew where he was, for I'd rung him at his flat—2A Romney Court, Hampstead—and asked if I might speak to him.

"This *is* Collinson," he had said, and at once I had rung off. I left him to imagine that someone had cut us off, not that it worried me what he thought or imagined.

Maybe you're wondering why I was anxious about those varied characters in the drama that Alice Stonhill had out-lined in Bill's office, so perhaps I'd better explain. When Bill tells a client that his office is like a doctor's consulting room or a priest's confessional box, he's as near right as makes little difference. But there *is* a difference. When circumstances arise that make it imperative for the law to cast a wide net, detective agencies are by no means sacrosanct. Were there to be a murder, for instance, and it was discovered by the police that a party or parties somehow connected had been clients of the Broad Street Detective Agency, then Bill would have been in a dilemma. If he refused to say what he knew about his client, he might have been called as witness at an inquest or even the Old Bailey, and refusal to speak there might mean contempt of court.

It was a ticklish matter, as you see, and Bill wanted to run no risks. Very little of his business comes from private clients and that the question of murder should arise is a remote contingency indeed. But now it had arisen and there was just an outside chance that he might find himself having to betray the confidences of a client. If that client was a murderer, then it might seem that he wasn't worth a moment's worry. But there'd probably be publicity and that would do the agency no good. That was why Bill had described the case as dynamite. It was a case, in fact, that wasn't worth the risk. And yet the fact remains that it was an intriguing case, and that was why he had been loth to let it go. That was why he had temporised and told Alice Stonhill that he could do nothing unless some new and dangerous situation developed. That also was why he had partly covered himself by urging her to go to the police.

Now I wasn't directly concerned. I wasn't a director of the firm, and I was prepared to stick out my neck. That case had intrigued me enormously and there were things I felt I just had to know. Besides, as I pointed out to Bill, I was the safety valve between him and the law. At the first sign of danger, I could become the go-between. All I had to do was to see George Wharton and reveal as much of the facts as we thought discreet. That sort of thing had worked before and there wasn't a reason why it shouldn't work again. And just one other thing, even if you think it a bit tricky or machiavellian. Couldn't we always plead that it had been in the interests of the client himself that we had privately approached the law? It was up to us to protect his interests, and the contract never said a thing about just how those interests were to be protected.

But to get back. There was one other character, and perhaps the most important of all, about whom I knew comparatively little, and that was Camille Wesslake. On the Monday then, before going to Broad Street, I went to Somerset House and saw a copy of Wesslake's wedding certificate. It was a Register Office marriage and the witnesses seemed to have been supplied. But that didn't matter. What interested me was that the bride's name was given as Constance Gedge, and her age as twenty. Her father was a Henry Gedge, tobacconist, of 29 Prentiss Road, Kilburn.

There are mannequins and mannequins. Bernice had told me that girls of quite good family make a useful living at the job, but Constance Gedge seemed to have come up the hard way. Doubtless she had changed her name to Camille as being more attractive, and I rather guessed there'd been a different surname too, for you can't play tricks on a marriage certificate. Maybe the wedding had been the secret one it appeared to have been, because Wesslake hadn't wanted the family to know of his wife's origins. And that made me give an involuntary chuckle. I could just see Camille Wesslake withholding information after a concentrated attack by Aunt Alice!

I didn't go on to Broad Street after all but back to the flat instead. It's only rarely that Bernice does any detective work, and when she does, she just loves it. George Wharton is a pet of hers, and she likes Bill too. I never let Bill pay me a cent unless I'm on a definite job for which he'd have to pay an operative, but he wormed Bernice's birthday out of me and now sends along a far too expensive present. The last time, in April, it was a bottle of scent that must have cost him a pretty packet.

"I'm on a job for Bill Ellice," I told her that morning, "and we'd like you to do something for us. Find out all you can about a Camille Something-or-other who used to be a mannequin. Two years ago she married a man named Peter Wesslake. I'll write it all down for you."

I did, and I told her just as much as she had to know.

"One of the high-class dress establishments," Bernice said. "That seems to rule out the big stores."

She shook a dubious head, then had an idea.

"It was just over two years ago when there was that big dress show at Olympia. They had an awful lot of mannequins. I think I could see the Miss Youngs who ran it all."

"Fine," I said. "There's no great urgency but I'd like it this week. Bill said it was a job right up your street."

So that was all settled, but the first thing I told Bill when I did get to Broad Street was what he was supposed to have said. Liars don't always need good memories; what they need is a good note-book.

Quite a few things had happened. Palton had rung up the office to say that he was wasting time at Millside. The summer-house had been a wooden one, and it was so completely gutted that nothing much but ashes was left. Anything that might have been of use to him had been removed apparently by the insurance people. But he'd taken a statement from the married couple about what happened on the night of the fire. His view was that they were decent, reliable people and in no way concerned. But one thing he had learned from them which seemed interesting. Wesslake had had the big and only window of that summer-house fitted up with thick curtains. In other words, if he had set off that fire by the old candle trick, then when he left the summer-house he'd only to draw the curtain and nothing could be seen. A significant rider was that there was a Yale lock and he had the only key.

That information I'd specially asked for had been furnished by the Upmans, and what gaps there were could be easily filled in. Drina Wesslake—you remember she had the money—owned a house some ten miles west of Winstode—The Orchards, Merridale. That had been the Wesslake home, but immediately after the divorce Wesslake had bought Millside and made a new home with his new wife. David Wesslake was at the moment staying with his mother and sister at Merridale.

"I rang Wesslake," Bill said, "and he agreed we ought to have a statement about the night of the fire from David, and from Collinson. I told him that our man'd be ostensibly a representative of the insurance company. Palton's probably down at this Merrivale place now. Then he's seeing the Camille woman."

"About this fire," I said. "I know you told Wesslake that his claim was reasonable. Was that eyewash?"

"Partly, yes," he said. "He charged up to the hilt—modern replacement values—for everything there was."

"He didn't stand to lose a single thing from the fire?"

"Nothing," Bill said, "unless he pleaded that he suffered inconvenience by no longer being able to work there."

I thought that over and then came to a decision, and it seemed to me a mighty important one.

"Remember what I told you about that P.E.N. congress and Wesslake becoming a new member. Nothing curious about that has occurred to you?"

"No," Bill said. "Should it?"

"I don't know," I said, "but I don't like the look of the pattern."

"What pattern?"

"The sequence of things. Begin in November when Drina Wesslake tried to bribe Camille to get a divorce. Next came Wesslake's becoming a member of the P.E.N. Club, in February. *And*, when he'd discovered that there was going to be a congress in Copenhagen. Then came the shot in the woods and then that cocktail business. That was quite recently, and the next thing that's going to happen is that next Friday Wesslake's going to Denmark. All that convey anything to you?"

Bill pursed his lips and shook his head.

"Let me put it this way," I said. "I want to get rid of my wife. I hear that the P.E.N. Club, of which I'm entitled to become a member, is having a congress at Copenhagen, and as my mother was a Dane, I've every reason for wanting to go there. Or so it would seem. Around all that I am building a murder scheme. I stage two accidents which scare the wits out of my wife, but they're only in preparation for the real attempt. I want to get her away from Millside for a holiday with my Aunt Alice. I know what I'm going to do when she's there. I'm going to do the thing properly but it won't be suspected—the way I've planned it, it won't be suspected as murder at all—but if it is, I shall then be in Denmark. If by some million-to-one chance the murder looks like being pinned on me, then Denmark's a good place to disappear from."

Bill had been looking a bit puzzled. All he could say was that I seemed to be assuming rather a lot.

"Put yourself in Wesslake's place," he said. "The P.E.N. Club arranges everything for its members for a week's congress. Wouldn't you have said to yourself, 'Dammit, why shouldn't I join? Here's a fine chance to get to Denmark. About time I went there and looked people up.'"

"Why didn't he join before?" I asked him. "The P.E.N.'s been going now for donkey's years."

"Has there been a congress in Denmark at all recently?"

That got me.

"I was afraid you were going to ask me that," I said. "Still, it was a good theory—while I was telling it."

"Wait a minute," Bill said. "Let's not waste it. Let's suppose it's true. What then?"

"Then there's a danger point between now and next Friday. That's when Camille's due for extinction. If the police knew what we know—knew it for a certainty, I mean—they'd have her guarded night and day."

Bill took a turn round the room.

"Well," he said, as he came back to his chair, "even if that theory's true, and you won't mind me saying I don't think it's true at all, then we're in the clear. We've advised the client to go to the police. And refused to take the case. If anything should happen—again I say I'm certain in my own mind that it won't—then our conduct is what you might call scrupulously correct."

I hope I'm a good loser, and I gave in.

"You're right, Bill," I said. "But all the same you don't mind if I do a little grubbing around on my own?"

"It's a free country," he told me dryly, and whether or not there was a twinkle in his eye I don't know.

I'll say frankly that I grubbed around so little because I now honestly believed that Bill might be right. There was also the reason that there was so little that I could do. Men are prepared to pay for their hobbies, whether it's stamp-collecting or darts or the dogs. My hobbies are the study of my fellow men and the solving of a mystery that happens to intrigue me, and you could even put crossword puzzles into that category. Those hobbies I'm naturally prepared to pay for, and more than once I've paid Bill for the use of an operative. But I didn't feel like doing it in this case. I should have felt something of a fool if I'd had a man sent as bodyguard to the Malfroi Arms.

But I did do a thing or two. I went to Prentiss Road and found that Camille's father—he was a widower—was no longer there. The one-armed ex-soldier who'd bought the business from him, thought he was now at Eastbourne. That looked to me as if Wesslake—or Camille with his money—had got the father out of the way. I don't say she was ashamed of him—the new man described him as a nice old boy. But maybe Wesslake was, and to have Gedge stay on in London wasn't to his liking. Maybe he had intended to do a Pygmalion act with his young wife and didn't want the intrusion of home influence.

On the Wednesday afternoon Bernice came triumphantly home.

"I've found out about the Camille," she told me. "She was a Camille Grace and worked for Raumur in Bond Street."

"What's Raumur?" I said.

"A most expensive place," she said. "Calls itself *Raumur et Cie.*"

"Pseudo-French," I said, and sighed. "How much did it cost you?"

"I'll be fair," she said. "The difference between the costume they're making for me there and what I could have got it for elsewhere is only about ten guineas."

"I'll pay," I said. "And what else did you find out?"

"How did you know I'd found anything else out?"

"Just because."

"Well, I did find something out," she said. "It was another mannequin I managed to talk to. Madame Raumur was out and we had a cup of tea together. She was a bosom friend of this Camille's and I've sort of half-promised to let her know where she's living. Camille sort of left the shop and Sybil—that's her friend—hasn't heard a word from her since."

"You'll have to dodge that somehow," I said. "But what did she tell you about Camille?"

"She said she was a good girl. I suppose she meant chaste. She said she'd begun as a work-hand and gradually worked her way up. She was very good-looking apparently and had a very good figure. Sybil said anyone would have taken her for a real lady."

"Did Sybil have any suspicions about marriage?"

"Well, I think she did. She mentioned the husband of a Mrs. Wesslake who used to be a customer. It appears he came in once or twice without his wife. He was a fair-haired, rather thin and rather good-looking man of forty or fifty, Sybil thought."

I said it was all we needed to know, and it certainly threw a good light on Connie Gedge. I could picture her trying to be smart and attentive under Madame's eye. A girl with ambitions in her job and probably looking after her face and figure and watching customers and learning how to speak and gesture and walk. So to the manne-quin's job, and the entry of Wesslake and his roving eye. A call or two on some pretence or other, and then absolute discretion. Everything continuing outside the shop from then on, and Camille saying never a word to Sybil. Then the sudden leaving, and Sybil being dropped like a hot brick.

But all that was what I might call of academic interest. The Thursday came and I was still restless in spite of the abandonment of that theory. Palton's report had come in, and he had discov-ered nothing fresh. The night of the fire had been a cold one and the lounge and its fire were on the opposite side of the house from the summer-house. What had first been noticed was at about ten o'clock there seemed a curious glow when the curtain blew a bit aside at a window. By that time the fire was furious and as the near-est fire-engine was six miles away, nothing could be done.

Friday came. I turned up at Broad Street at about eleven o'clock and I induced Bill to do something—to ring Mrs. Stonhill at the Malfroi Arms. I listened in on an extension wire.

"Oh yes, Mr. Ellice," she said, and quite chirpily. "How are you?"

That took Bill back a bit. He said he was quite well and hoped she was. She said she was.

"Everything all right down there?"

"Absolutely all right."

"And has our friend departed?"

She caught on at once. He'd gone, she said, and the Westmin-ster flat was shut up for three weeks.

"The secretary's gone?"

"Oh yes," she said, and made no bones about mentioning the name. "Deen's having a holiday I'd like to have myself: going round the country as far as Scotland in motor-coaches."

"Sounds attractive," Bill said. "Did you learn all this from our friend?"

"Oh yes," she said. "He came down on Tuesday morning and stayed all day."

That was that, and I'll say this for Bill that he didn't turn to me and use the I-told-you-so reminder.

"That lets us out," he said relievedly, and I couldn't help but think the same. But that morning I did something of which I ought to have been ashamed. Perhaps it was just out of pique because a good theory had gone west, or maybe it was because I hate loose ends. At any rate it occurred to me that we had only Alice Stonhill's word that Peter Wesslake had left for Denmark.

That P.E.N. brochure had said that it was up to members to arrange their own transportation, but it gave a choice of shipping companies. I tried the likelier one which was a stone's throw from Broad Street. It was after lunch when I went there.

"I believe a friend of mine has left for Esbjerg on the boat from Parkeston Quay this morning," I said to the clerk. "He's a Mr. P. Wesslake. Is there any means of checking up?"

He looked up his list. The Wesslake in question had definitely booked by that boat. If I came back in an hour he'd be able to tell me if he had sailed. The boat had already left.

I came back in an hour and he told me that the Mr. Wesslake had definitely been on board. He reminded me that I could get into touch with him by telephone. All I had to do was to ask for a call to him on the *Kronprins Frederik* now between Parkeston and Esbjerg. I allowed that to gratify and astonish, and thanked him warmly and left.

Life went on. A few days slipped by and then I did something else. I was at Broad Street and Bill was out, and so entirely on my own I rang the Malfroi Arms. I'd made it a person to person call and in ten minutes I had Mrs. Stonhill on the end of the line. I had my pipe in my mouth and I lowered the pitch of my voice.

"Good morning, Mrs. Stonhill. I'm ringing on behalf of Mr. Ellice. He's away for a day or two but he asked me to wish you many happy returns of your birthday. I believe it's on Saturday."

"But how perfectly sweet of him!" she said, and her laugh was a little musical ripple. "Thank him very much for me, will you?"

"I certainly will, Mrs. Stonhill. But one other thing he asked me to mention. Whether you had heard anything from . . . pardon me a moment. I've got it written down here . . . Oh yes. Ask Mrs. Stonhill if she's heard anything from our friend."

There was a moment or two before she answered.

"Yes," she said. "Tell him we've heard twice. Just a formal note to say he'd arrived and a rather longer letter this morning."

"Thank you, Mrs. Stonhill. I'll just take that down."

I went through the motions of repeating it and thanked her again and then rang off.

On that same Thursday night Bernice was to make a chance remark that was to change the whole complexion of things. The weather had been none too good for those last days of May, and in rain or drizzle London and a flat are none too pleasant. It was cold enough too, to make one uncomfortable. Yet so warm as to make a fire seem an extravagance.

"This is very boring weather," Bernice suddenly remarked. "I wish we could get away somewhere for a few days. Are you really dreadfully busy?"

I said I was a long way from it. Things were quiet in Bill's office and nothing had turned up at the Yard. I hadn't seen George Wharton for best part of three weeks. And then the idea came. It couldn't help coming.

"What about a few days at the Malfroi Arms?" I said, and you can guess the way I manipulated the conversational pendulum. The telephone number was in my notebook but I made a show of looking it up in the directory. It was Mrs. Laddon, wife of Major Laddon the proprietor, who spoke to me.

"I think—in fact I'm almost sure, Mr. Travers," she told me. "Hold the line just one minute, will you?"

It was sure enough and there was a bedroom on the first floor. The weather had kept visitors away, she said; that, and the lack of petrol. In another fortnight the hotel would be crowded. I said we'd be down on Friday at about tea-time. That was the very next day, and Bernice was at once talking about packing.

In the morning I saw Bill and when I told him about that ten days' holiday—Bernice had thought it had better include two week-ends—he gave me one of his wry looks.

"You needn't worry," I told him. "It's an absolutely unofficial holiday—no snooping, no prying, no nothing. Bernice is taking her knitting and some books and I'm going to play golf, and each Saturday night there's a special dance, not that I dance. Rest and gaiety, that's the programme. Which reminds me. Are you throwing your hand in on that Wesslake job?"

"That's what it'll come to," Bill said. "Palton's still digging away and hoping for a break."

"There you are then," I said. "I'd like Bernice to meet Alice Stonhill. Bernice has a lot of charm, Bill—you know that. I wouldn't be surprised if she got to know the whole Wesslake family. Something might crop up that'd give Pal ton his tip."

I don't say that Bill's reactions would have made an Eskimo shiver, but they weren't too enthusiastic, and I knew he was regarding me as an *enfant terrible*. But he was much more at ease when I left. Nothing should happen, I assured him, that should connect him with the Wesslakes. That was tactful of me. I could have accused him of mental wobbling. Hadn't he given it as his convinced opinion that nothing would happen to Camille Wesslake? Now he was scared stiff that it would and the presence of the insignificant Traverses at the Malfroi Arms would somehow implicate the agency.

I took a bus to Charing Cross and walked along to the Yard. When I enquired about George Wharton, they told me he was up north attending some conference or other. I thought that wasn't too nice of George. If I'm not Johnny-on-the-Spot whenever he happens to want me, his voice and look ooze pain and reproach. But the afternoon post, and just when we were leaving for Winstode, brought a picture-postcard from him to Bernice. He hoped to see us when he got back, he said, but meanwhile he was up to the ears in work. Bernice—I said George was one of her pets—was almost snappy when I said that George always came back from conferences with the red marks of table napkins still round his neck and about him the scent of seven-inch cigars.

PART II
AT THE MALFROI ARMS

CHAPTER 4
SETTLING IN

I'D BEEN a bit precipitate as you may have guessed. That's nothing unusual with me and I've warned you about it already. I believe in the Frenchman's adage that the only virtue in mistakes is to make them quickly. When George Wharton or Bill Ellice asks me a question, I usually give an immediate answer. How I see it is that it's my immediate reactions that they want. Bill is forbearing and long-suffering and takes my hits with the misses, but when a theory of mine explodes, George is always ridiculously exasperated. Once in such a moment he told me with his heavy irony that at a second's notice I could solve the problems of all the ages, and he instanced the *Marie Celeste*, The Man in the Iron Mask, and the larynx of Balaam's ass.

It's half an hour's crawl from King's Cross to Winstode and before we were half way there I knew that a diplomatic minute or two was ahead of me.

"I think we're going to like it at the Malfroi Arms," I said.

"It ought to be lovely," Bernice said. She's a mightily attractive woman, and I ought to know; and though she hadn't yet got that new creation from *Raumur et Cie*, there was about her a look of the most absolute chic. At forty she looks not much over thirty, and she's even-tempered and sympathetic and—well, she has the virtues I've often wished to possess.

"I think you're going to have an especially interesting time," I went on.

"But why me especially, darling?"

"I suppose I ought to have told you," I said, with just a tinge of apology. "But I think you're going to meet a certain young wife of the name of Camille Wesslake."

Her eyes popped open. There was a slight frown, and no more. You see what I meant about even temper? Some women would have flushed, their lips would have clamped together, and then I'd have heard something like this.

"And so that's why you suggested the Malfroi Arms! And all the time I was thinking. . . ."

"You mean the woman Sybil was telling me about?" was what she did say.

"That's the one. She's a grass widow at the moment. Her husband happens to be in Copenhagen for a conference."

There's another excellent thing about Bernice. Don't mistake me. Bernice isn't perfection. She's untidy and she's apt to get flustered at times, but it's not my Pharisaical place to tell you her faults, especially as in our skeleton cupboard most of the bones are mine. But this other excellent thing about her is that when I'm on a job she never asks questions. Mostly those jobs are highly confidential and she takes that for granted. Even on those rare occasions when she also has done a job of work, she has been content to keep herself to the job itself and to know little or nothing of what lay behind it. That was why I could tell her what I wanted her to do, and only, as I truthfully said, because I was sure it was something she would love to do. Alice Stonhill, for instance, she would find both charming and amusing. There might be points of interest about the ex-wife and her reactions to Camille. There was the younger generation as represented by the daughter, Nelda, and David, the son. And I didn't tell Bernice how to do things. I tried to make her feel that it was a job she could do far better than anyone else, and as things turned out, I wasn't to be far wrong.

The hotel car met us at Winstode Station. The Malfroi Arms is just over a mile to the south of the little town and about five minutes' walk from the golf course, and it lies back some hundred yards or so from the London Road. The main building is two-storied and has a special wing for the staff, and there is also quite a large annexe about fifty yards farther along the drive and near the swimming pool. That annexe has the one floor only and it's handy for two sorts of people: the elderly who dislike climbing stairs and the quietly disposed who go to bed early and might be disturbed on dance evenings by the noise of the band in the dance-room of the main building.

The hotel has a farm of some forty acres attached, or should it be the other way about? I don't know which way it is but I do know that the farm makes for plenty of milk and eggs and fresh vegetables and poultry, and hence, one might say, the rather stiff prices. It also has downy beds and comfortable lounges, and most of the things, in wet weather or fine, that one could wish for by way of diversion. There's quite a large swimming pool, as I said, two hard tennis courts, a croquet lawn and a putting green, and all absolutely first class. There's the shade of trees and plenty of comfortable garden chairs, and flower beds everywhere to cheer the eye. Indoors there's a billiard room, a card room, a room for table-tennis and a nursery-room for young children. The bar is a private one but it has a public look, if you know what I mean, with dart board and everything complete. There's a lot of old furniture about and some excellent prints, and the general scent of the place is a decidedly handsome and titillating mixture of pot-pourri and roast beef.

The desk clock said four o'clock when I signed the book and handed in our ration cards. I had a quick look at the entries and saw that James Collinson had arrived on the previous day. The receptionist said that as it was a blustering day and none too warm, tea was in the main lounge. Had it been warm weather it would have been served on the long verandah that occupied the whole of the south-west front. Our bedroom was on the opposite side overlooking the annexe and the swimming pool, and a fine large room it was, with bathroom and lavatory alongside.

We had a quick polish up and then came down for tea, and I had that queer zero-hour feeling that generally comes when one arrives at the scene of some new case. Major Laddon was waiting for us in the hall. He was a little man of about sixty, and neat and precise in speech and manner. I liked him. He was the sort who could make you feel that you were the only people to whom he would offer so kindly a speech of welcome.

"I'm sure we're going to be very comfortable," Bernice told him.

"Anything you want, don't be afraid to ask for it," he told us. "If you think I can do anything, let me know. That's what I'm here for."

"I'd like to fix up a game or two of golf," I said, "but I suppose I ought to apply to the club secretary for that."

"Not at all," he said. "There's a Mr. Collinson staying here—James Collinson, the famous author, you know—and he was mentioning the same thing. I'll see you get together. Here he is, by the way, just coming in."

Collinson was a sandy-haired man who looked just about his forty-two years. He was broad-shouldered and loose-limbed, and as he came towards us I was thinking how curiously jerky his walk was; the walk of a man whose mind is so alert that he doesn't mind how his legs carry him. Laddon hailed him and did the introductions. Collinson had a pleasant voice and a quite nice smile.

"Surely we've read some of Mr. Collinson's books?" Bernice said, and that's always a capital opening gambit.

"Of course we have," I said, "and enjoyed them very much too. The Elizabethan age happens to be a favourite one of mine."

"I'm very glad," he said, and I liked the way he said it. And I wasn't sorry that my own name had conveyed nothing.

"You're staying just for the week-end?" he asked Bernice, and then we somehow found ourselves moving in the direction of what I hoped was tea. I mentioned golf and in a moment we'd fixed up a game for the Monday morning. The course, I gathered, would be hopelessly crowded on the Saturday and Sunday.

The main lounge was a large room and a friendly fire was burning in the open grate. The main hotel, I should have said, has eighteen bedrooms and the annexe six, and if they'd all been occupied there'd still have been room enough in that lounge for all who wanted tea. But now there weren't more than a dozen people in it, and I was glad of that, because the fewer the guests the easier it is to get acquainted. Not that we were going to force our acquaintance on anybody. We were going to be the shy but friendly sort, with the hope that other people would make their own advances.

Collinson gave us a smile, said he'd be seeing us again, and then moved off to a table by the fire. We steered for a table in the far corner where the whole room was under our eyes and where we could talk with no risk of being overheard. Mrs. Laddon came in with our waitress. She was a much bigger woman than her husband; white-haired and smartly dressed in black. She was most friendly too and wanted our likes and dislikes in the matter of food.

"What a charming looking old lady that is by the fire!" Bernice said.

"She really *is* charming," Mrs. Laddon said. "She stays with us quite a lot. A distant relation of my husband, you know."

She moved on through a door that apparently led to the kitchen. Bernice was asking if the very young looking woman was Camille Wesslake. I said I expected she was, and I gave my horn-rims a polish and had a good look at her. There was nothing one could construe as rude about that: from where we sat we looked naturally straight ahead, and that was where the Stonhill table happened to be. And the look showed us the back of James Collinson and the faces of Alice Stonhill and Camille Wesslake in profile.

Camille looked far more mature than her twenty-two years, and she was certainly an extraordinarily good-looking woman. To me she looked the old-fashioned Gibson girl type, but there was nothing old-fashioned about her. From where she sat I couldn't see her make-up, but she had black hair coiled on the top of her head, full lips, a nicely shaped nose, and teeth that showed even and white when she smiled.

"That's a lovely dress she has on," Bernice said. "But, of course, she knows how to wear it."

That was a remark that I'd call feminine.

"Good-looking, don't you think?" I said.

"Very. And she has a nice quiet manner."

Our tea arrived and there we could sit comfortably over it and discuss those three people at that fireside table. Bernice said Alice Stonhill looked most spry and vivacious for a woman of eighty and she also said she still had a lovely complexion. Wrinkles naturally and that slightly yellowish ivory ageing, but still that beautiful peach colour in the cheeks.

"I think she must have taken over the grooming of Camille," she said with a little frown. "It's rather unusual nowadays to wear a formal frock like that at tea. You'd have expected a girl like Camille to wear a skirt and jumper. Something informal. It was different in the older woman's day."

I suppose that was logical enough, and it wasn't my policy to question it. But just then Camille got to her feet, and she was just a bit taller than I'd thought. She was, in fact, just about the same height as her husband—about five feet seven or eight. I didn't tell Bernice so but it seemed to me that she had an uncommonly good figure.

Alice Stonhill remained seated. Collinson had risen too and she was looking up at the pair of them and making some amusing remark, for they both laughed. I had a sudden idea.

"Pretending I'm fetching something," I told Bernice and made my way across the room to the door by which we'd come in. Collinson, as I'd hoped, hailed me. I turned in my tracks and joined him.

"You don't know Mr. Travers," he said to his aunt. "He and his wife are staying for some days. This is my aunt, Mrs. Stonhill, Mr. Travers. My cousin, Mrs. Wesslake."

I gave the usual how-do-you-do's and what I hoped was my best smile. I didn't let my eyes linger on Alice Stonhill though I had seen her quick astonished look. Somewhere, she was telling herself, she had seen me, and at any moment she would remember where.

"Are you down here for long?" I asked Camille Wesslake. She gave a quick look towards the older woman, as if on so simple a question she was not sure of her ground. Alice Stonhill, I somehow felt, was still regarding me.

"A week or two yet," Camille said. It was shyly spoken. The voice was not unpleasing and yet it lacked charm. So pretty a woman should have had a voice to match. Hers—and if you know me, you know that I hate snobbery as much as the devil hates holy water—was a voice that didn't come off a de luxe record. It even had a faint cockney intonation, though maybe there I was wrong.

"Fine," I said. "Mr. Collinson has been good enough to offer to put up with me at golf. I'm hoping that both you and Mrs. Stonhill will be meeting my wife. Mrs. Stonhill may possibly remember her," and I gave her what I hoped was a really charming smile. "At the moment she's only Mrs. Ludovic Travers, but she used to be Bernice Haire, the classical dancer."

"But of course I remember her," Alice Stonhill said. "I saw her in London and I believe I saw her in Nice. Wasn't her partner a Brazilian?"

"Carlo Manchez," I said. "He's dead now, poor chap. A first-rate man and an admirable partner."

"Then I simply must meet your wife," she said. "I'm quite excited at the thought of it."

I gave my diffident smile and said that it was nice of her to say so, and I hoped we'd all be meeting again. Then I went upstairs and down again, and so back to Bernice.

"Darling, you shouldn't!" she told me when I'd mentioned the talk at the fire-side table.

"I think I was right," I insisted. "This is a tough world. You can't always be loved for yourself alone."

"But I'm now a thoroughly domesticated person," she said. "It won't be in keeping. I shall look positively dowdy."

I said the usual things and then it was time to make a move. Collinson and Camille had gone for a walk, as we were to be told, but Alice Stonhill was still at her table, and now reading a book. I presented Bernice.

"My dear, you must stay here and talk to me," Alice told her, "I insist on it. When your husband told me who you were, it was almost a shock. A pleasant shock, of course, though just a little nostalgic. It's not true, you know, that people of my age live on nothing but memories. Which reminds me. I'm sure that somewhere or other I've met your husband too."

"That's queer," I said. "I seemed also to remember you."

Our eyes met and somehow I knew that she'd remembered and that she was wondering if I would remember too, and that she wished I wouldn't remember.

"The world's a small place," I said sententiously, and added that I'd leave Bernice with her.

"James and my niece-in-law have gone for a walk," she said. "Or they may have gone to the golf course. He's teaching her golf, you know."

"And you hardly know whether to approve or disapprove?" I asked roguishly.

There was a quick, apprehensive look, then she smiled.

"How did you know?"

"I didn't," I said. "I was actually being what I know now is unpardonably rude and sending you back to the age of Mrs. Henry Wood. Or should it be Mrs. Braddon?"

"Perhaps you're right," she said. "I still have a certain prejudice against women playing what I regard as men's games. Which is hopelessly antiquated of me."

"Not a bit of it," I said. "Though I love driving a car I often wish the internal combustion engine had never been invented."

"Yes," she said slowly, and frowned. "Nothing now seems so musical as the clatter of horses' hoofs on a London street." Then she shook her head. "But Mrs. Travers, I'm sure, is much more sensible. Sit here, my dear, and if you have any knitting or sewing, for heaven's sake fetch it. Nothing like doing something while you talk. It gives what I might call a gracious inconsequence."

"As a matter of fact I'm knitting my husband yet another pullover," Bernice said. "Ludovic, darling, you might fetch it for me, will you?"

I fetched it. Talk was in full spate, and I just gave a smile as I deposited it on the table. Then I put on a hat and coat and made my way towards the golf course, and behind me I knew that everything was in uncommonly good hands.

The secretary's office was closed and the professional was somewhere on the course. I walked over a few holes but saw no sign of Collinson and Camille Wesslake. Then it began to rain and I made my way back. I was in time to see two new arrivals by the hotel car: a youngish married couple and an elderly looking man who seemed to have trouble with his eyes, at least he walked what I might call tentatively, and with a stick, and was wearing dark glasses.

When I came downstairs the desk was momentarily deserted and I had a look at the book. The couple had registered as Major and Mrs. Pew of Banbury. The elderly man was H. T. Ferotti of London, and in spite of the name he was down as British, and from my bedroom window I had seen the porter escorting him to the annexe. As I moved away from the desk, Laddon came along.

"More guests?" I said.

"Only yourselves and one other couple," he said. "There's also a Mr. Ferotti who's staying for the weekend. He's leaving on Sunday night or very early on Monday morning."

We talked for a minute or two and then I went on to the lounge. Bernice's needles were clicking and Alice Stonhill was embroidering what looked to me like a table-mat. I had a good reception and Bernice insisted that I should look at the embroidery. It was really exquisite.

"Just something to do," Alice Stonhill said off-handedly, and then Bernice was saying there were things she had to do upstairs.

"Then leave your husband with me," Alice told her, and with never a touch of archness. "He struck me as being very intelligent and it's never too old to improve one's mind."

Bernice left us. I took the easy chair and stretched my long legs, and was trying to concoct some charmingly flippant opening. But it was she who spoke, and her tone had no trace of flippancy. It was quiet and direct.

"Mr. Travers, I've remembered where I saw you last. I think perhaps you've remembered too."

"Yes," I said. "I think I have. It was in a detective agency. I'd an appointment there and I was in your way in the corridor."

"I'm going to ask you an unpardonably rude question," she said. "Your business had nothing to do with your wife?"

I looked suitably astounded. Then I smiled.

"I assure you, Mrs. Stonhill, that there isn't a man more happily married than myself. My business was about a young nephew who happens to be having domestic trouble. I was only a kind of go-between and peace-maker."

"I'm glad to hear it," she said. "About your wife, I mean. You have a very delightful wife, Mr. Travers. Unaffected and unspoilt, and wholly charming."

"Yes," I said. "I think I have. But about your own business, Mrs. Stonhill. Believe me when I say that I'm not in the least inquisitive. All I will say is that the very little I've already been fortunate to see of you tells me that you had good reason for going to Broad Street. May we leave it like that?"

"That's considerate of you," she said. "And may I ask that you forget that you saw me there? Or have you mentioned it to your wife?"

"But I didn't see my wife," I pointed out. "I remembered the circumstances just as I was coming back just now to the hotel. And I can assure you that I'd never dream of telling her. After all, I have a secret too. She knows nothing whatever about that nephew business."

Most admirable lying, as you've observed, and every word of it near enough to the truth. She seemed grateful.

"Then we'll both share the secret that we have a secret," she told me with what she meant to be an intimate kind of roguishness. "But you were very frank with me and I'm grateful for it, and I'll be frank with you because we have this secret. I also was being what you called a go-between and a peace-maker."

That was all, for James Collinson and Camille Wesslake were coming in. There was something in the way that she smiled when he held open the door for her that made my fingers go suddenly to my glasses, and to the other Wesslake complications I knew there was suddenly added yet one more. There was no mistaking it, from the way he smiled back and the way his fingers held her own for just a quick moment. Then as they came towards the table they were what they seemed and no more.

I had a word or two and then went up to change. And I felt just a bit deflated when Bernice wasn't surprised at the news that James Collinson and Camille Wesslake were in love with each other.

We dressed for dinner—I'd found out beforehand that that was done—and I ought to say that the meal was so good that it would have been almost *lèse-majesté* to have eaten it without a wedding garment. The only man who hadn't dressed was Ferotti, and he was wearing a dark lounge suit. Not that he didn't look distinguished enough in a foreign sort of way, with his hooked nose, dark hair grey at the temples and his closely cut beard that began well below the ears and curved round chin and mouth.

He was at a corner table by himself and with his back to us, and I suppose there were twenty of us altogether. There was a good fire and everything was decorous but friendly, with people smiling a good-evening at us as we passed their table and we doing the same to them, which was all as it should be. Not that we weren't rather a mixed lot, even if Aneurin would probably have labelled us all as vermin. There was a pear-shaped dowager, for instance, Pekingese and all complete, and a bibulous-looking gentleman who kept snapping his eyes as if wondering what the devil he was doing in that particular galley. There were two spoilt children who, at one word of reprimand from their parents, behaved much worse than before. There was a very chatty table of six, and of course, the Wesslake table of three, with Alice Stonhill talking vivaciously and gesturing with little fluttering motions of her hands. There were the couple who had arrived that evening, and another couple almost certainly on their honeymoon, and, of course, there were the two Traverses, no longer able to be shy and retiring in a corner seat, but placed at a table almost plumb in the centre of the room.

Coffee was in the lounge and there we retired when the meal was over. We were wondering where to park ourselves when Camille came over and asked if we wouldn't have coffee with the Wesslake trio, so we joined them at a really cosy niche not too remote from the fire. I contributed to the gaiety by insisting on brandies. Alice Stonhill asked if she might have kümmel. She was wearing two marvellous rings that night, one of three large diamonds and the other a square-cut emerald. I thought that either would have fetched a thousand at Christie's. Camille was wearing a fine, if rather old-fashioned, diamond and ruby bracelet, and afterwards I learned it had been a present from her aunt. All I knew was that it went well with her scarlet gown, just as the gown itself so admirably suited her dark hair.

Collinson suggested a game of rummy and a waitress brought us a card table where we sat, which would be much more informal than the card-room. It was quite good fun and I scooped the pool for a total of one and sevenpence. Then Collinson reported that it had stopped raining and he and Camille and Bernice went for a short stroll round the grounds before we turned in.

"We've had a lovely evening," Alice Stonhill told me. "It's almost resigned me to tomorrow."

"Even I begin to regard birthdays somewhat mournfully," I said truthfully.

"But I'm not mournful," she said. "It's the fuss and the bother, if you know what I mean. But there, I'm just a silly old woman. I ought to have crawled into a corner and had my birthday all alone, and then reappeared, restored to normality."

"Like a chrysalis," I said. "Or would it be a butterfly? At any rate, good for another twenty years."

"I don't want twenty years," she told me. "I've had a good life. No children, perhaps, but that's my only regret."

"Isn't Camille rather like a child?" I said, and I admit it was something of a silly remark. But she didn't appear to think it so. In fact, she actually began telling me quite a deal about Camille; how to have her was in some ways like having a daughter. Camille wasn't of what one called good family, but she was genuine and sincere, and just as a mother brings up a daughter from childhood, so she was bringing up Camille from that paradoxical childhood that had begun with marriage and an entry into a wholly new life.

"I hope she'll live to profit by it, and be grateful," I said sententiously.

"I know she will," she said. "She's greatly improved already, and most grateful, though gratitude's not what I wish. I know she's very fond of me, and that's much more."

"As you're fond of her."

"Yes," she said, and nodded to herself, and there was my chance to have introduced the subject of Camille's husband.

But the others came back then and the opportunity was missed; not that I was worrying, for I knew there'd be chances enough.

"We just walked round the swimming-pool and on to the main road and back," Camille told us.

"And did that swimming-pool look cold!" Collinson said.

"I thought swimming by moonlight was great fun," I said.

"Well, I've a bathing costume I can lend you," he told me. And what should Alice Stonhill do but take him seriously.

"James," she told him severely, "you'll do no such thing. I won't have Mr. Travers risking pneumonia on a night like this."

I thanked her gravely, and then Bernice had to cut in with some quip or other to my derogation and on Collinson's behalf. It made a foolish but pleasant moment before we went up to bed. The following night was not to be nearly so foolish.

Chapter 5
EIGHTIETH BIRTHDAY

I'M A QUICK dresser but Bernice takes her time, especially when on holidays. Breakfast was from eight o'clock till half-past nine, which meant that the fashionable time was as near nine o'clock as makes no difference; at least, so Bernice argued. I was clad and in my usual inquisitive state of mind by eight, so down I went for a breath of air before the meal.

I had never had a good look round the hotel grounds, and it was just as well that I decided that morning to have a thorough exploration. It was a grand morning and the night porter told me that the weather forecast had been good, and altogether I was on top of the world. I could admire the huge wistaria that ran along the hotel front, even if most of its blooms had faded to a dirty grey. I could nod commendingly at the cunning way the low annexe had been made to fit its surroundings. Then the swimming-pool surprised me, even if I could get a bird's-eye view of it from my bedroom, for it was much more sheltered than I had thought. All round it were thick hornbeam hedges through which entry arches had been trained, and here and there the hedges were recessed to admit garden seats, some of which were shaded by some really magnificent elms. Here and there were hydrangeas in tubs, and the diving platform was gaily painted, and altogether it was a really attractive and secluded place. Then beyond it and the annexe were two acres of woods, large oaks mostly, and not too much undergrowth. Through the wood went a main circular path that curved round to the main road and so to the hotel again, but it was a natural path that would be mighty sticky on a wet day. I stepped from dry spot to dry spot, and I saw that beyond the wood the immense kitchen gardens began, and after those were the farm fields, the nearest being a meadow in which were four Jerseys.

On a seat by the hard tennis courts I smoked a cigarette and lingered out my time, though when I got back to the hotel well before nine o'clock, Bernice pretended perversely to have been waiting for me. The Wesslakes had had breakfast and maybe it was that that had put her off her stroke. Not that we had a frigid meal. It was a good meal and full of all sorts of anticipations and schemes. I said we ought to hang around and watch the arrival of the other Wesslake trio, and since a vantage point was the putting green, I borrowed Collinson's putter for Bernice and at eleven o'clock she and I were ostensibly amusing ourselves. We were only just in time. A big and rather old-fashioned Daimler drew up at the front door. A chauffeur in cerise livery nipped out and opened the door. James Collinson and Alice Stonhill appeared as by magic. Drina Wesslake—or Drina Farman as she now called herself—stepped straight into smiles and handshakes.

Let me own at once that if there is a Parker more frenziedly nosey than myself, I have yet to meet him. I whispered to Bernice to disappear and I took up a position of vantage behind a large clipped holly. But let me state at once that all I saw and surmised at that inquisitive moment is far less than I tell you now. The thumbnail sketches of those three important people were filled in from later acquaintance and dissection, but it seems convenient to give them as a kind of first impression.

Drina Farman was tallish, elegant and with a hard, aggressive voice that seemed to come from quite a way down. She was dark-haired and wearing a black and white check costume that had *Raumur et Cie* all over it, and her hat was one of those weird contraptions that seems to have been acquired solely for the purpose of making other women speechlessly jealous. She must have been about forty-five, and she looked all of it, but in her younger days when her face was less hard, she must have been a good-looking woman in a statuesque sort of way.

Nelda, the daughter, was slim, blonde, the kind that pecks at food to preserve the figure. Her nails were coloured and she was wearing some kind of sandal or toeless shoe that showed her painted toe-nails, and her lips were a scarlet rosebud. She wriggled her body a bit and seemed to me to be oozing a deal of sex. She had a high-pitched laugh, and yet for all the up-to-the-minute womanliness, she seemed to be much of a child, and probably a spoilt one at that. The last I saw of her was when she took Collinson's arm as they walked into the hotel.

David was a surprise. I knew he was an art student but I wasn't prepared to have the fact so violently thrust upon me. He had his father's hair but very much more of it, and he wore it brushed back from the forehead as his father did, but still with a difference, for it was clipped across at the neck to give him the look of a pianist or composer—until you noticed that his fair hair was also allowed to grow a good three inches below the ears, so that if his face hadn't been rather sallow, he'd have looked like a stage Spaniard. He was good-looking, also like his father, but whereas Peter Wesslake had been of the hearty type, the son seemed to regard life with a certain cynicism or even boredom—at least, so I judged from the pouting irony of his lips as he watched his mother and Nelda greet Collinson and Alice Stonhill, and the languid, off-hand way he himself greeted Collinson. But he smiled most charmingly at his great-aunt, even if he did seem to be patting her shoulder in a way that had patronage mingled with the affection.

The five disappeared into the hotel. I turned back to the putting green and Bernice reappeared from nowhere. I wondered aloud where Camille could be and whether it had really been tactful to exclude her from the arrival scene.

"I think we can leave that to Mrs. Stonhill," Bernice told me. "Surely you know enough about her to feel that she'll have had all this organised to the very last detail. She'll produce Camille at the exact moment."

"I expect you're right," I said. "The trouble is that I shan't be there to witness it."

"People are sensible nowadays," she reminded me. "After all, an ex-wife needn't feel crushed. It was she who divorced Wesslake. It's Camille I'm sorry for."

I said once more that she was probably right and, knowing just how little Bernice knew, the last thing I wanted was to argue the point. She couldn't even begin to guess that Drina had tried to bribe a new divorce, and I know she'd have been disturbed or even scared if she'd heard what Alice Stonhill had told Bill Ellice.

So we finished our putting and then I suggested mid-morning coffee. One or two people were already having it on the verandah and Ferotti was one, and he actually spoke to me when we went by his table.

"It is an excellent morning," he said, and there was something decidedly Italian about his intonation.

I agreed, and Bernice gave him a smile. We ordered coffee, and just as it came, in trooped the five Wesslakes. I let them get settled and then we left our table and went over to theirs.

"I hope we don't intrude," Bernice said, and she was speaking to Alice Stonhill, "but may my husband and I give our very best wishes."

I mumbled some addition or other and Alice Stonhill was saying it was most sweet of us both. Then she introduced us to the three newcomers. Drina was gracious, Nelda was very friendly, and David called me sir, even if he still kept that irritatingly ironic smile. I said we wouldn't intrude another moment, but I did manage to look as if I missed someone.

"Camille's lunching with some friends in Winstode," Alice told me sweetly. "She'll be with us all for dinner tonight."

We said happy birthday again and went back to our table. Bernice was a bit cock-a-hoop.

"I told you she'd do it," she said, and referring to Alice Stonhill. "Camille's been smuggled out of the way and won't appear till the official birthday dinner tonight."

"But where's the point?" I said. "Those two women have to meet some time or other. People can't stay in the same hotel as members of the same family and perpetually be doing what you call smuggling acts?"

"But Drina isn't staying after tonight."

"You didn't tell me that."

"Darling, I did. It was just before you went to sleep."

"Tell me again," I said. "I probably *was* asleep."

"There's nothing to tell," she said. "Drina's going back to her home some time tomorrow morning and the two children are staying on for at least a week."

I gave a grunt but made no comment. What I was thinking was that I might have to work fast.

In the afternoon we went for a walk as far as Winstode and had tea there. We walked home by a roundabout way and it was almost time to dress when we got back to the hotel. Each Saturday night, as you may remember, there was a dance from nine o'clock to midnight, and a few people—carefully selected, I imagine—would come in from the neighbourhood and have dinner and dance. Dinner was at seven prompt since the dining-room was also the ball-room and would have to be got ready after the meal. We were in on time and found the dining-room almost full. The Wesslake table was now a special one with a huge bowl of roses in the middle. Alice was at the head and facing her was Collinson. Camille was on his right and Drina on Alice's right. David was opposite his mother, and that left Nelda facing Camille. Camille was wearing a black gown with a lot of red trimmings, and round her neck was a sort of pendant with a ruby and diamond centre. I have to be vague because I saw only the flash of it in the light as I passed. Nor do I know what went on at the Wesslake table beyond what I could guess from occasional bursts of laughter, for Bernice said it was her turn to sit facing that table.

I do know that there was a special menu. Laddon must have had a considerable affection for Alice Stonhill—I didn't judge him the sort that would try a flagrant ingratiation—and at the end of the main course there was a little ceremony. I know that Alice Stonhill wasn't expecting it, and I certainly was not, but in came the champagne and Major Laddon with it.

"Ladies and gentlemen, I'd like you to drink to the health of a very charming lady. She's still a very young lady even if today—I know she won't mind my revealing it—is her eightieth birthday. I wish, and I'm sure we all wish, that we shall be here again on an even greater occasion, in twenty years' time. Ladies and gentlemen, will you see that your glasses are charged, and drink to the health and happiness of Mrs. Stonhill."

There was almost a babel as the healths were called. Then there was another surprise. Immediately the folding doors were back. The dance band had come especially early and they broke into "Happy Birthday." We joined lustily in, and it was followed by, "For she's a jolly good fellow." We sat down, the doors were folded to, and somebody bleated out, "Speech!" One or two others took it up.

I swivelled round in my seat as Alice Stonhill got to her feet. She was as poised as if she were going to open a bazaar, but there was nothing unnatural about the charm of her smile.

"Thank you, Major Laddon," she said quietly, "and thank you, all of you. But why all this fuss should be made about an old woman, I don't know, because my conscience is warning me that I've done nothing to deserve it. So perhaps you'll permit me, on this special day, the privilege of returning the compliment. Ladies and gentle-men, may I too wish you all that same health and happiness."

She gave a little bow and a smile and sipped at her glass. The applause was deafening as she sat down. Collinson was all smiles and giving her a gentle congratulatory pat. Bernice dabbed at her eyes and I thought she was going to cry, and certainly there'd been in that little ceremony—badly though I've described it—the kind of natural simplicity which, especially if one happens to be in a senti-mental mood, lies so often at the basis of tears. In that moment too, I felt a quick urge of affection for Alice Stonhill. Even in her poise and the dignity with which she had held herself, there had been a kind of frailty, and in the quiet, clear voice there had been even for me nostalgic memories of some vague Victorian or Edwardian past.

After the meal we made our way outside. Coffee had been in the dining-room and as we passed the Wesslake table, people were crowding round it to offer personal congratulations. It was a fine night though overcast. The moonlight—a capital thing at a dance, or so I seemed to recall—would be none too good, but there seemed no likelihood of rain. Garden seats had been brought out beneath the wistaria and Bernice and I sat there and watched the ebb and flow of guests. I wondered if Alice Stonhill would be at the dance. Bernice said she thought she could find out. I found my cigarette case empty and went upstairs to replenish it.

That was how I came to hear the extract from a family quarrel. It was when I was coming back and along the corridor towards the head of the stairs. The voices were coming from what I soon found out was David Wesslake's room.

"I think it's disgusting. It's worse than that—it's revolting!" That was Nelda Wesslake. "And if you're going to spend the week making goo-goo eyes at that woman, there's going to be a first-class row."

"Oh?" The voice had a drawling contempt. "And who's going to make this—what you call—row?"

"That's my business. Perhaps Aunt Alice. You wouldn't like that, would you?"

"My dear, it's a matter of supreme indifference. In the first place I have no intention of making what you so wittily called goo-goo eyes. I think that was the expression. Besides—"

"You make me sick." The voice aped his drawl but it had venom in it. "To hell with you!"

I moved quickly on and it was as well that I did for I heard a door slam behind me. As I went down the stairs I was feeling a bit cynical too. If there was anything in what I had heard, it was that David Wesslake, in the opinion of his sister, was making an exhibition of himself over Camille. Not that that was any great business of mine; all it did was to add to the complications.

There was plenty of room to dance. There was even space enough for small tables and chairs at each end. Alice Stonhill had a comfortable special chair and Collinson was with her a lot of the time. Bernice and I were there also and by special request, and Drina sat out a dance or two with us. Collinson and I were in agreement with Alice Stonhill—die-hards all—that modern dancing is a mournful business compared with what we were pleased to consider the old. Bent-backed men with vacuous expressions hold trance-like women, and the couples shuffle wearily with hesitating steps as if the whole thing were a penance to be grimly performed. Now in my young days—

But you don't want to hear about that. What I'll say is that my function at that dance was to try to give a little gaiety by being the producer of iced lemonade and long drinks. But Bernice loved it all, as did the younger generation. Camille was always dancing, and maybe because it kept her from too close or dangerous a contact with Drina. Collinson did have a dance or two and Drina Wesslake danced most of the time, but a goodish bit of the evening I was alone with Alice Stonhill.

"Now this is a waltz," she said to me once. "Why don't you have it with your wife? Dance it in the old way."

"For one thing," I told her, "I'm a menace on any dance floor. And if we did try the old way we'd be too conspicuous."

"I wish you would," she said. "I can watch, or read my book."

"What *is* the book?"

"That's a secret," she said.

"But haven't you and I agreed that we've no secrets from each other?"

"But this is a realty dangerous secret. It might even make you laugh at me."

"So it *is* Mrs. Henry Wood!"

"Oh no. Not Mrs. Henry Wood."

Then suddenly she gave a mischievous little smile. She lifted the evening wrap and showed me the cover of a book.

"*The Case of the Laughing Lady*," I read, and my eyebrows lifted reprovingly. "So that's the secret. You're a detective novel fan."

"And an unashamed one." She gave me a determined nod at that. "I simply love them. My husband did too."

"Yes," I said. "And didn't someone tell me that Mr. Collinson writes them—you know, as a sort of relaxation?"

Nelda and Drina came back. I told them to go away and dance again because we were talking scandal. They took it as amusing and left us to it, and in the very strictest confidence I was told about the Colin Lake books and about Peter Wesslake. Unhappily there was nothing that I didn't already know.

It was about ten o'clock and we had been unaware of the movement around us as other than a background. People danced and they went in and out. Doubtless they sat out dances in the grounds, but who went out and who came in I had no idea. Sometimes I'd glance around and catch sight of Bernice, maybe, or one of the Wesslakes, but if they hadn't been there I wouldn't have known because of the movement itself. But I did see a waiter making for Collinson. Collinson apologised to his partner and the waiter seemed to be speaking confidentially. A look of concern was on Collinson's face. He was passing our table and I got to my feet.

"Anything the matter?"

He frowned, glanced at Alice Stonhill, then decided to speak.

"It's Camille. She's had a slight accident."

It could have been little more than a quick glance that Alice gave him, but in the tenseness of the moment it seemed to me like a long, level look. Then she picked up her wrap. I draped it over her shoulders and we went out to the hall.

"Where is she?" Alice said.

"In her room. Mrs. Laddon and David are with her."

"What happened?"

"I don't know," he said. "But we ought to go and see."

There had been an impatience in his voice and we went up the stairs. The door of Camille's room was ajar and they must have heard us, for Mrs. Laddon came out. There was a cough behind us, and I turned to see another man at our heels—a shortish man whom I'd seen dancing.

"There you are, doctor," Mrs. Laddon said, and drew back to let him go through. Then she was asking us to wait. A minute, and David Wesslake came out. Alice Stonhill and Collinson began questioning him together.

"I don't know what happened," he told them, and was gesturing bewilderedly. "All I know is I'd been dancing and then I went out to get some air and I thought I saw someone like Camille going towards the pool. Then I thought it couldn't be and then—well, I thought it might be, so I went that way myself. When I got near the pool I couldn't see anyone at all and then I thought I heard a noise so I went through and there she was, lying right on the edge of the pool. Then I thought I heard someone moving away, and I didn't know what the devil to do, it all happened so quick. Then I picked her up and brought her in here. Mrs. Laddon happened to see us and she took over and sent for you, James, and the doctor."

"Yes, but what happened?" Collinson was firing at him.

"Good God! how do I know?" David told him angrily. "The light was bad for one thing. I didn't even see her lying there at first. I just saw something and then I saw it was Camille."

"Is she badly hurt?" Alice asked him.

"I don't know. I do know one thing, though. That pendant she was wearing has gone. So's her bracelet."

Collinson and Alice Stonhill looked at each other. Alice gave a sigh. There seemed a sudden relaxation of the tension.

"What was that noise like?" Collinson asked, and much more quietly. "You know, when you heard something moving away."

"Just a sound." He frowned. "Like feet. Someone moving away quickly."

"It was quite dark?"

"I just told you so. It was a changing sort of light. One minute it'd be a dim sort of moonlight and then it'd be almost dark. The clouds kept going across the moon."

The doctor came out with Mrs. Laddon, who beckoned Alice in.

"How is she, doctor?" David was asking.

"She'll be all right," the doctor told him. "A nasty blow on the back of the skull but nothing fractured. You carried her in, didn't you?"

David told him what had happened and in a moment there was a kind of quick conference. The attacker, it seemed, had been after her jewellery and had followed her to the pool. As David hadn't heard him, he'd guessed which way she was going and had nipped across the putting green. Probably he'd emerged from one of the hedge archways, stunned her, and then dragged or carried her through to the seclusion of the pool surround. There he'd taken the jewellery and David had heard him slipping away. When Camille was well enough for questioning, we'd know a good deal more.

Collinson was looking a bit restless. Something seemed to be at the tip of his tongue. He gave a quick shake of the head, and I knew the question he asked was not the one that had been in his mind.

"How is she, doctor?"

"No great harm done. She'll be all right in the morning. Better stay in bed for a day or two. It's the shock that counts in these cases. I'd rather she wasn't questioned tonight."

I went down with the doctor if only because it might have been too pointed to have stayed. Then I went back to my old seat in the dance room and nobody seemed aware of anything. Bernice and Drina came over at the end of the dance.

"Aunt Alice hasn't gone?" Drina asked me, and as if I'd been guilty of some spiriting away.

"Just temporarily," I said mendaciously. "Can I get you a drink?"

"Not at the moment," she told me, and her eyes were going round the room. Bernice refused one too, and then two men came up to claim them, and I was alone again. But only for a minute. Alice Stonhill came back.

"You're not to scold me," she said. "I said I would stay till eleven o'clock, and I'm determined to."

"The patient all right?"

"The doctor's given a draught," she said, and then there was a slight disturbance in the room. The bibulous gentleman was trying to make his way out but his legs were betraying him and he staggered into a couple and rebounded into another, and he was trying to apologise, and his speech was a bit thick.

One man was soothing him and beginning to lead him persuasively towards the door. Ferotti had come forward as if from nowhere, but went back to his seat when he saw the situation well in hand.

"What a horrible man!" Alice whispered as the bibulous one was steered by our table. "I shall really have to speak to Major Laddon."

The last word had trailed away, though it was only afterwards that I remembered that.

"My God—no!"

That was what she'd said, and though it seemed like a full minute, it must have flashed to my brain as quickly as she said it. And it had been only a whisper, spoken to herself. Her lips were still parted as I looked at her.

"Anything the matter?"

Her hands trembled, then she forced herself to smile.

"Nothing at all. Nothing. . . . I was just thinking about Camille."

"Don't you really think you ought to go to bed?"

I asked her gently. "It has been an exciting and trying day, you know. We're none of us so young as we were."

She slowly shook her head, and then suddenly was on her feet.

"I think I will, after all. . . . Please don't come. I prefer to manage by myself."

I was putting the wrap round her shoulders again, and I stared at her back, for the remark had been abrupt to the point of rudeness. But she gave me a smile of thanks as I held open the door and then I watched her go up the stairs. But the poise wasn't back again. Her hand was on the rail and she was moving like a woman both very old and very tired.

On a sudden impulse I went outside. The clouds were low and a thin moon was shining somewhere behind. But there was something I felt an urge to verify. The light was much the same as it had been when David Wesslake had caught sight of Camille, and he must have lost sight of her, as he said, almost as soon as he had thought he had recognised her. So I went the way the thief had presumably gone: across the bowling green, along the back of the tennis courts and so to the far side of the swimming pool. The concrete surround was clear, in spite of the comparative darkness of hedge and trees, and I went through the nearest arch. I struck a match or two and looked at the concrete surround again where David had said he had found Camille lying, but its hardness had left no trace of dragging.

What did I expect to find? Perhaps I hardly knew, for it had been based on something else that was far from certain—why Alice Stonhill herself had been so suddenly perturbed. And the next morning's events were to prove even that particle of certainty to be utterly wrong.

CHAPTER 6
THINGS STILL HAPPEN

EVERYTHING COMES, as they say, to him who waits. It was my policy not to intrude, for sooner or later I should know everything that was happening, and I should know it from Collinson or David Wesslake, or even Alice Stonhill herself. I even said nothing to Bernice. When we went up to bed at half-past twelve, she was what I might call tired and happy. I pretended to be tired too, though I was still wide awake an hour later, and that was when the scream came. It was a strange, squeaky sort of scream. Then it was repeated, and it was shrill.

Believe it or not, but Bernice didn't wake. I was out of bed and into the corridor and round the bend in a matter of seconds, and I hadn't even grabbed a dressing-gown though some instinct had made me grab my glasses. Doors were opening. At her door stood Alice Stonhill, clutching her night-gown about her.

"A man! There was a man in my room!"

Her face was contorted and the voice was like a querulous shriek, and cracking as if her old larynx couldn't stand the strain. As I ran near her, I saw her begin to sag, and my arms just caught her as she fell.

The light was on and I laid her on her bed, and then almost at once the room was crowded. Voices were babbling and Drina Farman was trying to take charge. Laddon's voice was heard. I drew back and had a look at the open window. That was how the intruder had left, and I looked out. The moon was still as uncertain but there were the long branches of that ancient wistaria making as perfect a ladder as a thief could wish.

I slipped unobtrusively from the room and went back for a dressing-gown. When I returned, the room was empty but for Laddon and his wife and Drina.

"Just a faint," Mrs. Laddon whispered. "Poor darling, she'd had a trying day. And this dreadful business coming on top of everything."

"Anything missing?" I whispered to Laddon.

"Not a thing. I've checked up and her jewellery and her bag are still here."

Drina held the smelling salts beneath the nose again. She looked almost gaunt and certainly much older in her dressing-gown. She drew back and almost at once Alice Stonhill's eyelids fluttered. Her eyes opened and she blinked. A minute and she was aware of us. Drina bent over her.

"There, darling, it's all right."

Alice struggled as if she wanted to sit up.

"No, darling, just lie quiet."

"I don't want to lie quiet," the older woman told her.

And then suddenly she *was* sitting up.

"My jewellery! Did he get it?"

"Everything's all right," Laddon told her gently. "Everything you were wearing is still here."

She let out a breath. She even let Drina ease her down in the bed again. I nodded to Laddon and we went out.

"I don't think I'd question her tonight," I told him. "Put a camp bed in the room and let someone sleep there with her."

"I doubt if she'd have it," he said. "Mrs. Stonhill can be a very obstinate woman. If the window's shut and the door left open she should be all right." Then he was shaking his head. "An extraordinary business. Most unsettling. We've been here all the time and never had anything happen like it. It gives the place a bad name."

I said that all the same he'd better report at once to the police. In the morning they could try the room for prints and examine that wistaria. Then I went back to bed.

What I had in mind was to examine that wistaria for myself before any of the staff were up, and it was thinking of that that made me sleep so restlessly. I wanted to be up at the crack of dawn, and the consequence was that at every half-hour or so I was waking and looking at my watch. The last time I woke I could hear birds beginning to twitter, so I got out of bed and took a peep out of the window. It was getting nicely light and I was just about to slip on a dressing-gown when I saw something moving. A man was coming past the annexe towards the swimming pool, and he too was wearing a dressing-gown, and he had on white tennis shoes. As he went through the arch of the hedge, I knew he was James Collinson.

I drew back to the side of the window and watched him, and there flashed through my mind that chance remark of the Friday night. Collinson had said that the mere look of the water was enough to make one shiver. And there'd been no sun since then and that water would still be like ice, and yet, and at an unearthly morning hour, he was evidently about to have a swim. But he didn't go in at once. He looked up at the hotel windows as if with a fear of being seen, and then he had a quick look at one of the garden seats, and I knew that he too was wondering how Camille could have got to the edge of that swimming-pool.

Then all at once he slipped off his dressing-gown. He didn't dive in as one might have expected, but slithered in. He was below water, and in a second I was expecting him to reappear, and spluttering a bit and shaking his head and rubbing the water out of his eyes. But he didn't. To me it seemed a long minute before his head came up and when it did it was a goodish distance away from where he'd first gone under, and almost half the length of the pool from where Camille had been lying when David Wesslake had found her.

Almost at once Collinson was under again, and again it seemed a minute before he reappeared. A third time he went under, and a fourth, and he seemed to be working his way along the side that lay by the main clipped entrance arches. But the fifth time he was under for only a second or two. He drew in to the side and his hands went to the stone surround as if to draw himself up. Then he changed his mind, and swam back to where he had left the dressing-gown and shoes. Standing on the very edge of the pool he slipped off his shorts and wrung them out, and with them gave himself a quick wipe down. Then he put on the dressing-gown and the shoes, and with another quick look at the hotel windows, made his way through the arch again and in a moment or two I had lost sight of him.

Very quietly and thoughtfully I got back into bed. What I had just seen seemed to me of tremendous moment. Collinson had been looking for something at the bottom of that pool, and he had been looking for it stealthily. And, whatever it was, he had found it. When he had left the water he had taken a something from *inside* his bathing shorts and had slipped it so quickly into the pocket of the dressing-gown that I'd never had a chance to see what it was. As for the stealthiness—well, there was the hour of the morning, for one thing, and there was that business of swimming all the way back to where the shoes and the dressing-gown had been left. In other words he hadn't wanted to let wet footmarks reveal that someone had been in the pool, and that too was why he had wiped the superfluous water from himself with the bathing shorts.

As for what he had been looking for and what he had found, there seemed to me to be only one answer—the jewellery of which Camille was supposed to have been robbed. What then had Collinson suspected? One possible thing only, it seemed to me— that that story of David Wesslake's was a fake. It was he who had struck her. He had even tried to drown her, but had been in some way disturbed when he had dragged the body to the edge of the pool, and at the deep end. But he had already thrown both bracelet and pendant into the water to bolster up the story he had planned to tell. At some time or other he also planned to recover the jewel- lery, and now Collinson had forestalled him.

And there was one way I could test that story. If I abandoned my idea of examining that wistaria, I could sit at the window and read and smoke and watch for the appearance of David Wesslake. For he too would have to be early at that pool. At any moment he might be there, and with that I quietly drew up a chair, found the previous day's paper with its crossword I'd had no time to solve, lighted a cigarette and settled down to watch.

For two hours I sat there and never a thing happened. Then Bernice stirred so I quickly moved back the chair, yawned artisti- cally and made play with drawing the curtains.

"What's the time, darling?" came the muffled voice from under the sheets.

"Half-past seven," I said.

"Heaps of time before we need get up. . . . Besides, it's Sunday."

"You lie on," I said. "I feel like getting up. Don't worry about my early tea. I'll have a cup downstairs." By pure chance I looked out of the window again.

"Good lord!" I said. "There's Nelda Wesslake. She's going to swim!"

"Her mother told me she was a magnificent swimmer," Bernice said from the warmth of the bed.

"But this time of morning! That water must be like ice."

"Not if you dive in straightaway," she told me complacently. "It's when you go in gradually that you feel cold. And, darling, I think I'll have a couple of aspirins. Bring me some water too, will you?"

I lingered at the window as long as I could, and just as I moved off, Nelda dived into the deep end. I hurried across to the wash-basin and the aspirins weren't there. Then Bernice said I must have moved them off the ledge, or were they in her case? They weren't, and she said they *must* be. Then I was told to look in her handbag, and there they were. By the time I'd brought her a glass of water I was already too late at the window, for Nelda was slipping on a bathing wrap and in a minute was scampering back to the hotel.

I let out a sigh and began to shave. It was lucky the razor wasn't a cut-throat, the way I kept losing myself in thought. And I could tell myself that if it hadn't been for the sheer bad luck of those aspirins and Bernice's forgetful untidiness I might have had some answers. Now all I had was one more puzzle. Had Nelda suspected what Collinson had suspected? Certainly the brother and sister weren't on such loving and trustful terms that David could have confided in Nelda and sent her to recover that jewellery. And why should Nelda suspect that David had tried to kill Camille? What she guessed or knew was something very different—that David was in love with her and was making a kind of public ass of himself.

Then I thought of something. I finished my shaving, had a quick wash and went bathless back to the bedroom.

"Darling, I hate to disturb you," I said. "But could you tell me something? You danced with David Wesslake last night—"

"And a very good dancer he is."

"I know," I said, and for speed's sake. "But did he tell you anything about himself? His relationships, say, with his mother and sister?"

"I really can't think," she said. "It's this head-ache. Ask me again later. I'm sure there were a lot of things he told me if I could only remember them."

That was that. I made my way downstairs, scrounged a cup of tea and then went out to the wistaria. Laddon must have seen me for he joined me there.

"No doubt about how he got up," he said, and I'd seen that already for myself. The bark was abraded and in one place a foot had crushed a cluster of dying blossoms.

"Yes," I said. "And what are your ideas about the job? To me it rather looks like a kind of inside one."

"I disagree," he told me rather sharply. "My staff are absolutely reliable."

"But what about those extra guests that came in last night for the dance?"

"They were all accounted for. Inspector Smallacre and I went into it thoroughly last night after that business of young Mrs. Wesslake."

"I expect you're right," I said. "All the same you must admit one thing. Mrs. Wesslake's jewellery was valuable, and what I'd call noticeable, and she'd worn the pendant only for the special occasion of last night. Mrs. Stonhill also wore very valuable jewellery. Am I right in thinking that it's generally kept in your safe?"

"It is."

"Then how could a thief have had foreknowledge? He must have come by chance, so speak, to have an exploratory look. Wasn't it just a bit too lucky that he should have spotted two women wearing stuff that was a burglar's dream? What's your safe like, by the way?"

"Oldish, but pretty strong."

"Don't let me decry it," I said, "but mightn't a modern cracksman bust it like a matchbox? In other words, wouldn't it have paid him to have *tried* the safe?"

I hadn't had time to be too logical, but I knew I'd made him uneasy. The time had come, as the walrus said, and I took his arm and led him along the drive. I told him, to his considerable amazement, just who I was and what my job was. I assured him I wasn't at the Malfroi Arms for any purpose but a quiet holiday, but, provided he was prepared to keep both me and my job a close secret, even from his wife, I was prepared to do a bit of underground work, solely, of course, with his interests and those of the hotel at heart. And just then, by a piece of apt timing, who should arrive but Inspector Smallacre.

The name had rung a vague bell. In my job, and after twenty years of it, one has an unsuspected circle of acquaintanceship. All sorts of people, from inspectors to constables whom I'd long forgotten, come up and address me by name. Maybe that's because of my height and leanness and huge horn-rims. And now Smallacre's eyes were to pop.

"It can't be," he said. "But it is."

Out went his hand with a, "How are you, sir?"

"Just crawling along," I said, and he grinned. But that was only for a moment. The next look was one remarkably like consternation.

"You're wrong," I said, "I just happened to be here—on a holiday. Major Laddon here will confirm. That's why I'd rather no one knew just who I am, so to speak."

Laddon popped in with what we'd been discussing just before Smallacre's arrival. Smallacre kept nodding.

"Could be," he said. "I've been wondering a lot about that myself. But one thing just doesn't seem to me to fit in. That attack on Mrs. Wesslake was a dirty job. The one who did it might have got anything from a five-year stretch to a seven. Then why did he hang around till one in the morning and then have the nerve to try that other job? And how did he know Mrs. Stonhill's room?"

"That'd be easy," Laddon said. "He'd only to watch her go into it. And it's in the book, of course, once he knew her name. And he'd know it from what happened at dinner. The birthday party, and so on."

"How *is* the lady this morning?" Smallacre wanted to know.

"Mrs. Stonhill's quite recovered. It was only a fainting fit, you know, though everyone's insisting she stays in bed for a day or so. Give her a few minutes warning and she can see you."

"And the other lady?"

"She seems all right too. A bad headache but I think she'll see you. The doctor's coming in a minute or two."

"I'm keeping out of all this," I said, "but if Inspector Smallacre's agreeable, I'd like to hear anything he picks up."

"Where shall I find you?"

"I'll be hanging around after breakfast," I told him, "and I'll follow you outside to your car. But there's just something you might do for me. When you question Mrs. Camille Wesslake, will you remember one special thing. Ask her if she definitely and distinctly heard sounds coming either way. You know: David Wesslake following her in one direction or the man who attacked her coming from the other. Will you do that?"

He saw the point. At any rate he gave a grim sort of nod and told me he certainly would.

It was after nine o'clock when Bernice at last appeared for breakfast. The headache was only a little better, she said, but the meal would probably bring the blood down from the head provided the meal was a good one. I could have made a remark or two about that, but I didn't. What I did say was that I was hungry and I didn't mind who knew it.

Nelda Wesslake was the only one at the corner table.

"You're looking very blithe and bonny this morning," I said as we were passing. Truth to tell, she was made up to the nines.

"I've had a swim," she told me triumphantly.

"Good Lord," I said, and shuddered, and as we went on I was wondering why on earth she had told me that.

A moment or two and she had gone. Bernice and I were well into our meal before I began divulging the night's happenings.

"But how dreadful!" she said, and gave a ferocious scowl. "It's all this crime there is about. Men going to lonely houses at night and tying people up and robbing them. Something really ought to be done about it."

I said nothing and she was giving me a look. Something was dawning on her.

"Darling, you don't mean it's anything to do with . . . with why we came down here?"

"Could be," I said. "It certainly wouldn't do you any harm if you kept your eyes and ears even more open."

"Yes," she said, and frowned to herself. Something was remembered.

"What was that you were asking me in the bedroom this morning?"

"Chiefly about David's relationships with his sister and mother."

There was more frowning and then something came.

"I don't think he and Nelda get on too well. Not that that's unusual. Brother and sister of that age very often don't. But I do know that she simply hates her father."

"Why?"

"My dear, can you ask? The divorce and all that. And she loathes Camille."

"Arguing from that," I said, "it follows that Nelda sympathises with and likes her mother."

"I wouldn't say that," she told me with yet another frown. "Just before the divorce, Nelda had an affair at only seventeen with a dance band leader and the father made a frightful scene. I rather gathered that after the divorce Nelda thought her mother would be more amenable, but she wasn't. Drina keeps her under her eye but Nelda's still hanging round the band leader."

"David told you that?"

"But of course! Who else could have told me?"

"And what about him? Any personal grievances?"

"Well, I don't think he has a lot of use for his father." Then there was something else she was wondering. "Tell me, if you can. I've been puzzled about it and I think it might fit in. Is the Wesslake man tired of Camille? I mean tired enough to want to divorce her?"

"Assuming he is, how does it help?"

"Because I think David doesn't like him either. I think he's a bit mad about Camille himself."

"Could be," I said. "And what about David and his mother?"

"That's all very involved," she said. "I think the mother can't manage him except by holding the whip hand about money."

"Yes?"

"Don't hurry me," she said. "I've got to think."

What thinking produced was interesting enough. Drina knew he was spending far too much time in England and neglecting his Paris work. David wanted a car of his own but Drina had made a completion of his studies an essential condition, and she held the purse-strings.

I left it at that. For the moment it was all I wanted to know. For one thing it fitted a brand new theory, or rather a modification of the old. If David Wesslake had that jewellery, then he could surreptitiously dispose of it in France, and there would be his car. To his mother, a lucky night at some casino or other would be sufficient explanation. That was a good theory, or so it seemed at the time. Maybe David's goo-goo eyes at Camille had been part of a scheme—to ingratiate himself sufficiently to make it ludicrous for her to suspect him of what had happened at the swimming-pool.

But I did put just one other question.

"What about Camille and Drina? How did they react to each other?"

"They were most correct. Sort of frigidly polite," Bernice said. "I like Camille but I think I'd be just a bit afraid of Drina. I think Camille's afraid of her too."

I told Bernice to lie low, it was a dull morning and maybe she might read or knit on the verandah, and if any of the Wesslakes approached her, that'd be all to the good. As for myself, I might be anywhere till lunchtime, but a visit to the golf course might be as good an excuse as any for a possible absence. With that we parted company. Bernice went upstairs and I got my pipe going and took up a strategic position to watch for Smallacre's reappearance.

He wasn't so long as I'd thought, and just short of ten o'clock I saw him emerge with Laddon. I moved off along the Winstode Road and there he overtook me. I hopped into the car and a few yards on he turned into a side lane and pulled the car up.

"Mrs. Stonhill first," I said. "Did she see the man clearly enough to identify him?"

"She didn't," he said. "All she saw was a moving shape between her and the window. She'd left the window just open at top and bottom and it must have been the sound of him easing it up that woke her. She said she was simply paralysed with fear but she made a kind of gurgling noise and then he bolted through the window. Then she shrieked and switched on the bedside light."

"And what about Camille Wesslake? Did she see the man who attacked her?"

"She didn't see him at all. And about that question we were going to ask her, she didn't hear anything either."

He frowned. "Well, perhaps she did—just faintly. A sort of sound behind her and that's all she knows. Something hit her and out she went."

"Any finger prints in Mrs. Stonhill's room?"

"Never a one. Not even on the bottom of the window."

"And why did Camille Wesslake go to the swimming-pool?"

"Now there's something rather peculiar," he told me. "I had the idea she wasn't telling me all the truth. When I asked her that, she said she was tired and didn't want to be questioned any more."

"Yes, but what *did* she say?"

"Just the old story—wanted a breath of fresh air and wasn't going anywhere in particular. Just happened to go that way."

"Yes," I said. "That sounds a bit odd. That swimming-pool's a secluded place. Not a bad spot to meet somebody by appointment, so to speak."

"If so, it's somebody she isn't going to give away," he said. "My idea is that you're right. She wouldn't have gone all that way for a breath of fresh air."

"And alone."

"Yes," he said. "And alone."

I let out a breath.

"Well, if she decides to keep her mouth shut or tell lies you can't do a thing about it. Perhaps I might try a bit of questioning myself when she's up again and see how she reacts." And then I put the plain question.

"Let's get down to brass tacks. You see the implications of all this? If she was lured there, it couldn't have been a supposed gangster who lured her, it must have been someone she knew."

"Then what about the man in Mrs. Stonhill's room?" he asked me. "He must have been the same man who attacked Mrs. Wesslake."

"You'd certainly think so," I said. "In fact, it looks a certainty. But it doesn't explain why Camille went to the swimming-pool."

He did a bit of scowling and then suddenly moved the car on.

"I think I'll have another look round that swimming-pool," he told me. "Maybe I'll get some new ideas."

* * * * *

We circled round and came out to the main road again. He drove the car into a side entrance I hadn't known about and past the big garage and round the back premises. Just as I was getting out of the car Laddon came hurriedly up.

"I'm glad you've come," he said. "You must have driven pretty fast."

Smallacre didn't get him.

"I only rang you about five minutes ago and they told me at the station that you weren't back."

"But I haven't been to the station," Smallacre told him bewilderedly.

"Then how did you know?"

"Know what?"

"Who the man is," Laddon told him triumphantly. "One of the guests is missing. You know him, Mr. Travers. The man who called himself Ferotti!"

CHAPTER 7
THE BIG QUERY

"How DO you know he's gone?" I was asking him.

"The chambermaid found the room empty," Laddon said. "That was just after you left."

"Just a minute," cut in Smallacre. "Who *is* this Ferotti?"

Laddon explained. Smallacre said he'd ring for his sergeant and go over the bedroom for prints. Laddon and I waited for him out of sight behind the annexe. I didn't want to be seen and we didn't go into the room because it seemed that he ought to have a look at it first. Laddon told me he'd had a look himself but had touched nothing, not that that was to matter.

Ferotti had gone—vanished, skipped it, or what you will. That annexe bedroom was as bare as a chicken carcass when the tits have finished with it and not a scrap of paper or a single trace of anything remained to show he had ever been there. The chambermaid had even found the bed almost as neat as when she had finished making it on the Saturday morning.

"It was something Mr. Collinson told me that made me send her along specially," Laddon told us.

"That's the tallish man I was talking to last night?" Smallacre asked him.

"That's the one. Mrs. Wesslake's cousin. Nephew of the old lady."

"And what was he telling you?"

"It was rather confidential," Laddon said uneasily. "I don't see why it should be so now, though."

"Get him here," Smallacre said. "If it's anything important I'd like to hear it at first-hand."

Smallacre and I tried working out how Ferotti could have got away. *When* he left was easy enough, for that had to be just after one-twenty in the morning when Alice Stonhill had scared him down that wistaria. But there were no trains from Winstode till seven-thirty on a Sunday, so unless Ferotti had had a confederate handy with a car, he must have taken to the road with the hope of thumbing a lift. Unless he'd stolen a car from the hotel garage.

That was the question Smallacre was intending to ask as soon as Laddon got back with Collinson. Collinson, by the way, gave me a quick enquiring look. Smallacre, duly primed, told him that I also had noticed something suspicious about Ferotti.

"And what was it you happened to notice, sir?" he asked Collinson.

"Something that wasn't really in keeping with what I'd seen of him before," Collinson said. "I suppose a lot of this is really my fault. I ought to have gone to Major Laddon last night."

What he'd seen was something remarkably peculiar, and, in view of subsequent happenings, at a very interesting time. It was at about a quarter past ten when the waiter approached him in the dance room, and it was fairly easy to work out the timings from there. Collinson was dancing at the time, but just after the preceding dance he had gone out for a spot of air and had strolled along the drive towards the front gates. Then he heard hurried footsteps approaching, and he halted where he was—on the grass verge. The light was particularly poor with clouds across the moon, but the man—Ferotti, it was—passed near enough to be definitely recognised. It was that short, neatly trimmed beard that gave him away for one thing.

"What was unusual about that, sir?"

"One or two things," Collinson said, and as if he hadn't noticed the impatience. "He was supposed to have trouble with his eyes and walked with a stick, but when he passed me he wasn't wearing his dark glasses and he had the stick in his hand and he was fairly hurtling along. You know, a sort of trotting walk."

"And you didn't mention the matter?"

Smallacre was pretty resilient or Collinson's look would have shrivelled him.

"Should I have? If we made a fuss about every eccentricity that came to our notice—"

"Now, sir, don't take me wrong," Smallacre told him placatingly. "I see your point. This Ferotti was acting in a peculiar way but it wasn't any business of yours—not then."

"That's exactly it. All I did was notice what I've just told you, and then I didn't think about it any more. I did turn back to the hotel, sort of puzzled, if you know what I mean, and then another dance began and before I'd been dancing a couple of minutes, the waiter fetched me. After that the whole thing slipped my mind, what with seeing to Mrs. Wesslake and so on."

Smallacre shook his head and said it was a pity Collinson hadn't mentioned it to him that night.

"I know—but I didn't. Then came that other business of Mrs. Stonhill and then I began putting two and two together. After breakfast I thought I'd mention the matter to Major Laddon but he was with you. Then I did tell him."

"To go back to when you returned to the dance-room, sir. Did you see Ferotti there?"

"I can't say that I did."

"Did you notice him at all during the evening?"

"Oh, yes," he said. "He was sitting at one of the tables most of the time. The far end from where Mr. Travers and my aunt were sitting."

"I saw him there," I said. "I remember the waiter bringing him a beer. And I know he was there when the fraças began. That was much later, though. Somewhere around a quarter to eleven."

"Fraças?" asked Laddon.

"A man was a bit tight," I said. "He barged into some couples when he was trying to make his way out. He wasn't being objectionable or anything like that; it was just that his legs didn't function properly. I do remember that Ferotti got up from his table as if he wanted to lend a hand, and that strikes me now as rather peculiar. There were plenty of able-bodied men to handle the situation without a man with Ferotti's disabilities thinking it necessary to help."

"I'm afraid that was Colonel Holster," Laddon said. "We've had trouble with him before."

"Let's get back to what Mr. Collinson saw," Smallacre told us. "If Ferotti was coming along the drive *towards* the hotel, what does that mean exactly?"

"Probably this," I said, "and little as I know about it, the times do fit. *If* Ferotti robbed Mrs. Wesslake and *if* he was the one Mr. David Wesslake heard running away, then he went along the back path by the tennis courts and round to the main road."

I'd deliberately emphasised those *ifs* and Collinson promptly rose to it.

"Of course it was Ferotti who robbed Mrs. Wesslake! David said he picked her up straightaway and carried her to her room. I didn't know it but that was probably happening while I was walking along the drive. It fits in almost to a second. Ferotti was running back to give himself an alibi."

"Maybe you're right, sir," Smallacre told him. "Not that he'd want an alibi all that bad. I don't reckon anyone would suspect a guest."

He made a gesture of annoyance.

"Something I'd almost forgotten to ask. Are there any cars missing?"

Laddon was all of a fluster.

"I'd better go and enquire. There are only three cars here."

"They're still there," Collinson said. "I saw them myself when I was servicing my own car this morning."

Laddon looked relieved. If Ferotti had stolen a car belonging to one of the dance guests, then the hotel would have heard about it. Besides, those cars had all gone soon after midnight.

"Well, I think that's all we need trouble you for, sir," Smallacre told Collinson. "I don't think you need blame yourself for not speaking sooner than you did. You weren't to know what was going to happen."

I made as if to leave with Collinson but was called back. Then Sergeant Blews arrived and got to work finger-printing, and we watched him and talked at the same time. Smallacre was anxious to hear just what Laddon knew about Ferotti. Laddon looked rather uncomfortable when he told us he knew virtually nothing at all. As it happened it had been he who had taken a call from a man who said he was Mr. Ferotti's secretary, and the secretary had asked if there was a room available from the Friday, May 28th, till the following Sunday evening or Monday morning. Mr. Ferotti, he said, would prefer a room in the annexe as his eyes were rather weak. That was all, and the room had been booked.

"A hundred to one the secretary was Ferotti himself," I said. "You'd never connect him with the Ferotti who arrived, and who had a foreign intonation."

"The main point's this," Smallacre said. "If he knew about the annexe, then he must have done some previous reconnoitring. What about it, Major? Ever had anybody like him here before?"

"Not to my knowledge."

"Well, did you have any conversation with him when he arrived here, or yesterday?"

"Just the usual," Laddon said, and then frowned. "I remember he told me he'd been naturalised a good many years and he'd had business interests in Brazil."

"He was a Brazilian?"

"Originally, yes—or so I gathered."

"And what about that beard of his that everyone keeps mentioning? Was it real, do you think?"

"Most decidedly it was," Laddon told him, and rather testily. I agreed. It was closely trimmed, for one thing, which meant that it simply couldn't be attached artificially to the face.

"Black, I think you said?"

"Not black," Laddon told him, and again I agreed. "It looked black at a distance but when you saw it closely it was sort of streaked with grey. So was the hair."

"That was grey at the temples," I added.

Laddon remembered something else. Ferotti had said he would be away either on the Sunday night late or very early on the Monday morning—by the eight o'clock from Winstode—and asked if that would be an inconvenience. Laddon had assured him that it wouldn't.

We'd been watching Sergeant Blews with a growing anxiety. Now he straightened his back and gave an exasperated shake of the head.

"Never a print here, sir, except that chambermaid's."

"Keep on trying," Smallacre told him, and then I was thinking back and trying to recall something, and I was sure I was right.

"When Ferotti arrived here he was wearing gloves—yellow, chamois gloves. I remember he was wearing them when he had a coffee on the verandah yesterday morning."

"Probably wore 'em all the time he was in here," Smallacre said disgustedly, and as if Ferotti had been hitting below the belt. "And the devil of it is that everything he handled without gloves—spoons, forks and so on—was washed up long ago." Then his eyes popped a bit. "That means he's got a record!"

"Not much use to us if we can't get his prints," I said. "I hate to be pessimistic but I don't think we shall. This job was planned far too carefully. The room was booked by telephone, Major, and you had no checking address. He booked for only a short weekend, which meant that he didn't have to produce a ration card which would have his name and address and identity number. As he was British he didn't have to show an identity card."

"You say the job was planned," Smallacre told me. "I don't see it, not unless he had a confederate planted here. How could he know about the jewellery?"

"This is a high-class hotel," I said. "It advertises extensively and it mentions its charges. It's the sort of place where there's almost bound to be someone with valuable jewellery. Ferotti came on the off-chance. He stood to lose nothing but his weekend expenses, and as things turned out, he had a lot of luck. He blundered right into those birthday celebrations. And he knew there'd be a dance on the Saturday night because it's mentioned in the hotel brochure. A dance might mean strangers. It'd certainly mean a certain amount of movement or excitement to act as a cover-up. And something else," I went on. "He took care to emphasise that he was leaving late tonight or early tomorrow. I'd say therefore that his original hopes were to commit a possible robbery on the Sunday night and be away before it was discovered, then there'd be only a faint chance of his being connected with it. Then that birthday and the sight of the jewellery changed the schedule."

Smallacre frowned and nodded. I asked what about the *Police Gazette*? Had there been any recent description of anyone resembling Ferotti or using his methods? Smallacre said he couldn't recall any, and then was asking, pertinently enough, what Ferotti's description was. And that soon led us into deep water. The only thing on which we could rely was his height, and I thought that was five-foot nine, allowing for the slight stoop. Laddon didn't even agree with that. He put him at only five-foot seven. As to age, I mentioned sixty-five at least. Laddon thought he was younger. As for the rest, the dark glasses concealed the eyes, the slight stomach bulge might have been artificial and the somewhat plump cheeks induced by pads.

"How could he eat with plumpers in?" Smallacre wanted to know.

"It's been done," I said. "But if you enquire you'll find that he sat at a far corner table and generally with his back to the room, so he could have slipped them out. But one other thing he did have, and that's a bald patch nearly as large as a tonsure on the back of his head. And his nose was rather aquiline. Maybe that could have been faked, but I doubt it."

That was about all. Smallacre said he'd have a word with Ferotti's waiter, and, in fact with every single guest who'd spoken to Ferotti. When he mentioned getting a description of Mrs. Wesslake's missing jewellery, Laddon said he could help. And he also had something interesting to add. Laddon had seen most of Mrs. Stonhill's jewellery since it was usually kept in his safe. Mrs. Wesslake had also kept there the ruby and diamond bracelet which Mrs. Stonhill had given her. The pendant, which matched it, had been a loan for the special birthday occasion. But Mrs. Stonhill had also lent Camille a single-stone and quite valuable diamond ring.

Camille had worn it above another one that had been a present from her husband, but the Stonhill ring had fitted so tightly that Ferotti had been unable to remove it, even if he had tried, and that had also saved the ring below it. It had been the work of only a second or two, of course, to slip off the bracelet and pendant.

"Talking of that," I said, "I still don't see why David Wesslake found Camille Wesslake lying on the very edge of the pool. If Ferotti carried or dragged her there to try to remove the rings, that doesn't make sense. The light there wasn't any better than anywhere else. All he need have done was to get her out of sight just inside the hedge."

But Smallacre was agog to get on the telephone to his Chief, so I left him and Laddon to it and made my way round by the back of the verandah in search of mid-morning coffee. Bernice wasn't there, and then I caught sight of her on the putting green with David Wesslake and she was evidently trying to teach him some new kind of grip. I called to them and mentioned coffee and they called back that they'd had it. That suited my book. The sight of Collinson had given some new ideas, and there was a certain theory I'd had and with which I was now far from disposed to part.

I lighted my pipe and sat there thinking. In my game there's little that's too fantastic, and that's why I was thinking so seriously about James Collinson. By his own admission he was out of the dance-room at somewhere about the time when Camille was being attacked and robbed.

Nobody, or so it seemed to me, could possibly fix the exact moment when Collinson did actually leave that room. Suppose then it was he who had struck Camille! Suppose that story of seeing Ferotti was a fake, and merely produced to give himself an alibi! Suppose it was Collinson who had dropped that jewellery into the pool—he had taken it to give the impression of a robbery—and had then retrieved it at dawn the next morning!

I liked that theory, and I didn't. It was attractive in the sense that the unusual and plausible is attractive, but for all that it had too many holes. Collinson couldn't have guessed that Ferotti was a crook. If then he faked a story why should he have picked Ferotti for the faking? It is true he approached Laddon in confidence, but still I didn't see why he should pick on Ferotti. Besides, Collinson was ostensibly a man of excellent reputation; a man utterly out of keeping with that new theory. And if I'd been sure of anything in the world, it was that he was in love with Camille.

And yet something kept nagging at me and telling me that everything was far from as obvious as it seemed. Back of it all was a tremendous uneasiness, and then suddenly I knew what that uneasiness was. Ferotti, something had been telling me, was an obtrusion. He didn't belong. He was no part of the events that had brought me to the Malfroi Arms.

And yet he should have been. That attack on Camille Wesslake was a continuation, as it were, of the story Alice Stonhill had related in Bill Ellice's office. Two attempts maybe on Camille's life, and now a third, and all three attempts abortive. There was the sequence, and yet there was about them something that was wrong. Wesslake, or so we'd almost assumed, had made those first two attempts on his wife's life, even if, as Bill had insisted, they'd been no more than a warning and with no real intent to murder. Then, to maintain that sequence, it should have been Wesslake who had attempted to kill Camille, or once more to frighten, at the pool. But that was impossible, for Wesslake was in Denmark. *Or wasn't he?*

Something else occurred to me before I concentrated on that last question. Suppose Wesslake had never been responsible for those two previous attempts or warnings. If he had not, then Collinson or David Wesslake had been responsible, and neither had been without opportunity. And each had had the opportunity at the swimming-pool, and that would make the sequence unbroken. But there again something was wrong. Whereas it seemed that Wesslake had an excellent motive for killing his wife, neither Collinson nor David had any vestige of motive at all. *Or had they?*

I put that question aside and went back to the other: the question of whether or not Peter Wesslake was in Denmark. That made me face something else that had been all along at the back of my mind: *the question of whether or not Ferotti could possibly be Wesslake.* Now I thought it impossible. I hadn't seen him any too well at Broad Street, but surely no disguise could deceive the whole Wesslake family. Except perhaps for height, Ferotti and Peter Wesslake resembled each other in nothing whatever, and my mind's eye was now seeing them as two utterly different men. And there was one other thing. Whereas Wesslake-Ferotti might have tried to kill Camille, he had no reason for trying to kill his aunt, for that was what his presence in her bedroom would really signify. Everything I knew had told me that when Alice Stonhill died, Peter Wesslake would get never a penny of her money.

But there was a way to narrow things down. Remove Wesslake finally from a suspect list, and only Collinson and David Wesslake would be left. But don't get me wrong. I knew well enough that if Ferotti was genuine, then all Collinson or David Wesslake could have done was to fit his actions somehow into schemes of their own. For there certainly *had* been scheming. Collinson hadn't been searching at the bottom of an icy pool at the crack of dawn for the mere pleasure of the thing. But enquiry into that could come later. All I had to do was prove to myself that Wesslake was in Copenhagen. And I *could* do it. And then I knew I couldn't, for I had left that P.E.N. Congress brochure at the flat.

A minute or two later I went to the bureau and consulted the list of trains. Then I went to the putting-green.

"Didn't know you were a golfer," I told David.

"As a matter of fact, sir, I'm not," he said, and for once there wasn't that cynical droop to his lip. "Mrs. Travers has been giving me a lesson in putting."

"Well, I've got to run up to town," I said to Bernice. "I forgot those wretched papers after all and I simply must have them."

"But can't you go after lunch?"

"I ought to go now," I told her, and her look was asking what it was really all about.

"What a pity you didn't know before," David said. "Jim Collinson's just gone up to town in his car. He could have given you a lift."

"I wish I'd known," I said. "Still, there is quite a handy train and the walk'll do me good."

"Like me to come with you, darling?"

"I don't think I'd risk it," I said. "It looks to me as if it might rain before you got back."

It was just before one o'clock when I got to the flat, and after I'd arranged for lunch to be sent up, I had a look at that Congress brochure. There, as I had thought, was the name of the secretary:

Axel Dessau, 8 Bernstorffsgade. The telephone number was Palais 5983.

I asked for the number and was told that I'd be rung. Lunch arrived and I'd eaten it and got my pipe going when the call came, and that was sooner than I'd hoped. The voice was as clear as if it were speaking from the service extension.

"Is that Mr. Axel Dessau?" I said.

"Yes. It is Axel Dessau speaking."

I explained that I wanted to get in touch with an English author who was attending the P.E.N. Congress—a Mr. Wesslake. Could I possibly be given the name of his hotel.

"I think so. Just wait a moment, will you?"

The English, I was thinking, was uncommonly good, and then the voice came again.

"Mr. Wesslake is staying at the Metropolitan Hotel."

"And the telephone number?"

"Central 1003."

I thanked him warmly and rang off before he could ask for my name. Then I waited a minute or two and asked for the new Copenhagen number.

This time the wait was very much longer. When it did come, the voice at the end of the line was that of the desk secretary, and her English was none too good. Then she cupped the telephone and in a minute or so I was hearing a man's voice.

"I'm speaking from London," I said. "Have you a Mr. Wesslake"—I spelt the name—"staying at the hotel?"

"Just a minute, please."

I heard faint voices and then I was told that Mr. Wesslake *was* staying at the hotel.

"Could you tell me when he arrived?"

"Yes," the voice said. "He arrived on the twenty-second of May."

"Can I speak to him, please?"

"Just a minute," the voice said again, and I was wondering just what I should do if Peter Wesslake came to the end of the line. Maybe I'd better pretend to be speaking on behalf of his publishers, even if that might sound rather odd for a Sunday. But all I would need, of course, was to hear his voice and then I could get off the line at once.

"Are you there?" the voice came, but it was the same voice. "Mr. Wesslake isn't here at the moment. He has gone to Roskilde with an English friend."

"Then he was definitely in the hotel last night?"

"Oh, yes. Mr. Wesslake was here. But would you wish to leave a message? Mr. Wesslake will almost certainly be back for dinner."

"Thank you very much," I said, "but I'll ring him again. Probably tomorrow morning."

At twelve-and-six for each three minutes that hadn't been a cheap afternoon, and yet I felt it had been worth it. Wesslake was in Copenhagen. Ferotti was by now heaven knew where, but he was definitely Ferotti, and it was therefore he who had knocked Camille out and taken the jewellery. I, in fact, had again been the victim of my own too luxuriant imagination. Ferotti was an obtrusion into what had looked very much like a sequence. Everything was open and above-board with Collinson. Or wasn't it? Wasn't there still that matter about the swimming-pool and the something or other he'd found at the bottom? And, now I came to think of it, I was wondering too just why he also had had to go to town that morning in his car.

<h2 style="text-align:center">CHAPTER 8
RETURN TO NORMAL</h2>

I RANG the Malfroi Arms and asked for Mrs. Travers. It wasn't long before she was on the line and I guessed she'd been in the lounge. I said I was coming back by the train that got in at five o'clock and if she liked to come in by bus, we could walk back together.

"But it's raining," she told me. "It's simply coming down in sheets."

I said I'd take a taxi from the station and then I was asking what she'd been doing. Alice Stonhill, it appeared, had come down for lunch and Bernice had spent the afternoon with her in the lounge. David was upstairs, painting whatever it was he saw from his bedroom window. Drina had announced her intention of staying till the next morning and had gone out with Nelda. Camille was still in bed but the doctor was letting her get up the next afternoon. James Collinson she didn't know about, but he hadn't been in to lunch.

There was plenty of time to ring Bill Ellice at his house, and I found him in.

"Enjoying your holiday?" he said.

I said everything was fine but I didn't tell him I was in town.

"We've had a bit of excitement here," I told him. "You may see it in the paper tomorrow and you may not. Young Mrs. W. cracked on the head and robbed of some jewellery, and then an attempted robbery from a certain old lady's room."

I could almost hear him thinking that over.

"More than meets the eye?" was what he said.

"I don't think so. Just a job pulled off by someone posing as a guest."

"Anyone else robbed?"

"I see what you mean," I said, "and I still don't think so. There was a birthday party, you remember, and the jewellery was just a bit flaunted. But there's something I'd like you to do for me. You know what you advised that certain lady—that she should ring you at once if anything happened? Let me know if she does. That ought to be a test, don't you think, if she herself considers this robbery business tied up with what she told you."

Bill said he'd certainly let me know. I asked him about the Millside fire and how Palton was getting on.

"I took him off long ago," Bill said. "It was sheer waste of time. I think the gentleman's going to look down his nose when he gets the account. He's thrown a lot of good money after bad."

"Do something else for me," I said. "Send me a résumé of Palton's report."

Bill said it should be in the post first thing in the morning, and a minute or so afterwards I rang off. I looked out of the window and the rain was coming down. But it was no distance at all to Leicester Square, where I took the Tube to King's Cross. There I had a cup of tea, and then had the Winstode train almost to myself.

I spent that journey thinking about the Millside fire, for it was something on which I'd hitherto spent far too little thought. Now, the more I thought things over, the more curious that fire was to seem. Insurance companies can't afford to make mistakes. One might also say that they're always only too anxious to pay, for on prompt and satisfactory settlements depends much of their good-will. So if they knew that fire had been a fake, then a fake it had been.

Why then had Wesslake set fire to his summer-house? It couldn't have been with the hope of making money. Allow a profit of twenty pounds on the difference between the planted typewriter and his own, and another fifty, say, for appreciation of values on the furnishings that had been destroyed and a further thirty for oddments, and the total gain was only a hundred pounds. But that was more than counterbalanced by the loss of the summer-house itself. Though only of timber with a shingle roof it was a largish one and well-built—and it was pre-war. The difference between its original cost and its present replacement value was at least that hundred pounds. And if it wasn't replaced, then the Millside prop-erty had lost that much amenity value.

So Wesslake couldn't have been hoping to make money. Why then had he fired it? Could it possibly have been, as Alice Stonhill had hinted, as a part of yet another abortive attempt on Camille's life?

I began thinking that out, and the method I tried was one that has often paid me. I imagined, in fact, that I was writing a detec-tive novel, and its villain was Wesslake. How, I asked myself, could I make that fire the perfect, and for him, safe cause of his wife's death. One answer was an overturned lamp and a lock out of order and the summer-house so far from the house itself that Camille's shrieks had not been heard. But there'd been no lamp and a Yale lock couldn't very well jam, and Camille would only have had to break the window and her shrieks could have been heard a half-mile away. If Wesslake had stunned her, then even a burnt skull would have shown traces of the blow, and if he had drugged her, there'd still have been the stomach content.

Then, before I could produce new variations on the theme, I realised something that made me drop the whole thing. Camille had reported those two abortive attempts to Alice Stonhill. They were genuine, and they had scared her. But she hadn't reported that fire as yet another attempt. That had been Alice Stonhill's own idea. Presumably then, Camille had never thought of that fire as an attempt on her life. Why should she? She didn't use that summer-house, and she'd been with the three men in the house when it broke out. And therefore it hadn't been an attempt, and that brought me back to where I had been before.

There was nothing for it but to switch to Peter Wesslake and try to deduce just what sort of man he was. He was a spender, but so are many men of both charm and character. He was vain, and probably inordinately so, or he'd never have thought he could get away with arson. He was morally erratic or he would never have allowed himself to fall for Camille. He was unscrupulous or he would never have condoned that bribery of Camille for securing a divorce. *If* he had tried to scare her into that divorce, then it seemed to me his mind was pretty badly diseased; he was, in fact, a megalomaniac and a dangerous one. How much those devious and dangerous actions of his had been influenced by his profession and the success he had made of it, seemed to me a problem out of my depth, though I did think the opinion of a psychiatrist might be highly illuminating.

I'd got that far when I became aware that the train was stopping, and there I was at Winstode. The rain was coming steadily down and it was blowing half a gale. There was no taxi and I had to wait half-an-hour for a bus. The grounds of the hotel looked sodden and dreary and a pessimism was in my bones as I made my way along the drive. It wasn't helped when I turned aside to the garage and saw Collinson's car was still not there.

I went upstairs and changed into my other suit—the Sunday evening meal as at most hotels was supper and not dinner—and came down to find Bernice still in the lounge, and Alice Stonhill with her.

"Well, young lady?" I said quizzically. "How are you feeling now?"

She looked almost indignant.

"Perfectly well, of course. How ought I to be feeling?"

That rather hit me in the wind. I could only mumble something about a disturbed night. Bernice came to the rescue.

"We were waiting for you to come. Mrs. Stonhill's going to show us her presents."

Alice Stonhill spryly led the way upstairs. The presents were in a drawer and she took them out one by one. First was a woollen bed-jacket.

"This was from Drina," she said, and gave a little moue of amusement. "Now you know what an old woman I really am. This was from Nelda. A much more charitable view of me, as you see."

It was a charming little hand-bag in brocade, suitable, I imagined, to be carried with an evening gown.

"This," she went on, "came from my nephew, Peter. Camille's husband, you know. It arrived on Saturday morning. Very thoughtful of him. And rather sweet, don't you think?"

It was a piece of Copenhagen porcelain; modern of course, but exquisitely fashioned and with the sheer simplicity of all good art— just a goat, and a girl feeding it with a handful of grass and a young brother looking on. From what I knew of values, that present must have cost best part of forty pounds.

"Most charming," I said, and Bernice was positively ecstatic. "But how did he manage to buy it? I thought one wasn't allowed to take more than thirty-five pounds. Don't think I'm being curious," I went hastily on. "All I was wondering was how I could do something of the sort myself."

"Peter always has ways and means," she told me, and her lip seemed to me to droop. "I expect he has some arrangement with his Danish publishers."

There were three of his own books, beautifully bound in leather, from James Collinson, and then came something more cumbrous—a framed oil.

"This was David's present," she said, and her look was somewhat quizzical. "It's my cottage at Ashenby. He painted it specially for me."

Bernice didn't look at me but said heroically and unblushingly that it was rather nice. I thought it an emetic. Bold colour doesn't appal me, nor does modern perspective—I like Matthew Smith and Stanley Spencer, for instance—but that picture was something outside my conceptions of what might be even impudently allowed to call itself art.

"It's very modern," I said. "And just a bit beyond me, I'm afraid."

"Yes," she said, and smiled almost maliciously as she held it at arm's length. "It isn't even what in my day would have been called daring. But there," and she smiled to herself as she put it back, "we mustn't allow ourselves to be dogmatic, if that's the word.

My husband, who knew a great deal about painting, always said the junk of today might be the sensation of tomorrow." The smile became impish again. "But for goodness sake don't tell David that."

There was a last present—a really beautiful jade figure of a swan.

"Now, that's really lovely," Bernice said. "Don't you think so, Ludo?"

"Perfectly charming," I said. "It must have been given you by someone of exquisite taste."

"It was Camille," she said, and I seemed to catch a something mischievous in her look.

The voice of Jacob and the hands of Esau, I thought. Camille may have bought it but it was Alice Stonhill who had chosen it. And in some uncanny way she guessed what I was thinking, or so it seemed.

"I never could resist jade," she said as she closed the drawer. And then Bernice was asking how Camille was, and the two women went off to her bedroom and I made my way downstairs.

As I passed by the desk, Drina and Nelda came through the door. Drina gave a vicious shake to her umbrella. Nelda made a face at me, as much as to say that she'd been dragged out that afternoon against her will.

"What filthy weather!" Drina told me, and I watched her ramrod back as she went on up the stairs. A masterful woman, I told myself. Probably pampered and spoilt from her youth up. Selfish, peevish, and liable to cut up pretty rough if baulked. But whether the sort of woman to have cracked Camille on the skull was quite a different matter. But Ferotti had done that, so why start new theories? And yet I wondered.

It was something, maybe, in line with the tag about Satan and idle hands. The weather kept me to the lounge and I had nothing to do but think, and a new theory was coming in spite of myself. Suppose Ferotti had *not* committed that assault and theft. That answered Smallacre's reasonable objection—that a crook, after one successful theft, would never have the nerve to wait till one in the morning in order to try another.

Suppose then that that first business was a coincidence and nothing whatever to do with Ferotti, then Camille had been somehow lured to the pool and had been attacked by the one who had lured her there. *If* David Wesslake's story was correct, and *if* he had really found her body on the edge of the pool, then the one who had attacked her had intended murder. The theft was only a kind of red-herring. But for David's unexpected appearance, Camille would have been found drowned in that pool.

If that were so, and if David Wesslake's story was a fake, then he was a suspect, even if he hadn't intended murder but only the theft of the jewellery. That was his only possible motive, but when one came to his mother, there was a something that was very different. She hated Camille—possibly with good cause—and had tried to bribe her into a divorce. When Camille had stood her ground, Drina must have hated her still more. And as I saw her again in my mind's eye, it seemed to me that she was more than capable of giving that crack on the skull. And motive was more than there. Think of how things, from her point of view, had deteriorated. Bribery had failed, and now Alice Stonhill had Camille well under her wing, and Drina could say goodbye to the hopes of getting back a husband.

There's something of an avalanche quality about a theory. Once it starts, there's no telling where it's going to end, and that was how it was then. If Drina had struck that blow, then there must have been a weapon. It must have been something heavy and hard: something that would sink in water. Drina had thrown it into the pool, and either James Collinson had seen her or else he must have suspected her. And that weapon must have been something that would tie up Drina with the attack. That is why he had recovered it from the bottom of the pool.

And if that were so, just what could I do about it? The answer seemed to be precious little, except perhaps to keep an eye on Camille when she recovered and to think out some cunning lines of conversation with Collinson. And that reminded me of the golf that had been fixed for the morning, and then I was wondering if he were back from town.

It was not till after supper that night that I got a chance to mention that. The four at the Wesslake table seemed to me to be particularly quiet that evening. After the meal, David and Nelda went out together—to play billiards, I learnt; an unholy alliance that would probably end in a dog-fight.

"Mr. Collinson hasn't gone away?" I asked Alice Stonhill. "I only ask because we'd fixed up some golf for the morning."

"Oh, no," she said. "He had a dinner engagement in town. I think he said he'd be back late tonight."

It was certainly late when he came back. I know, because I was up early and I spoke to the night porter.

"Mr. Collinson back?" I said. "We're supposed to be playing golf this morning."

"Oh, yes, sir; he's back," he said. "Got back about one. Not that I reckon you'll get a lot of golf."

He was right. It was still blowing half a gale, and there was rain in the air. Soon after breakfast it came steadily down. But something happened before that. While I was at the desk the postman brought the letters. I asked the porter if there was anything for me. He waved a hand to indicate that I could look for myself.

There was a letter for Bernice but nothing for me. I noticed a letter for Collinson with Danish stamps—an air mail letter bearing the Saturday postmark. There was a postcard for him too, a picture one with a view of Edinburgh Castle. The porter had disappeared for a moment so I unblushingly read it.

> *May 29th.*
>
> *Having a fine time and weather pretty good. Going on Inverness Monday. Don't forget that reprint business with L/V.*
>
> *F. D.*

That would be Francis Deen, Peter Wesslake's secretary, I thought to myself. L/V would be Laud and Varden, who published the Colin Lake novels, but I wasn't particularly interested. What I'd have liked to know was what was in that letter from Copenhagen. I didn't know Peter Wesslake's writing, but the letter would certainly have to be from him. But maybe he was also writing about business.

Nelda Wesslake came down the stairs in a bathing wrap and plimsolls.

"Making a habit of it, are you?" I said.

"I hate to feel frowsty," she said. "A swim before breakfast always bucks you up."

Then she was giving me a pert look and asking why I didn't try it myself. I said I wasn't of the Spartan breed. I only went in when the water felt warm to my toes.

"Just like David," she said, and gave a pout of contempt.

"What about Mr. Collinson?" I said. "Why don't you rope him in?"

"He's as bad," she said. "And yet they're always running down the present generation and trying to make out what wonderful people they were when they were young."

"Hypocrisy is one of the privileges of age," I told her, and she gave a little sniff as she went out.

I waited a minute or two and then made my surreptitious way by the tennis courts to the far side of the pool, and took a peep from behind the hedge. But Nelda didn't seem to me to be looking for anything. All she did was swim from end to end with a crawl stroke, and she seemed to be timing herself, for when she reached the near end, she pulled herself up and had a look at the wrist-watch she'd left on the concrete surround. Then she had another go and timed herself again, and then she came out. I was wishing I could swim one length of that pool in the time she took for two.

Bernice was early for breakfast and we were finishing it when Collinson came in, and David and Nelda with him. He came straight to our table.

"How's Mrs. Wesslake?" I asked.

"Practically recovered," he said. "She's coming down after lunch. But about our golf. I don't think it looks too promising, do you?"

He said he'd just been to the garage, and when he came out it was raining.

"That reminds me," I said. "I always like to know if there's any racket one can work more or less legitimately, but how did it come about that you happened to get petrol? I thought the new basic only began today."

"Mine isn't a racket," he said, and smiled. "I've had petrol all along. Just happened to be writing a book that meant touring Warwickshire, so I applied on the off chance, and they gave me it. Quite generous too."

"Good," I said. "That gives me an idea. I'll start writing a book about the French Riviera."

He laughed, though it wasn't much of a joke, and went back to his table. He'd had his letters in his hand and he began opening them. In a minute he was reading something to Nelda and David, and I guessed it was extracts from their father's letter. As we left the room, Drina came sailing majestically in, and she gave us both a very gracious good morning.

Bernice went up to do some tidying. I took my newspaper to the verandah, and the rain, as I said, was now coming pitilessly down. A few minutes and Collinson appeared again, and he still had his letters in his hand.

"Been looking for you," he said, and was waving a letter at me. "Not an unmixed disaster, this rain. I have to go to town straightaway, so we couldn't have played."

"Better luck when you get back," I said.

"I don't think you'd better count on me," he said. "I might be away for two or three days. I mightn't even be able to come back here at all. Just a rush job of work and I can't afford to turn it down."

I said it was bad luck, and that was that. But I'm a suspicious kind of cuss and I couldn't help wondering. The upshot was that I rang Bill Ellice.

"I'd like you to do a private job for me, Bill. Collinson—you remember him—has had a sudden call to town and I rather think he'll be leaving here at once. I don't guarantee that he'll be going to his flat but I'd like a man to pick him up there if he does. And I'd like him watched for at least twenty-four hours. Can you do that? The address is: 2A Romney Court, Hampstead."

He thought it could be done, and I reminded him to let me know if Alice Stonhill rang the office. That finished, I had the rest of a wet morning on my hands. I did a couple of crosswords and then Bernice and I had coffee and it was then that I saw Drina's big Daimler coming along the drive. I remembered too that Alice Stonhill had not been down for breakfast, but even then I don't quite know what made me go upstairs. A porter was already bringing down the luggage and I heard Drina's voice saying she'd be down in a minute. I went quickly by her room and then peeped unashamedly from round the corner, and I saw her go into Alice Stonhill's room. The door closed after her.

I knew I was taking a risk but I slipped into the bath-room on the near side. I put my ear against the communicating door.

"I'm not going to quarrel with you," Drina was saying stridently, "but I still think it was sheer bad manners to have done what you did. But I'm warning you. I shall never meet that woman again."

"I wouldn't be too sure, my dear," Alice told her quietly. "As for bad manners, I don't consider that you're a judge. But there, as you say, there's no need to quarrel."

"And I'm warning you of something else. If you think—"

"Please don't. I'm an obstinate old woman, Drina. When I'm threatened I'm apt to take it rather badly."

"I'm not threatening. I'm telling you that if Peter wants to come back to me, then neither you nor that woman shall stop him."

"But how can we stop him?" There seemed a deliberate malice in the question. "This is a free country. If Peter wants to live with a woman other than his wife—"

"You're insufferable! . . . What right have you to interfere with other people's business!"

Nelda's voice was heard.

"Mother, are you coming?"

I drew back. Nelda passed the door. I looked furtively out and then moved off down the stairs. Bernice was still on the verandah, and from there we watched Drina's departure. Alice stayed at the door. David and Nelda had a last word at the window of the car, and then off she went. The two didn't stay to wave but went back to the hotel, and that wasn't because of the rain, for now it was just merely spotting.

"The cat's gone," I said. "Wonder what the mice will do?"

Bernice gave a quick sh! Alice Stonhill was coming towards our table.

CHAPTER 9
COLD PASTORAL

I DO NOT know if you remember that June of 1948, but if you do, your feelings won't be particularly kindly, for it was a month of rain and winds and thunderstorms. Of the few fine days, most were over-cast, and the rare days of sun flattered only, as it were, to deceive.

As for what occurred at the Malfroi Arms during that last week of our stay, I shall mention only those happenings which seemed to have importance, and it seems that unless I relate them in diary form, they will read very much like shreds and patches. To begin then with the Monday afternoon.

Camille Wesslake came down for tea and she looked to me to be absolutely normal. She said she was feeling fine and described the doctor as a fuss-pot. There was a violent thunderstorm shortly after tea but it didn't give her a head-ache. I would have liked to ask her for her own version of what happened on the Saturday night, but Alice kept her too closely under her wing.

Inspector Smallacre appeared between tea and dinner and I managed to see him before he left. He told me the Yard had a man on their books whose methods were very like those of Ferotti. He showed me a photograph cut from a copy of the *Police Gazette* but I didn't see any resemblance, and perhaps because the much aliased gentleman concerned was wearing a somewhat bushy beard. He had been posing at the time as a French count, so Smallacre said, and his idea was that the beard had been shaved off after his last coup and allowed to grow and be trimmed again in readiness for the Malfroi Arms affair.

The Tuesday was dull in the morning and I managed to get a game of golf with the aid of the club secretary. After lunch David went off with painting materials and Camille went with him, and I gathered from some malicious remarks by Nelda that David had discovered something local and was all agog to get it on canvas while the sun was out.

Thunder was in the air and it had given Bernice a head-ache, and that was why she preferred to stay with Alice Stonhill instead of joining me in a walk. Nelda was there at the time and I know now that she deliberately waylaid me when I was ready to start off.

"I'm going for a walk too," she said, and what could I do but suggest we should go together. She said she would love it if I didn't go too far, so I said that four or five miles was my limit.

"There's a wizard walk in a book I bought," she said. "I've got it with me. All field paths and things."

I said that was just up my alley and off we went, and she was to be responsible for the route. I knew later that she'd meant to make no mistakes, and we never set a foot wrong. A quarter of a mile along the main road we went over a stile and from then on I lost my bearings. But she knew where we were, even if she was doing a considerable deal of talking. The talk took an amazing turn.

"Do you think parents have a right to interfere with their children?" was the question that began it.

I said rather heavily that it all depended. Privileges demanded certain returns—loyalties, for instance. That was more or less threshed out and on the usual hackneyed lines—that children didn't ask to be born, and the duties lay wholly with the parents, and that on reaching what I might call the age of reason, children had a right to their own lives. I agreed that if the children were in a position to support themselves, that latter was a reasonable argument. Then I heard things.

Nelda said it was wholly her mother's fault that she hadn't been able to support herself. She had wanted to qualify for a job but her mother had kept her under her wing. That divorce had been the excuse, and about it Nelda was exceedingly bitter. It was plain that she hated both her father and mother, and even more than she hated Camille. Her cheeks flushed angrily when she confided in me that her mother was angling to get her father back.

"There seems nothing you can do about it," was all I could say.

"But there is," she said, and then she actually stopped in her tracks. "I like you, you know. I'm sure I can trust you. Promise you'll never say a word."

"Finger wet, finger dry," I told her with just a touch of flippancy.

"Then if I want to get married, have my parents a right to stop it?"

I moved on and was apparently deep in thought. I pointed out that she was under age and, or so it seemed to me, the parents surely had a right to run their eyes over any proposed man.

"But what if they're prejudiced?"

I said that didn't alter the fact that she was still under age. She bit her lip at that.

"Is one forced to tell one's right age? I mean on the certificate or whatever it is?"

I said I didn't know the exact position but I rather thought the whole thing might even be null and void if false statements had been made. And that was when she said we'd forget the whole thing. But she added a something before we did forget it: that it was her father who'd make the trouble.

"But how can he? Didn't the courts give your mother your custody, so to speak?"

"I'm sure something's going to happen," she said. "He's going to get a divorce from Camille and coming back to mother. It's simply revolting!"

The talk petered out from then on and nothing particular happened till we were, as I judged, well on the way back to the hotel. We were going across a meadow path and Nelda kept looking almost expectantly ahead. At the end of the path we came to a wood and at the end of a fairly wide ride I could just see what looked like farm buildings.

We turned a bit to the left and Nelda was grasping my arm.

"There's David!"

There was the easel and the folding stool, but David wasn't painting. His arms were round Camille and she seemed to be struggling. She got to her feet and her hand slapped David clean across the mouth. She snatched up her coat from the ground and began running away from us along the ride. I pulled Nelda back to the bushes, and I was unreasonably angry.

"You came deliberately round this way," I told her. "You guessed something like this was bound to happen."

"How could I?" she said, and brazened it out. Then the lip curled. "I did know he was here but I didn't know—well, what we saw."

"Then you were luckier than you guessed," I told her. "All the same, I'd rather you kept quiet about it. I'm not having myself dragged into any affairs like this. You understand that?"

"Perfectly," she told me, and with a cool resentment.

I looked out. David and the impedimenta had gone; he, as I guessed, in pursuit of Camille. Nelda and I went on, and we didn't exchange ten words till the hotel was in sight again. Then she made the advances.

"I'm sorry. I oughtn't to have done what I did."

"I was a bit abrupt too," I told her.

"And if I forget it, will you forget that other thing . . . that we were talking about?"

I said it was a bargain and then we crossed the main road and went in at the drive gates. Bernice met me outside the hotel. There'd been a telephone call for me from Bill Ellice. He'd asked if I'd ring him as soon as I got in.

"Sorry I was out, Bill," I said. "Any news?"

"Yes," he said. "I'll skip the early details, but your man boarded a plane this afternoon at three o'clock for Copenhagen."

"The devil he did!" I said, and then was having to modify the surprise. It had rather startled me, I said, but now I came to think things over it wasn't so extraordinary. He and Wesslake still had literary interests together and something had arisen which couldn't be settled over the telephone.

That was all for the Tuesday, except that, judging by Alice Stonhill's attitude that evening, I was sure that Camille had not told her what had happened that afternoon in the wood.

On the Wednesday it was raining again. Nelda went off early and Bernice was told that she was spending the day in town with a school friend. In the middle of the morning I had an unexpected call from George Wharton. He said he'd rung the flat and had been given our address. I told him Bernice had been feeling a bit run down and so we'd decided on a short holiday and we'd be back in town on the Monday morning. I suggested he might bring Mrs. Wharton to lunch at the Malfroi Arms on the Sunday. George said he couldn't because his daughter and son-in-law and the baby were arriving for a week's holiday on the Friday night. I said we'd like to see them, and George said he'd fix it up. He told me to give his love to Bernice, and that was that.

The Thursday morning brought a sensation, though Bernice and I were merely aware that something curious was happening. Bernice was later than usual for breakfast and when we went to the dining-room, all the Wesslakes were there except Nelda. Even Camille, released from the oppressive presence of Drina, was not only there but making a very good meal. Towards the end of the meal, David left the table and came back almost at once, and very excitedly. I couldn't hear what the excitement was all about, but Alice Stonhill laid her napkin aside and she and David went out together. A moment or two and Camille was following them.

We went on with our meal and when it was over Bernice went upstairs as usual. I cast an unobtrusive look round but the only thing I noticed was that David was doing some telephoning. It was a horrible morning with a gale blowing and rain lashing against the windows, so I adjourned to the small lounge where a maid was actually lighting a fire. Bernice came in and reported that all she'd noticed upstairs was that Camille was in Alice Stonhill's room. Then we saw a car coming along the drive. I went out to the entrance hall and was in time to see David dashing across to the car, and he had a bag in his hand.

About half-an-hour later Alice Stonhill and Camille came in, and it seemed to me that they were trying to behave as if nothing had happened. I went on with my crosswords and later we had mid-morning coffee. The lounge, I should say, was uncomfortably full, so there wasn't much chance for talk, and those two obstreperous children were being a bit of a nuisance. Just before midday Alice Stonhill was called to the telephone, and we didn't see her again till lunch. During that meal I made an excuse to go upstairs. Nelda's room, as I had guessed, was empty.

That was why the news in the later afternoon was no great surprise. I got it through Bernice who'd been given it by Alice Stonhill. Nelda had gone from the hotel that morning before anyone was up and had left a note behind her to the effect that she was going to stay with a friend in town. What lay behind that had been guessed and David had gone post-haste to town to try to stop the marriage, but as he had known only the name of Nelda's boy-friend, he had been able to do nothing. Then towards tea-time a telegram had come from Nelda, simply announcing that she was just married and was going away, and hoped to see everybody in a week's time.

Nothing was said to me by either Alice or Camille. David didn't return to the Malfroi Arms that night.

*   *   *   *   *

On the Friday morning Alice Stonhill left the hotel in a private car, and she had no luggage with her. Afterwards I discovered that she'd gone to Drina at Merridale, which is only ten miles west of Winstode, and she didn't return till just before dinner that night. Just after lunch I had a surprise. Bill Ellice rang me.

"Just had a commission from a certain old lady," he said. "She rang me up from a place called Merridale. A great-niece got married yesterday on the quiet and we're to find out where it took place and where the honeymoon's being spent."

"What's the man's name?" I asked him.

"Pedro Moroni—that's a stage name. Runs a band known as Pedro Moroni and his Morons. One of the haywire sort of shows. Just concluded a contract at the Paliceum. Does some work occasionally for the B.B.C. . . ."

"The client didn't hark back at all to what she mentioned on a former occasion?"

"Not a word. You'd have thought she'd never been here, except that she addressed me by my name and asked me how I was. By the way, she's in cahoots over this with a Drina Farman. That's P. W.'s wife, isn't it?"

"His ex-wife."

He said he'd meant to say that, and that was all. Or nearly so, for at the very last second I got in a question.

"I suppose you don't happen to know if J. C. is back yet from Copenhagen?"

"I don't," he said, "but if you'd like me to I could easily find out."

I told him to go ahead.

Between tea and dinner that evening, I managed to have a talk with Camille. It was something I'd been longing for a chance to do, but it turned out to be most disappointing. What had been intriguing me was the situation that had developed. Camille was refusing to give her husband a divorce, and in that determination she was being strongly backed by Alice Stonhill. But if Camille was in love with Collinson—and everything told me that she was—then surely she ought now to be only too willing to grant a divorce in order that she herself might remarry. But was Alice's determination too strong? Or would Camille rebel as Nelda had rebelled? And was it to do with that interplay that Collinson himself had flown to Copenhagen to see Wesslake?

But to get back to my talk with Camille. I introduced Collinson's name and she didn't rise at all. I mentioned her husband and Denmark, and her replies were obvious to the point of inanity, and finally the only thing I could conclude was that Alice had warned her to keep very quiet about any matters that even remotely concerned the family. Then when we talked about general topics, I found her not only uninformed but woefully dull. Let me repeat that I'm not snobbish. Camille Wesslake was merely an example of the impossibility of building Rome in a day, and Alice Stonhill still had a woeful way to go before she could shape a Camille who would fit easily into no matter what society groove. Camille's veneer was in fact so thin that it would have been better if there'd been none at all. Then she would have been only a very pretty woman who could be both friendly and charming, and without the least pretension. Camille, I thought, might be an admirable housekeeper and all that, but when it came to that other important side of marriage—what I might call the two chairs before a cosy fire—she would have driven me frantic in a month. But again don't misunderstand me. I quite liked Camille, and I had an enormous sympathy for her, but all the same I couldn't help wondering if a marriage with James Collinson the intellectual would stand as long a strain as even the first effort with Peter Wesslake.

There was one other piece of news that night and it was given to us by Alice herself—that she and Camille were leaving the hotel in the morning and going to Ashenby. She gave us a very pressing invitation to come one day to lunch, but Bernice reminded her that we ourselves were going back to town early on the Monday, and thereafter I'd be very busy. Later that night I looked up Ashenby again, and confirmed what I thought I knew—that Alice's cottage, The Briars, and Drina's house and the Malfroi Arms made a triangle, and almost an equilateral one at that, with the sides roughly ten miles long. That wasn't important at the time, though it did seem to me to put the present wife, Camille, far too near the ex-wife, Drina.

So to the Saturday morning and the departure of Alice Stonhill and Camille, and with them, by the way, went the balance of

David's luggage. We saw them off in the hired car, and the farewell was almost an affectionate one, if only because Alice seemed to have grown really fond of Bernice. The three women agreed to meet some day in town, and there was an interchange of telephone numbers.

The car moved on and with them the whole heart went out of the rest of our stay at the Malfroi Arms. It was as if that intriguing Wesslake family had been our personal guests at our own house, and now they had gone and the house was unbearably empty. That afternoon Bernice and I went to the cinema at Winstode and had tea there, and came back to find quite a lot of new arrivals. But we weren't in the least interested. All we were doing was filling in our time till the Monday morning.

On the Sunday I walked into Winstode and saw Smallacre. He had nothing new to tell me. No replies had been received to the broadcast request for any driver of car or lorry who had given a lift in the early hours of the morning to a man of Ferotti's description. The case, in fact, seemed to be out of Smallacre's hands, and even if the Yard should make an arrest, he was guessing that there'd be in it little kudos for himself.

The Monday morning came—another wet and blustering day— and Bernice and I returned to town. After lunch I went to see Bill Ellice, and the first thing he told me was that James Collinson had returned by air from Copenhagen on the Thursday morning, which meant that he'd had just one complete day in which to talk to Wesslake. That seemed definitely to make it purely a business trip, though I couldn't help wondering why Collinson had never returned, even for a meal, to the Malfroi Arms.

"What about the happy couple?" I said.

They were at the Sussex Hotel at Eastbourne, he told me.

The marriage had taken place at the Register Office, Paddington, with two of Moroni's band as witnesses. Moroni's name, so Bill had dug up, was Alfred Hawden, and he'd once had a combination which played under the name of Alf Hawden and His Music. He was about thirty-five and his general reputation seemed pretty good.

Nelda had described herself as a spinster of twenty-one, but that wasn't my headache or Bill's As far as he was concerned, he'd done the job and he'd got his cheque, and that cheque had been Drina's. I did tell him the rest of the news from the Malfroi Arms, and I was rather surprised when he said a something I ought to have seen for myself.

"It looks to me," he said, "as if it might be rather convenient now if the old lady were to fade out. If she has this Camille under her thumb, and Camille wants a divorce to marry Collinson, there's going to be a head-on collision if the old lady doesn't give way."

"You're not implying that Alice Stonhill's in any danger?" I said.

He looked surprised that I should rush so fantastically ahead. People didn't go murdering other people for the reasons I'd implied. Camille was of age. Alice Stonhill didn't have her incarcerated at The Briars. If she wanted to go to Collinson, she could do so, and live with him till a divorce came through.

"I rather think the old lady intends to leave her a goodish bit of money. Maybe Camille hates losing that."

"But Collinson's got money."

"I know," I said. "But maybe Camille wants some insurance this time against a second failure."

"It still doesn't add up to murder," Bill told me, and I had to admit that he was right.

The days went by and I thought less and less about the Wesslakes. We spent a very pleasant evening at George Wharton's house, and naturally everybody wanted to know what sort of a time we'd had at the Malfroi Arms, and that was how the Wesslake family came to be mentioned. Then when the following Saturday came, I did remember that that was the day the P.E.N. Congress was ending, and that Peter Wesslake had proposed to stay on in Denmark for a further week.

That week went by and I think Bernice and I hardly mentioned the Wesslakes at all, except once when we wondered how Nelda had survived a possible facing of the family when she got back from her honeymoon. Bernice also said, but none too heartedly, that she really ought to ring Alice Stonhill and try to fix lunch in town, and either a matinee or a tour of the shops. But nothing came of it, and the Wesslakes became something that had receded to the far backward of our minds.

And then came a certain evening—Monday the 28th of June. It was a rainy evening and Bernice and I were in the flat, and I remember she was winding wool on a patent gadget she'd acquired and I was reading James Collinson's latest book—*Elizabethan Comedy*. I had just remarked to Bernice that it was a book she'd certainly like, when the telephone bell shrilled. Bill Ellice was on the end of the line.

"You'll be dropping in in the morning?" he asked me in his mild way.

"I think so," I said. "Why? Anything on in particular?"

"Mrs. Drina Wesslake's coming in," he said. "She wouldn't tell me why; merely said it was something urgent and she wanted to see me personally."

"What time's she due?"

"Eleven o'clock."

"Right," I said. "I'll be there long before that."

PART III
THE CASE REOPENS

CHAPTER 10
DRINA WESSLAKE

THERE WAS no need for me to leave that inner door ajar for a quick sight of Drina Wesslake. As for her voice, it was always a bit strident, and it came to me clearly through the three-ply of the panel against which I had my ear.

"You're Mr. Ellice?" she began as soon as Bill had her seated, and then, without waiting for a reply, she said she recognised his voice.

"It was my aunt—aunt by marriage, I should say—who recommended me to come to you originally, Mr. Ellice. We were most satisfied with what you did about my daughter."

"I hope everything turned out well?"

"Such things never can turn out well," she told him severely. "But I've come about something quite different. Not even Mrs. Stonhill is to know that I've consulted you."

"Mrs. Stonhill?" Bill asked diplomatically.

"My aunt," she told him impatiently. "The one who recommended me to consult you about my daughter."

"Of course," Bill said. "Very stupid of me. And this business you wish to see me about this morning is—what?"

"You give me your assurances that it's most confidential?"

Bill repeated the old, old formula, even if it sounded like something perfectly new and fresh.

"Then it's about my husband—my ex-husband. I'm very much worried about him. He was very definitely in Denmark till the first week in June, but he's never returned to England."

At Bill's request she enlarged the information and we heard all about the P.E.N. Congress. Regular letters or postcards had been received from him; and his cousin, a Mr. James Collinson, had seen him in Copenhagen during the Congress week on a matter of business, and Wesslake had then told Collinson that he was staying on in Denmark for another week as he had originally planned.

"He should have been back on the twelfth," she said, "but no one's heard a word from him. Even his secretary hasn't heard a word, and he was expecting him back at his flat on the fourteenth at the very latest. There's work that urgently needs doing. Deen is almost frantic."

"Deen?"

"Frank Deen, the secretary. He's been with my husband for very many years."

Bill asked unblushingly for particulars and took down the address of Wesslake's flat.

"Now, Mrs. Wesslake," he said. "What enquiries, if any, have you made yourself? One moment," he said, as she began a quick interruption. "I'm referring to the Shipping Company. Or did your husband fly to Denmark?"

She said she didn't know, but she was rather under the impression that he had gone by boat. She knew he'd left England on the twenty-first of May.

"Then, of course, you don't know if he had a return ticket or a single?" Bill told her.

She didn't know, and he hastily said that that was one of the things he'd soon find out. Then he was asking if the secretary had made any enquiries.

"He rang me yesterday," she said, "and asked me what he ought to do and I said he was to do nothing. I'd handle the matter myself, I told him. Don't you agree that I was right?"

"Undoubtedly," he told her. "I think we can soon clear this matter up for you. You'd like us to begin at once?"

"Very definitely so."

"You wouldn't object to our questioning the secretary?"

"Certainly not."

"And one other thing. There might be all sorts of reasons for Mr. Wesslake's staying on in Denmark. One, at least, mightn't be very pleasant—"

"What do you mean?"

"Frankly this, Mrs. Wesslake. You want me to be frank?"

"Of course I do," she told him impatiently.

"Well, he might have met some lady or other in Denmark. A discovery like that might have upset you."

"Not at all," she said grimly. "I want to know why he hasn't come back to England, and where he is now. That's all, and I'm prepared to pay for it."

"And we're prepared to do all we can. But just one other frank question. Do you know of any reason, financial or otherwise, why he should deliberately avoid coming back?"

"There is none," she said tersely. "That's why I'm so uneasy. He ought to have been back and he isn't back. And why hasn't he written or telephoned? Any entanglement such as you mentioned wouldn't stop him doing that."

Bill agreed. As he said, it should be the other way round. If anything had been designedly abnormal, then one would have expected Mr. Wesslake to make it appear normal.

There seemed nothing else to do but agree on terms. When Bill mentioned a possibility of enquiries having to be made in Denmark, she seemed surprised.

"But isn't that just where you've got to make enquiries?"

Bill said that as the clients' interests were always his own, he'd had expenses in mind. And what if Mr. Wesslake should be in England?

"He can't be in England," she said. "In any case, something must have happened in Denmark because I didn't receive an answer to a letter I wrote to him during the last week of his stay."

The client is always right. Bill said that everything possible would be done. Terms were agreed on without a word of haggling, and she gave an immediate cheque for the retaining fee. Then she had a last remark to make.

"About Deen, the secretary. I'd rather he didn't know that I'm making this sort of enquiry. I wouldn't trust him not to talk."

"I think we can get over that difficulty," Bill told her. "I'll see him myself as, say, a business associate of Mr. Wesslake. Leave everything to us and rely on our tact and discretion. It's the kind of thing we're always accustomed to handling. And what about reports? You'd like them rendered confidentially. . . ."

I drew back then for the interview seemed to be virtually over. I waited till I could hear them leaving the office, and in a minute or two Bill came back and I went through.

"What'd you think of her?" I asked him.

"She's still a fine-looking woman. A bit on the dictatorial side. Genuine enough, it seemed to me, as far as what she wanted us to do."

"What comes first?" I said. "Ring up the United Shipping Company?"

Bill said I'd seen them before and they were right on our doorstep, so why shouldn't I slip round while he concocted some yarn or other for Deen and arranged an interview. So round I went. I waited in a small queue because I wanted to speak to the same clerk who'd seen me before.

"You remember my calling about a Mr. Wesslake," I told him when my turn came. "He'd sailed on the *Kronprins Frederik* for Esbjerg on May the twenty-first."

"Yes?" he said, and I thought there was something peculiar about his look.

"Well, he should have come back on the twelfth or thirteenth of this month and he was to get in touch with me. I wonder if you could tell me if he really is back?"

He hesitated for a moment and then there was an amused ironic droop to his lip.

"Mr. Wesslake returned on the *Parkeston* on the twelfth."

My eyes popped, and not because of the news but because he hadn't needed to look up his files.

"Either you've got a remarkable memory," I said, "or someone else has been asking about Mr. Wesslake."

"Put it down to memory," he said.

"Yes, but look here. Suppose Mr. Wesslake owes me a devil of a lot of money. If other people are after him too . . ."

He cut me short.

"Sorry, sir, but we're not allowed to give information of that sort. All I can tell you is that the passenger you're enquiring about used his return ticket on a certain date."

There was nothing to do but thank him and leave. But I wondered just who had been enquiring. If Drina, then she had been both a fluent liar and a remarkably good actress in Bill's office. If Deen—and he seemed the likeliest person—then he'd been deceiving or withholding information from Drina. According to Drina, he had been in touch with her and had been very worried about Wesslake. The information I'd just obtained was open to him. He could have telephoned for it and could then have telephoned Drina. But he hadn't done that very obvious thing, and that seemed to me to be highly peculiar. It was certainly something I must mention at once to Bill.

I got back to find that Bill had made contact with Deen and had fixed an appointment at Bridge Mansions at two o'clock. He seemed most interested when I told him that Wesslake had definitely returned, and even more so when he heard what I'd discovered. And he agreed with my arguments.

"I'll try to get Deen to throw light on it," he said. "But there's another interested party—the wife. Why shouldn't she have enquired?"

"Or Collinson," I said, "if it comes to that. And that reminds me. Wesslake sent letters and postcards home. He must have mentioned the actual boat and the sort of crossing he had. If so, everyone would have known it, including Drina."

"Not necessarily," he said. "If she was the ex-wife, don't you think the others would have kept her a bit out of things? And would it have been tactful to have discussed the ex-husband when she was there?"

"Was it tactful to ask her to those birthday celebrations and be in the company of the new wife?"

"Leave it," Bill said. "I'll see what I can get out of Deen."

I struck another iron while it was hot. Whatever happened with Deen, I said, it looked a certainty that someone would have to go to Copenhagen. I'd rather like to do that job myself. It wasn't for the sake of a pleasant trip but because I thought I could handle things, and I'd already made contacts there over the telephone. Bill said he'd be mighty glad if I did go, and maybe I'd better see at once about a seat in the next day's plane.

I went back to the flat for lunch, and to break the news to Bernice. It was from there that I did my telephoning, and when I'd fixed things up at the airport, I ventured to ring Drina Farman. I always thought of her as Drina Wesslake, but Farman was how she'd signed Bill's two cheques.

"Mrs. Farman?" I said in my special bass voice. "This is Mr. Ellice's confidential secretary. He wishes me to tell you that he's already begun work and has obtained certain information. Is it correct, for example, that one of the reasons why a particular gentleman went to Denmark was because some of his late mother's relatives might still be there?"

"I think perhaps that was one of the reasons," she said. "In fact, I'm sure it was."

"Then could you give me any information? His mother's name and birthplace, for instance? And any relatives you happen to remember?"

She asked me to hold the line and I had a wait of at least five minutes.

"His mother was Ilse Jensen of Roskilde," she said. "Shall I spell it for you?"

The client is always right, so I let her do the spelling.

"She was a very charming woman," she told me. "I knew her quite well, of course."

"And any other likely relatives?"

"She had one brother. His name must have been Jensen, of course, and I seem to remember his Christian name was Mogens."

I was glad she spelt that for me. When I asked what he was, she said he was quite a famous artist. She didn't remember where he had lived but if I waited a moment she'd try to refresh her memory from the map.

There was another longish wait and then she was telling me that the place was called Tisvilde.

"And what exactly was his father? Use Jensen's father too, of course."

"He also was an artist, and he wrote books. We had one or two in the house but when my mother-in-law died I got rid of them with a lot of things of hers we didn't want."

I thanked her and rang off. A hasty cup of tea and I was hopping a bus for Broad Street. Bill had only just got back.

"Deen's a quiet, intellectual sort of chap," he told me. "Very frank, or so it seemed to me. He's been with Wesslake some fifteen years, so he must be pretty good at his job. He took me for what I said I was, or if he didn't he concealed it remarkably well. He says he didn't make enquiries at any shipping office."

"Why didn't he?"

"Well, according to him, Wesslake could be very secretive at times, and he didn't say how he was going to Denmark. If anything, he went out of his way to give Deen the impression that he was going by air. Deen did ring the two air-lines and found Wesslake hadn't come back from Denmark that way."

"I wonder if you thought of something," I said. "Did Deen leave for his holiday before the twenty-first?"

"He did," Bill said. "I asked him and he says he left on the Tuesday and Wesslake was leaving on the Friday. Deen spent that Friday and the Saturday in Oxford. He was due back from his holiday, by the way, a day or so before Wesslake was supposed to return. There was a first draft of a film scenario to get ready, and he showed me what he'd done."

"I wonder," I said.

"Wonder what?"

"Whether it was by design that Deen was sent on that holiday before Wesslake started on his own."

"What design could there be?"

"To keep Deen from checking up on how Wesslake actually went to Copenhagen."

Bill didn't see the point and neither, to tell the truth, did I, at least in all its implications. It was just that something was warning me that somewhere everything wasn't just what it seemed. I dropped the whole thing and asked if Bill had formed any idea of what Deen really thought of his employer.

"He couldn't have been more open," Bill said. "Mind you, I do think he was trying to give me the impression that he himself was the one who held everything together. I was ostensibly a business acquaintance to whom Wesslake owed money, and Deen didn't scruple to say that Wesslake was very secretive and even touchy about his private affairs. He admitted Wesslake was far from careful where money was concerned and he hinted that if it wasn't for the work he put in himself in making money, Wesslake might have had to reduce his personal expenditure pretty drastically."

"And how'd he find Wesslake as an employer?"

"He didn't," Bill said dryly. "The work he did and the ideas he contributed—according to him—made him almost a partner."

That wasn't quite answering the question, but it did make me ask something else.

"Let's suppose something, Bill. Let's suppose Wesslake is dead. Did Deen give you the idea that that mightn't make any difference to the Peter Arden books. That Deen, for instance, knew enough of the technique and so on to go on writing them himself?"

"I suppose that's what it amounted to," Bill said, and then was giving me a rather peculiar look. "You're not implying that if Wesslake should happen to be dead, then Deen might have engineered it?"

"You've got to look at things from all angles," I told him. "And it's much nicer to get the cash and the credit for books that you've practically been writing for someone else. But let's go back to Wesslake, the man. What else did Deen say about him?"

"That he was an excellent employer and the work wasn't too onerous and he paid quite well."

"Sounds to me as if Deen was contradicting himself," I said. "But you ought to know. You saw him yourself. But about tomorrow. This is what I've done."

Everything was fixed up and it was the sight of the travellers' cheques that reminded Bill of something.

"Deen told me something else he'd done in the matter of Wesslake's non-arrival," he said. "Though Wesslake was secretive about the way he was going to Denmark, he did give Deen the job of getting the £30 travellers' cheques and the hundred kroner he was allowed to take. That bank was the first place Deen thought about when Wesslake didn't turn up because the regulations are that if the bank supplies you with the currency, you have to hand back any balance left over and they make an entry in your passport. The bank said Wesslake hadn't been in at all."

That was all. I said goodbye to Bill and told him that I'd telephone from Denmark if anything sensational turned up, and if not, then I'd probably be back in forty-eight hours. But on my way home I was still thinking about Deen. It was true that you could get wrong ideas from second-hand reports, and yet I was still of the mind that Deen had rather contradicted himself when talking to Bill Ellice. First Deen had been anti-Wesslake and then pro-Wesslake; first subtly appreciative of his own work, and then quite satisfied with his employment. I wondered which came first, and whether Deen had realised that one of these attitudes had been the dropping of a brick, and if he had promptly eradicated one impression by presenting another.

Then I had to smile at myself. I do that sometimes when I realise where impetuosity has led me—that, perhaps, and an abnormal curiosity and a nervous dislike of unsolved problems. I could tell myself that whereas I often felt irritated by George Wharton's showmanship and love of having a finger in every pie, I myself was tarred with the very same brush. Perhaps I didn't trust Bill's summing-up of Deen because some latent vanity had been telling me that I could have conducted that interview far better myself. When I got to the flat some urge of conscience made me ring Bill in order to say as much, but he didn't happen to be in. When I rang him again in the morning, he was out on some other business, and by then, of course, I was feeling far less vividly the overnight twinges of conscience. And as things turned out, that was to be rather a pity.

One of the things you do not wish to hear about is a description of a trip by air to Copenhagen, so let's say that I got there at exactly four o'clock the next afternoon. The airport is quite a way from the city but there were plenty of taxis, and when I'd got through the customs, it didn't take long to get to the hotel. I'd reserved a room, by the way, by telephone, and at Wesslake's hotel—the Metropolitan.

I had some ersatz tea and two excellent cakes. Then I changed and went down to the hotel desk, and never had I felt so happy about making an enquiry. There was I in a foreign country where not a soul knew me. Even if it was the same girl at the desk who had answered my telephone enquiries of some weeks before, I was reasonably sure she'd not remember my voice. But it happened that I didn't have to speak to her at all. A gentleman in a dark lounge suit came up and hoped my stay would be a happy one. It turned out that he was the manager, and I guessed he was the one who'd given me the previous information about Wesslake. I hoped that he too wouldn't remember my voice, and I'm sure he didn't.

"Did the recent P.E.N. Congress make much difference to you here?" I asked him.

His English was quite good and I was wishing I spoke Danish half as well, for mine was limited to a phrase or two I'd acquired from a book I'd bought at the airport. What he told me was that the hotel was practically always full, but he had accommodated about twenty members of Congress. The hotel, as he pointed out, was in the Kongens Nytorv—that lovely square called in English, the King's New Market—out of which led the Bredgade, in which was the Congress headquarters.

"It was an English member who recommended me to come here," I said. "I don't expect you remember him—a Mr. Wesslake."

But he did remember Wesslake. He had been at the hotel for a fortnight and then, if he remembered rightly, was going to spend a further week in Fyen and Jutland. Mr. Wesslake, he said, was a very nice gentleman, and, he believed, quite a famous author.

I said that was so. Then I remembered that Mr. Wesslake had had an English friend, or so I thought, at the hotel. The manager's face lighted. The name was on the tip of his tongue and he was exasperated because he couldn't recall it. Then he checked up in his office and was able to tell me that the friend—Wesslake had shared a table with her—was a Mrs. Chrome.

That sounded interesting. I asked if she wasn't quite a good-looking woman of about thirty. Dark and rather tall. He shook his head. Mrs. Chrome was of middle age and rather short. But a very vivacious lady and also an authoress, or so he thought.

I left things at that, even if I did think that an elderly lady, however vivacious, was hardly the Congress stable-companion I'd have expected a man like Wesslake to choose, though it might have been, of course, that she had wished herself on him. What I did next was to take a stroll round the immediate neighbourhood and along the Bredgade. But I didn't call on Axel Dessau. I telephoned him after dinner at the hotel, but he wasn't in. But I left a message and that kept me to the hotel till he should ring me, and that was at about nine o'clock that night. I gave him my real name and I heard the same courteous voice. An appointment was made for nine o'clock the next morning.

After that I took, as recommended by my waiter, a stroll round the Tivoli gardens, but it was none too good a night and the place was a bit raucous for even the low-brow side of me, and after I'd had a beer in one of the restaurants, I took a bus back to the hotel. Almost as soon as my head hit the pillow, and before I'd had time to wonder what the next day would produce, I was sound asleep. And even if I had known what was to happen, I don't think it would have made any difference.

CHAPTER 11
DYING FALL

I FOUND the Congress secretary to be as charming and helpful as his voice had indicated. For my part I was perfectly open. I was employed by a reputable firm of private investigators to discover the present whereabouts of a Mr. Peter Wesslake, and I didn't conceal the fact that I was the person who had rung Mr. Dessau from London just before the Congress had begun.

"Naturally," he said, "I didn't come into contact with every member. Official delegates and guests of honour—yes, but not what one might call the ordinary members."

"There were debates?"

"Most certainly," he said, and spotted what I was trying to get at. "But I don't remember your Mr. Wesslake as a speaker. A lot of members, of course, never intend to take part in debates. Some, I'm afraid, regard the Congress merely as a means of having a holiday abroad."

He gave me a beautifully printed Program, as it called itself, of the Congress. It had a certain amount of general information and the programme itself. I said, and rightly, that members could have had a remarkably good time, what with conducted tours of North Zealand and Copenhagen, and various banquets, receptions and lunches, and evenings at the ballet and the Copenhagen Broadcasting House.

"Were there any official photographs of any of these functions?" I asked him.

"The newspapers had their own photographers," he said. "We made no arrangements for taking photographs ourselves."

Then he asked me to wait a minute, and when he came back it was with some newspaper clippings. Most were photographs or sketches of Congress celebrities, but there was one—not too well printed—of what looked like a very large number of members in the paved court of a castle or museum.

"Here's an actual print of that," he said. "It was taken on the Friday at Frederiksborg, Hillerod."

He smiled as he showed it to me. The photographer had been well above the crowd and, as there was bright sunshine that afternoon, everyone was squinting upwards. The perspective was unusual and amusing.

"That's you," I said, pointing him out. Then I spotted Wesslake. He was hatless and his hair looked white compared with the dark-hatted heads of most of the men and women.

"That's Mr. Wesslake," I said. "The view's rather an odd one but there he is. I recognise his hair."

"I think I remember him now," he said. "A man of medium height and about fifty or over."

"That's roughly it," I said. "And I believe he was often with a Mrs. Chrome, an English lady who was staying at the same hotel."

"I remember her," he said. "She spoke at one of the debates. Rather petite, and very alert. Lively, perhaps you'd call it."

The Program gave a full list of members. Under ENGLAND I found Phoebe L. Chrome, and her Copenhagen address the Metropolitan Hotel. I asked if he had her English address and he looked it up. The address from which she had written to ask for a hotel reservation was—The Retreat, Sedford, Nr. Braintree, Essex.

That seemed to be all I could do about Wesslake. I did mention that his mother had been Danish, and her father a certain Jensen who had been both artist and author.

"That would be Peter Jensen," he said. "You will see some of his pictures in the Hirschsprung Samling—the Hirschsprung collection of pictures which is near the Museum of Fine Arts."

"I think he had a son who was an artist too," I said. "A Mogens Jensen. Do you know if he's still alive?"

He seemed to know the name and no more, so I left it at that. When I thanked him he told me he was at my disposal for anything else I wanted to know. He also gave me a copy of the Program. But for the uncertainty of my movements, as I told him, I'd have been delighted to ask him to join me at lunch.

What I did was to make my way back to my hotel, and there I asked for a call to London. There was far from a long wait, and it was Bertha Munney's voice I heard. Mr. Ellice, she said, was out.

"Take this down as urgent, Bertha," I said, and was recommending Bill to interview Phoebe Chrome. I mentioned her as having been a companion of Wesslake's in Copenhagen, and that, like him, she'd left the Metropolitan Hotel on the morning of Sunday, June the thirteenth.

I enquired about a tram to take me to the Museum of Fine Arts, and when I got off it, asked a passer-by the whereabouts of the Hirschsprung Samling. Whereas the Museum was a huge building with—as my guide book said—a collection of sculpture, and pictures by the Old Masters, the Hirschsprung Collection of Danish pictures was housed in a single storied building that looked rather like the entrance lodge to a castle. All I wanted there was a catalogue and a quick look at a picture or two by Wesslake's grandfather. I found one or two at once—quite pleasant, if rather old-fashioned landscapes—but I also found two pictures by his son, Mogens, who was Wesslake's uncle. Each was a view of grassy dunes with glimpses of the sea and each quite competent and highly attractive.

I looked up the Curator, introduced myself as an English art critic, and asked if Mogens Jensen was still alive. He said that for all he knew, he was, though he must be getting to be an oldish man. He looked up his address—Lynghytten, Tisvilde, and told me that the best way to get there, if I didn't mind the expense, was to hire a private car. When I got back to the hotel, the manager arranged for a car to pick me up after lunch.

Tisvilde is a small town in the northwest corner of Zealand, just a few miles short of the coast, with its sand dunes that Mogens Jensen painted so well. I sat in front with the driver whose English was no better than my Danish, but a wave of his hand and the help of the guide-book map were enough to make me see the things that ought to be seen. When we left Copenhagen, the country was undulating farmland, with woods and an occasional lake. Then came the shores of Roskilde Fjord, and finally we came to heath-like country abounding in pines and firs, and the tang of them was lovely in the sun as we passed. I think it was just over an hour—and we'd travelled fairly fast—-when we got to Tisvilde. The driver got out to make enquiries, and then we went on through the little town towards the sea. A kilometre on, we stopped at a little villa. I knew we had arrived because that villa had a wing attached with a glass roof, and that meant a studio.

I went along a short path to the door. It was open, and I ventured to give a call. An elderly woman appeared, and she looked to me like a housekeeper.

"English," I said, and smiled and tapped my chest. Then I raised an enquiring hand. "Mr. Jensen?"

She shrugged her shoulders and her hands were gesturing what seemed to be a denial, and when she spoke I couldn't understand a word. I beckoned to the driver and he came to the door, and he and the elderly woman were talking nineteen to the dozen. Then he turned to me.

"Seek," he said, and pointed upwards. "Jensen seek. No see."

If Jensen was sick and couldn't see anybody, then I'd wasted my time.

"English?" I said, and waved back towards the town.

It is amazing what a little gesticulating and gibberish will produce. He had some more words with the woman, then beamed at me and pointed back towards Tisvilde. Off he went to the car, reversed it, and was driving back. And he must have given me a good character, for the woman was motioning for me to come in. She showed me into a kind of lounge, walls lined with low bookshelves and above them pictures by Jensen himself.

In about ten minutes I heard the car drawing up again. The driver had brought back a perfectly charming girl. Her English was as near perfect as makes no difference, and after that we got on like a house on fire. Mogens Jensen, it appeared, had had a stroke and was lying seriously ill upstairs. I explained about the P.E.N. Congress and wanted to know if a Mr. Peter Wesslake—a nephew of Jensen—had called to see his uncle.

And he had called. The old woman produced a card he had left. He too had come by car but his driver had had some English, and through the driver Wesslake had asked if the card could be given to Mr. Jensen as soon as he was sufficiently recovered. It was simply a visiting card with the Millside, Burnbury address, and on the back of it was carefully printed—"Your nephew wishes you a speedy recovery and hopes to hear from you then."

I asked when it was that the Mr. Wesslake had called. It took a good deal of argument before the woman claimed she knew. The date, she said, was Thursday, June the third, and in the afternoon. I also elicited the fact that the woman had been Jensen's housekeeper for over twenty-five years. Jensen, as far as she knew, hadn't been to England during that time. She had not known Ilse Jensen, though she had heard Mogens speak of her, and she did remember her death. But for being unwell at the time—he had apparently been delicate all his life—he would have gone to England for the funeral.

There seemed nothing else to ask, so I thanked the old housekeeper and the three of us went back to Tisvilde.

I treated the interpreter to an ice, and she told me about her stay in England. When I went back to the car I got her to explain to the driver that I wanted to go back via Roskilde, and that if it meant extra mileage, I was prepared to pay.

I also asked her what there was to see at Roskilde and she told me what I should have remembered, that there was a magnificent cathedral and in it the monuments of several of the Danish kings. When I said I might need the services of an interpreter, she advised me to look for any young pedestrian who looked like a student. That was all, and we parted with mutual smiles.

It was a long ride to Roskilde, which is about half-an-hour by train to the south-west of Copenhagen. I had coffee there and cakes, and the driver had a beer. The owner of the restaurant—the driver had told me somehow that it was the best in the town—spoke reasonable English, and he sent for his son, whose English was better still, to conduct me to the house where Peter Jensen had lived.

It was a middle-aged lady who opened the door. She was living there and she spoke good English too. And she was vastly surprised when I told her I had come to see the house where Peter Jensen had lived and worked; surprised because I was the second Englishman who had come for the same reason that summer. On her, too, Wesslake had left a card, but this time it had on it no writing, but he had told her, to her great gratification, that he was a grandson of the famous man.

I asked her what the date was, and she had to think back. But she was positive enough when she did remember it. It was on a Sunday, May the thirtieth, and Mr. Wesslake had called in the early afternoon. I asked if he'd been accompanied by an English lady and she smiled as she said he had. She had offered them tea but they had said they had not long had lunch, but she had shown them some of the rooms.

That was all I needed at Roskilde. I did have a quick look at the cathedral and then we drove back to Copenhagen. At the hotel I confirmed my temporary reservation for a plane the next afternoon, and by then it was time for dinner, and I had to call it a day.

I had breakfast early and had an immediate hunt through two of the nearest bookshops, and in the second I found Danish editions of two of the Peter Arden books, and the publishers were Martins Forlag. I was given my directions for the publishers' address and then took a bus to Raadhus-pladsen and walked the rest of the way.

I should have missed it but for a notice on the wall, for it was in a little courtyard off the main road. The principals were both away but a charming elderly lady saw me, and her English too was almost perfect. Again I made no bones about saying why I was there, and she was showing an immediate concern. Mr. Wesslake had called during his stay, though she hadn't seen him herself. He was very charming, she'd been given to understand, and his visit had been merely a courtesy one; a personal introduction of himself, so to speak, to his Danish publishers. I asked if she could find out the date, and at once she was pressing the buzzer and speaking to a probable secretary. The answer came almost at once. Mr. Wesslake had called on the Wednesday morning of his first week's stay.

I thanked her and assured her that Mr. Wesslake doubtless had some excellent reason for not returning to England on the date expected, and then I went back to the hotel. There was little else, it seemed to me, that I could do in Denmark, but I did make some more enquiries about Wesslake's likely movements after leaving Copenhagen. All I could elicit was that he had mentioned at the desk when he settled his bill that he was probably going to stay for a day or two in Odense. He had been recommended to try the Plage Hotel. I at once rang the Plage Hotel and made enquiries, and after some time was told that no one of the name of Wesslake had stayed there.

At seven o'clock that evening I was in Bill Ellice's office, and from there I rang Bernice to say I'd be home in about an hour. Then I went over everything I'd done in Denmark. Bill agreed that we'd discovered nothing, except to prove everything we were supposed already to know. Wesslake's sudden joining of the P.E.N. club was really—as we'd thought—solely for the purpose of a holiday in Denmark.

"One thing does surprise me," I said. "I regarded him as a man who'd want to hog the limelight. You know—the great Peter Wesslake. Yet he'd been so unobtrusive that Axel Dessau hadn't noticed him, and he hadn't opened his mouth at any debate."

"Why should he," Bill said, "if he was there simply for a holiday?"

"Just something that occurred to me," I said. "And there's another thing in that same context. When they filled in the form for hotel reservations, members were given space on the same form to fill in the names of their books, and so on. Wesslake simply wrote 'Author' on his form and left it at that. He didn't even mention either of his pseudonyms, which at least two other English authors did. Their names are here—look—in this official Program."

Bill had a look and said it still went to show that Wesslake wanted nothing from that Congress but the amenities it afforded. I said maybe he was right, even if it wasn't altogether in keeping. Then I was wanting to know what had happened at the interview with Miss—or was it Mrs.?—Chrome. It was Miss, he said, and he had seen her himself.

Her house, he said, was a tiny, arty sort of cottage, and she was just as my informants had described her. Her qualification for membership of the P.E.N. was the authorship of articles on spiritualism and black magic, and that was a bit of a bee in her bonnet. She had found Wesslake an excellent companion, and she confirmed that he had dodged practically every business session of Congress, and had cynically regarded the affair as an admirable excuse and opportunity for a holiday. She mentioned herself that visit to Roskilde.

"Nothing much there, then," I said.

"Wait a minute," Bill told me. "There's something to come yet. She left the hotel early on the Sunday, went to Esbjerg, stayed there a night and came back by boat on the Monday. She said goodbye to Wesslake in the hotel before she left Copenhagen, and she knew all about him staying on for a week in Fyen and Jutland. But he told her something else. When she asked if he'd run down some time and have lunch with her at Sedford, he told her that immediately on his return to England he was going to America. To Hollywood, to be exact, and he'd probably be there for at least two years."

My eyes had popped a bit at that.

"What was the idea?" I said. "Trying to impress her? If so, that's more like the real Wesslake."

"My idea is that he'd begun to find her a bit of a bore," Bill said. "He didn't want her pestering him in town, so he put her thoroughly off with that Hollywood yarn."

"But you're going to try to check up on it nevertheless?"

"I certainly am."

"Well, it's a forlorn hope," I said. "I can't imagine Wesslake keeping the news of a genuine, highly-paid Hollywood job away from all his family. Anything else have you done?"

What he'd concentrated on, he said, was to try to pick up Wesslake from the moment he'd landed at Parkeston Quay. Two men were on the job, questioning porters and so on at the Parkeston end and taximen at the other. He'd also rung Millside, though knowing it a waste of time. The Upmans had reported, as he'd expected, that they'd never heard a word from the master.

"I'd rather like to run down there myself tomorrow," I said. "I shan't find anything but I'd like to see the place. Especially that summer-house. I think I can find a perfectly good excuse."

Bill was all in favour of anything that might produce some information. It was a rather ironical situation, as he said. Drina Farman wanted her ex-husband found and Bill wanted to find him for her. But he also wanted Wesslake on his own account, in order to collect on that fire enquiry business. Sixty pounds would neither make Bill nor break him, but it was just as well in his pocket as in Wesslake's.

As I was thinking things over on my way back to the flat, it seemed to me that no harm could be done if I told Bernice what that trip to Denmark had been about. It turned out that she had guessed most of it. After all, she had heard from both Camille and Aunt Alice that Wesslake was in Denmark, and had gathered from the latter in particular that Wesslake wasn't all he should be. But it did surprise her to learn that Wesslake had disappeared.

"I wonder if you'd like to ring them up at Ashenby," I said. "Try to arrange a lunch in town and a show. I'll pay. I might even be induced to join the party."

Bernice rang at once. It was Camille who spoke. I had my ear pretty close and could catch what she said.

"That's awfully sweet of you, Mrs. Travers, and we'd have loved to come, only Aunty's been ill."

"I am sorry. What's been the matter?"

"A really nasty chill. She frightened me badly at the time, but she's getting over it now. She's still in bed, though."

I was making signs to Bernice to hand me the telephone. "We do hope she'll be quite better soon. Here's my husband, by the way. I think he'd like a word with you."

"Hallo, Mrs. Wesslake," I said. "So sorry to hear about your aunt. Give her our love, will you?"

"I will," she said, and seemed at a loss for further words.

"You're keeping fit yourself?" I asked.

"I never get ill," she told me with a laugh.

"That's fine," I said. "But what I was going to mention was this. I've got to see some people quite near Ashenby tomorrow, and I wondered if I might drop in."

"Do come in," she said. "Will it be for lunch or tea?"

"I don't think it will be either," I said, "though it's very nice of you to ask me. It'll probably be at about eleven in the morning. Just the briefest call."

"Can't Mrs. Travers come too?"

"Sorry, but it's absolutely impossible," I said, "or she'd have loved to come. Be seeing you in the morning, then."

"In time for coffee," she said, and we both laughed.

As I told Bernice, all I wanted was to study Camille's reactions to the disappearance of her husband. With Collinson the likely go-between, the two women at Ashenby would naturally be highly intrigued. While they wouldn't know that Drina had employed Ellice's office, they'd be interested in hearing from Collinson of Drina's reactions. In my view, they'd regard the whole thing as highly suspect; some new coercion perhaps, in that matter of a divorce, or some swindle in which Drina was playing a part. In any case it ought to be interesting to know just what the ideas were.

In the morning I rang Bill and told him of the change of plans. He said he'd run down to Millside himself as there was something he wanted to check at that end. I used some of the firm's petrol to drive my car to Ashenby, and it was just short of eleven o'clock when I drew up outside The Briars.

It was a thatched, half-timbered house set back from the lane, and as charming a place as one would wish to see. And it was larger than I'd imagined from that dreadful painting of David Wesslake's, with at least four bedrooms. A man was working in the front gardens which were dazzlingly gay in a sun which had decided to come through the clouds. A flagged path led to the front porch and at the side was a short drive with a garage at its end. As I came through the front gate I noticed the garden chairs and table set on the lawn beneath a gigantic beech, and it was there that we were to have our mid-morning coffee.

"You wouldn't believe it," was almost the first thing that Camille said to me, "but Auntie absolutely insists on seeing you. I made her promise she wouldn't keep you more than a minute."

She went up first to make sure, and in a minute was beckoning to me from the head of the narrow stairs. Alice Stonhill was sitting up in bed, and I was shocked at the sight of her. She was so frail that a puff would have blown that life candle out. But she smiled at the sight of me and her thin hand went out.

"So nice to see you," she said, and her voice was remarkably firm. "What a pity you couldn't bring that charming wife of yours."

"I ought to scold you if I had the heart," I said. "Here I am, leaving you at Winstode like a frivolous widow of forty, and now what do I find?"

"Just an old woman who oughtn't to be here at all," she said, but there was still a smile as she shook her head. "But there, I mustn't complain. This is only the second time I've been really ill in my life."

"And you're not going to be ill again for a very long time to come," I told her, and then Camille was saying that I would have to be going.

"Camille, you're a dragon," Alice told her.

"But a good dragon," I said.

"Yes," she said, and very slowly: "The best dragon in the world."

Camille tried to smile at me but there were sudden tears in her eyes. I quietly backed out but Alice was calling that I was to give her love to Bernice. I said I certainly would.

I went downstairs to an exquisitely furnished room with an open fire-place, and Camille joined me there almost at once. Or rather she winkled me out. Coffee was to be outdoors, she said, and we strolled across the lawn to the shade and shelter of the beech. The daily woman brought the tray.

"Just like old times," Camille said. "Mid-morning coffee at the Malfroi Arms."

"Where are the rest of the family?" I asked her.

David was in Paris, she said, and Nelda living at a London hotel. Her husband's work took him from one place to another, and they hadn't a settled home. Alice had seen her since her marriage, and so had Drina. Alice, I gathered, was of the private opinion that Nelda had found her milieu. Drina had done the cut-off-with-a-shilling act, not that the couple couldn't get along well enough without her.

"Now tell me what you thought of Auntie," Camille said, and I had to say that it looked to me as if she must have had a remarkably narrow escape.

"She's a queen now, compared with what she was. And it all started so ridiculously. You know: just her nose beginning to run and she was sniffing a bit, but she wouldn't go to bed. And then, before she knew where she was, she was running a temperature and absolutely delirious. I sent for the doctor and he had a nurse come at once. I think she must have had pneumonia, but he wouldn't say. I do know she was dreadfully ill, and, as I said, she's a queen now compared with what she was. She doesn't even need the nurse. In a day or two he's going to allow her to come down."

"This must have happened as soon as you got here," I said.

"It did. We'd only just got back."

"Well, she's a great soul," I said. "I'm glad she pulled through. You're very fond of her, aren't you?"

"I am. I never loved anyone so much in all my life."

"I think she feels that way about you too. I think she'd do anything for you, Camille. You don't mind my calling you Camille? After all, I'm old enough to be your father."

"I like it," she said, and flushed delightfully. "I like you too, Mr. Travers. I think you're so—well, so thoughtful and nice. Look at the way you spoke to Auntie just now."

"You give me another cup of coffee and stop flattering," I told her, and I was thinking nevertheless that Camille was far from finding me allergic. She was being utterly natural, with no worries about speech and poise. "And strictly between ourselves," I went on, "I rather like you, Camille. And so does my wife. I wish we'd lived nearer so that we could have helped."

She gave me my second cup and insisted on my having another biscuit. Something was at the tip of her tongue.

"Is there anything I can do now?" I asked her.

"Well," she said, and for some reason or other her cheeks were flushing again, "I'd like to tell you something. It's something that happened and I can't understand it."

"Something that happened?"

She gave a quick look back towards the house.

"It was the night when I brought Auntie up her hot milk," she said. "She'd gone to bed early because the cold was worse and I'd said she must have some hot milk and some aspirins. She wouldn't let me send for the doctor. So I took the milk up and, do you know, she was absolutely out of her head. She frightened me to death, and I simply flew downstairs to the telephone and spoke to the doctor and he came almost at once."

"But you said something happened."

"Yes, it did. It was when I went upstairs again and was waiting for the doctor."

She paused. She looked away for a moment before she met my eyes again.

"Promise you'll never say a word to a single soul. Not even to Mrs. Travers, or anyone?"

She was in deadly earnest and I said as earnestly that whatever she told me I'd keep to myself.

"Well, it was something she kept on saying to herself. It wasn't loud, if you know what I mean. It was more of a mumble as if she was delirious and talking to herself. I put my head down to hear it and I could just make something out. She was saying, all sort of over and over again, that Peter knew."

"Peter?"

"Yes, Peter. My husband. And she was saying something else, about not letting them do it. 'Peter knows,' she kept mumbling, and 'They shan't do it,' and all over and over again, and it gave me the willies. It made me feel I wanted to scream. I think I'd have fainted or something if the doctor hadn't come. He gave her an injection and she was quiet after that." She let out a breath. "But I was frightened!"

"Have you told your husband about this?"

Her cheeks flushed again.

"As a matter of fact he should have been back long ago from Denmark but we haven't heard a word. That's been a bit of a worry too."

"You mean he's disappeared?"

"We don't know," she said. "All we know is he hasn't written or done anything. Naturally I don't want to worry Auntie with it till she's properly well again, but if she doesn't do anything about it then, I think I shall go to the police. I think it's my duty, don't you?"

"Your husband'll appear long before that," I told her. "Let's hope so in any case. But about those words your aunt was muttering to herself. What could they mean? Just what did Peter know?"

"I can't think," she said. "I expect it was something silly, though. Something quite . . . trivial." She gave a little smile as she hit on that right word. "Perhaps I've been silly too. I oughtn't to have been scared."

"I think you'd every reason to be scared," I said. "But I shouldn't go on worrying. You've got it off your mind now you've told me about it, and now I'd forget the whole thing."

I glanced at my watch and pretended to be startled at the time. She walked with me to the car.

"Don't forget," I told her. "You've only to ring me at any hour of the day or night and if it's humanly possible I'll be along as quickly as the car'll get me here."

"I know you will," she said. There were tears in her voice and her eyes. I hurriedly slipped into the car and waved a final hand as it moved off.

There was nothing I could report to Bill Ellice. I had given my word not to divulge what Camille had told me, and it was a promise that I intended to keep. Naturally I had my own ideas. "Peter knows," was what Alice had told herself in that delirium, and what he knew I couldn't guess, unless it was who had struck Camille down at the swimming-pool. As for that other remark—"they shan't do it"—that was something incomprehensible, unless it was tied up with the remark that went with it—that more than one person had been concerned in that swimming-pool attack. And one other thing I did gather, that Collinson had been frequently to The Briars. When I had mentioned the other members of the family, Camille had not added his name. But I was sure that he had been a frequent visitor, and the strange thing then was that she had not told him what she had just told me. I was sure that I was the only one in whom she'd confided, and that was making me wonder just why. Maybe—and the theory didn't seem too outrageous—Camille herself had had a suspicion that Collinson was one of those people who comprised the they. "They shan't do it," was what Camille had said she had heard. Were Wesslake and Collinson in cahoots? Was—and it was far more likely—David Wesslake one of the they? Had he and Collinson been concerned in that attack at the pool?

Another week went by and Bill decided he wasn't justified in spending any more of his client's money. Here is the confidential letter he sent to Drina:

> . . . As I told you over the telephone, I can see nothing further that we can do, and as I said then, I do most earnestly advise you now to apply to the police. We know that Mr. Wesslake landed from the Parkeston on the thirteenth and we have the actual porter who carried his luggage off the ship to the train. We can prove his arrival at Liverpool Street, but can find no taxi that handled him or his luggage from then on. Perhaps, as he had only one large bag and one small, he took the Underground from the Station itself. At any rate, as far as our enquiries are concerned, he disappeared from then on.
>
> I am enclosing your account as requested. Please settle it at your absolute leisure. We can only regret that we have been unable to render the services we would have wished, and I would like to repeat that under the circumstances it would be a waste of money to continue enquiries.
>
> Believe me,
>
> Yours sincerely,
W. E. ELLICE.

Two days later the cheque came. With it was a short note to the effect that she was satisfied he'd done his best.

If, however, any new information should reach her, she would get into touch with him at once, and ask his advice. She remained, his sincerely, Drina Farman. Nothing was said about the police.

But no more information apparently arrived. July went by and the first week in August. And then something did happen, but not through Drina Farman.

PART IV
ENTER THE YARD

CHAPTER 12
THE PLOT THICKENS

I WAS IN bed and on the very edge of sleep when the telephone went, and I grumbled to myself about inconsiderate people as I switched on the light and hooked on my glasses. Then, and I really don't know why, I wondered if it could be Camille Wesslake who was calling. That was curious, for the Wesslakes had again faded into the far background of my mind.

"Hallo?" I said. "St. Martin's 229."

"Wharton here," came the familiar voice. "You got anything on hand?"

"No," I said. "But why?"

"Something's cropped up," he said. "Very much of a coincidence. Weren't you staying at that Winstode place with some people called Wesslake?"

I said we'd all been guests at the Malfroi Arms.

"One of them was an author—name of Peter Wesslake?"

"No," I said. "He wasn't there, but his wife and ex-wife were. And his two children. He was in Denmark attending a P.E.N. Congress."

"He won't attend any more," George told me grimly. "He's dead, so I'm told. Dead as mutton, and deader."

"Good God!" I said, and the words slipped out. "Where is he, George?"

"Lying on a slab, what's left of him. The thing is, can you be at the Yard at half-past five in the morning? I'll be waiting."

I said I'd be there and he rang off. I began setting the alarm clock, and then remembered a whole lot of things. Bill Ellice has a telephone at his bedside and I knew he'd even be grateful for being disturbed.

"Travers speaking, Bill," I said. "Sorry to disturb you at this time of night but I've just had some news. From Wharton. Peter Wesslake is dead. I gather they've just found his body somewhere, and I'm off there with Wharton first thing in the morning. What am I to do?"

I heard Bill's grunt, and waited.

"I think we'd better come absolutely clean," he told me. "We're in the clear. I take it he won't let the clients know where any particular information came from."

"I'll guarantee that," I said. "Thanks, Bill. I think we shall be doing right. But don't be surprised if Wharton drops in on you some time tomorrow. You might do worse than make a synopsis of all the reports."

Bernice was wide awake and insisting that she would get up too. Between us we got me away on time and I was actually early at the Yard. George was waiting with a police car and driver, and he and I sat in the back. It wasn't a good morning, and just a bit chilly. George was wearing his old blue overcoat with the faded velvet collar, and his weeping-willow moustache was more untidy than ever. But he seemed in quite a good humour. Usually at that hour, when his circulation hasn't got properly going, he's apt to be curt and even irritable. That morning he even began volunteering information, and that was almost a sure sign that he already had something up his sleeve.

I mention that because you can't work twenty years and more with George without learning a few of his tricks, and I deliberately say few because to know all his little subterfuges, devices and arts of showmanship would need a couple of lifetimes. My own idea that morning was that he was aware of the fact that he was sitting pretty. We were bound for Burnbury and Millside, so he had just vouchsafed, and that meant he was counting on dazzling the local police with what to them must seem powers of deduction incredibly uncanny. In me he had a fine source of information for the purpose. Not that I was inclined to be at all resentful. A superintendent of the Yard is a mightily important person who's got where he is by the hard way. George had a position to maintain and a legend to support, and I was all for him.

But first there was what he had to tell me. The local police had received by the first post on the previous day an anonymous letter which simply said a body was lying in what were known as Millside Woods, Burnbury. By the time the red-tape had been unwound and a search party could be organised, it was well into the morning. There were about forty acres of wood to search and the anonymous letter had given no exact indication as to where the body could be found, and it was not till two o'clock when the letter was proved to be true. The body, in an advanced state of decomposition, was found lying behind a holly clump, and as the June and July had been abnormally wet, grass was actually growing through it. But the blond hair recalled something to one of the local searchers; that and the fact that some of the wood belonged to Millside, and there'd also been local rumours about Wesslake's being missing. At any rate the body was photographed and then carefully removed to the morgue, and there the police-surgeon discovered that death had probably been caused by a shot through eye and brain. The bullet—from a small-calibre automatic—had been recovered, but the surgeon had requested the services of a Yard pathologist, and one had been sent down hot-foot.

Wharton had then got wind of what was happening, and the name of Wesslake rang an immediate bell. There was not only what he had heard from me; certain cross-references were vaguely in his mind and he made enquiries. The application of Smallacre's Chief to the Yard turned up at once, and, far later, another application, and this time from a Mrs. Camille Wesslake, through her local police in the matter of the disappearance of her husband. Then later that night the Yard was asked to take over the Peter Wesslake business, and that was why it had been almost midnight when George had at last been able to ring me at the flat.

"Suppose you tell me all you know about these Wesslakes," he told me when it was my turn to do the talking.

"There's not a lot of time," I said, "but I think I can surprise you. I've been up to the neck in the Wesslake affairs for the last ten weeks, and more. No less than three of them were clients of Bill Ellice, and Wesslake himself was one."

You can't often startle George but that certainly shook him. His usual reactions would have been to glare at me as if I'd been guilty of criminal collusion. Now all he could do was stare.

There was a good half-hour ahead of us and I told him most of what I knew, and that began with Alice Stonhill's call at Broad Street and ended with the failure to find the information sought by Drina Farman. That Camille Wesslake should have become alarmed at her husband's continued absence was only natural, I said, though it was news to me that she had applied to her local police. Wharton told me that the Yard enquiry into Wesslake's absence was still going on, and, as far as he knew, it hadn't begun till a few days before.

Wharton was quite reasonable about Bill Ellice, if only after I'd told him that Bill was at work on a confidential report. Those efforts on behalf of the Broad Street Detective Agency made a job of work for me. At the first opportunity I was to fill in all the gaps so that George could have before him a comprehensive summary of everything that was known about the Wesslakes. He even cajolingly told me that once he'd got that Wesslake history and background, the Case shouldn't take long in cracking. I like George to be cheerful so I didn't point out that I'd had that information all along, and that even the knowledge now of Wesslake's death and probable murder hadn't put into my head any quick and bright ideas as to who his murderer was. But there wasn't time for more talk. The car was drawing up at the back of the police-station, and out we got. George told the driver to wait.

I don't want to bore you with all the preliminaries that go to the taking over of a Case. I know it was well over an hour before George went to see what remained of Wesslake. I contented myself with the photographs. Corpses to George are merely exhibits, and, whether they're clean or messy, he never turns a hair. I look at the clean ones when it's necessary, but the others stay at the back of my mind and haunt my sleep, which goes to show once more that Scotland Yard must have some uncommonly peculiar reason for keeping me on its books.

But the photographs were grim enough, for all that seemed to be left of Peter Wesslake was bones and putridity and the poet's hank of hair. It would have been gloomy in that wood and maybe the flashlights had made the photographs even more ghastly, and I didn't linger over them long. Wharton had probably felt much the same about the remains themselves, for he was back in no time. What he wanted particularly to see was that anonymous letter.

Envelope and paper were of the cheapest kind, and the writing was large, round and infantile, with each letter carefully formed. It was the kind of letter, in fact, that is written by a right-handed person with the left hand, and to give an impression of a lack of what I might call advanced education—the letter, in fact, of one who had had only ordinary schooling and belonged to what used to be known as the working classes.

> Dear Sir,
> there is a body in the wood at Millside woods and I think you ought to know.
>
> A friend.

That was all, and with its eccentric use of capitals was a deliberate attempt to bolster up the manipulation of the writing itself. And in case you think that that was wide guessing or uncanny prescience on our part, let me say at once that the letter itself had never a finger-print. That was damning from the start. If that letter were what it purported to be, the writer would never have worn gloves.

Wharton wore gloves when he put it back in its envelope and the envelope into another one, for there was a vital exhibit from the word go, or so at the moment it seemed. In some queer way it made Wharton's earlier optimisms far better founded. That letter, in fact, might definitely have been written by whoever was responsible for Wesslake's death.

There was one other thing to see—the bullet that had been extracted from the skull. To me it looked quite small; little bigger, in fact, than bullets from a .22 rifle. The Yard specialist's decision was that it belonged to a French Lautrec.

"It must have been fired from pretty close quarters?" I suggested to George. "Any traces left around the actual point of entry?"

Decomposition had left no trace, George said. After all, the view by those who ought to know was that that body had been lying in that wood for about two months. And that French automatic needn't have been fired at close range. From ten yards it would have been deadly enough, provided it hit a vital spot.

There was one other thing to do in conjunction with the local police—to compose a carefully worded report for the Press.

"You people may be swamped with enquiries and information, and most of it from cranks," George said. "Just pass it on to me at the Yard, and don't enlarge on this report."

He gave copious thanks all round and left them with one last thing to chew upon.

"Your handling has been first-class," he said, "and we're duly grateful. I doubt, in fact, if we'll be here at all after today. The answers aren't going to be found down here, or my name's Robinson."

We collected the police-sergeant who was to act as guide and moved on towards Burnbury. We lighted our pipes and talked about everything but the Case. But only for ten minutes. The car had left the main road and turned into a lane on the left. We were skirting Millside Woods, the sergeant said, and after a quarter of a mile of twists and bends we turned right, and into a second-class road. The woods were still on our right, but almost at once the car was pulling up.

Those woods were of the usual chestnut, cut down every twelve years or so for hop-poles or fencing, and there was the usual interspersing of oaks with occasional beech, silver birch and ash, and here and there a nut or holly bush. The chestnut, so the sergeant said, was almost ready for cutting. The stubs were reasonably apart and there was practically no undergrowth. As for the hedge that surrounded that wood, it was of badly layered beech and full of gaps. The sergeant mounted the bank and stepped over, and we followed. It was cloudy outside and in that wood was a depressing gloom.

It was less than a hundred yards to where the body had been found, and pegs had been stuck in the clayey ground to mark the outline. Not that it had been necessary. A horrible, yellowish discoloration showed where the body had kept the light from the lush grass. In the air was the heavy smell of chlorine.

"I don't think we need keep you, Sergeant," Wharton said. "My man will drive you back and then he can come on to the house. Tell him I said so."

He waited till the sergeant had gone, then gave a grunt.

"Knees drawn up a bit," he said. "And no gun. Everything plain as the nose on your face."

"In fact, he was brought here."

George gave a glare, which showed he was getting well down to work.

"Of course he was brought here! Who the devil'd come to this ungodly spot for a rendezvous?"

Then he was getting on his haunches and squinting south, away from the road.

"Can't see where the wood ends that way. The house ought to be that way, though, on the main road. Let's see how far it is."

We dodged this way and that between the tall chestnuts, and making for what we guessed was the south-west. It took us five minutes to get to the main road, and the house was still a good hundred yards to the right.

"No one could carry a body all that way," George said. "It'd be a nightmare, especially in the dark. Where our car was, that's where it was taken. Only a hundred yards to carry it, and it's a back road too."

We moved on along the road to the house. It was a larger place than I'd thought, and a few hundred yards short of Burnbury village. It looked like a converted, half-timbered farmhouse with the low barn used as a garage. Its gardens occupied well over an acre and Wesslake must have spent a goodish bit of money on them. A brick path led between twin herbaceous borders to the front door. A youngish man opened it. Wharton introduced himself, and we were shown into a large and comfortable lounge.

"We'd just like a few words with you and your wife, Mr. Upman," Wharton said. "Nothing to be alarmed about."

I had a quick look round the room. It was comfortably furnished and the open fireplace was particularly fine. In a very large set of expanding book-cases were the Peter Arden books in their various English and foreign editions, and the Colin Lake books as well.

"Just sit down and make yourselves comfortable," Wharton said genially as Upman came back with his wife. He was red-faced and bucolic and evidently spent most of his time in the gardens. She was a pleasant-looking woman in the early thirties.

"Just a little information is all we want," Wharton told them, "and then in less than no time we'll be away and gone and you'll have nothing else to worry about. Now you, Mr. Upman: you've helped identify the body of Mr. Wesslake. The hair helped, I believe, and the suit of clothes."

"It was a tweed suit, sir," Upman said. "A greyish tweed. He often used to wear it."

"He kept it here?"

"You couldn't really say that, sir." He looked at his wife and she explained: "Mr. Wesslake kept his clothes all over the place. Some were at the flat and some at Millside. It was like a man spending his time travelling between two hotels. He'd take with him this and that, and he'd bring with him that or this."

"You think he took that tweed suit with him to Denmark?"

Upman frankly didn't know. Mr. Wesslake, he said had been at Millside from the Friday evening, May 14th, till the Sunday afternoon, and then he had gone back to town, and what he had with him in his bag, Upman didn't know. But he was of the opinion that that suit would have been taken to Denmark. Mr. Wesslake liked it, and it was reasonably new.

"He wrote to either of you when he was in Denmark?"

The Upmans looked surprised. There had been no need for him to write, for his instructions had been explicit beforehand. Besides, they hadn't been at Millside. They had been on their annual holiday. They left on the Tuesday morning for Southwold in Suffolk where they stayed with Mrs. Upman's sister, and returned, as also arranged, on the Thursday three-weeks in order to have the house ready in case Mr. Wesslake should decide to come down immediately after his return.

"I understand," Wharton said. "But now to something a little less pleasant—the contents of Mr. Wesslake's pockets. You saw what there was to see, Mr. Upman. There was a handkerchief, for one thing. It wasn't marked and it hadn't ever been washed. Were his handkerchiefs marked, Mrs. Upman?"

She said he was very particular, even finicky, about his clothes. All his handkerchiefs, as far as she knew, were linen ones with a W embroidered in the corner. You could buy handkerchiefs like that, with initials on, and they were the only ones of his she'd ever seen.

"That's all right then," Wharton said, and was producing a bulky envelope from his pocket. I'd seen its contents already. There were the bunch of keys which Upman identified, a gold pencil and some odd coins, and finally a wallet.

"I understand you've never seen this wallet," he was asking Mr. Upman. Mrs. Upman had a look at it, and she also had never seen it before. It looked cheap, she said, compared with the one that Mr. Wesslake always carried—a black one with the initials P.W. in gold on the leather.

Wharton could have told them some curious things about that wallet. Its contents were sixteen pounds in pound and ten-shilling notes. There wasn't a visiting card or an identity card or a scrap of identifying paper. But he was putting the things back in their envelope. Wallet and notes had both held prints and he wanted to know the likeliest place where he could get Wesslake's prints.

"Where did he usually work when he was down here?"

Then he heard the Upman version of what I'd already told him about the fire.

"Seems curious," he said, "a man wanting to work out there when he could be in comfort here. What sort of a man—purely as man—was he, by the way?"

Both agreed he was a good enough master, but with provisos. He was faddy, Mrs. Upman said, and you had to treat him the right way. The right way, Wharton elicited, seemed to be to let him always be right. Upman said in so many words that he had a good conceit of himself, and then was qualifying the remark. He wasn't much of a reader himself, he said, but he was given to understand that Mr. Wesslake had a right to think himself an important man.

"And Mrs. Wesslake?"

"She was very nice," Mrs. Upman said. "Very nice indeed. The easiest one to get on with that you'd ever wish to work for."

Wharton was duly gratified and then harked back to the question of prints. The desk at the far window was where Wesslake had worked after the fire, and his keys opened it. Wharton put on his gloves and began inspecting the untidy collection of papers and oddments that lay on the top. He dusted one or two and there were Wesslake's prints.

The keys were left in the lock and he came back to his seat. What he was wanting to know was when the Upmans had first become aware that their master was missing. Both said it was in the week after he should have returned. Mr. Deen rang up from London, and they thought that was on the Monday. A day or two later Mrs.

Drina, as they called her, rang. Mrs. Camille rang and then Mrs. Drina again; in fact there came a time when there was a whole spate of ringing. Finally Mrs. Camille told them over the telephone that they weren't to worry as she was having enquiries made. That, they thought, was just over a week ago.

That was all for the present with the Upmans. Wharton said he might have to spend an hour or two in the house and on the premises and if we could have a pot of tea and some bread and cheese at about midday, we'd be grateful. That was that. Wharton left the keys still in the lock of the desk, and I knew afterwards he'd arranged them specially to spot if they'd been disturbed. Then he was saying we'd go out for a look round.

On each side of the path stretched the lawn. To the right as one left the door, and set far back in the shrubbery that shielded from the road, was what was left of that summer-house. There were the blackened brick foundations on which it had stood, and the heap of ash that had been its walls and roof. George walked all round it.

"A funny idea wanting to work out there in the sort of spring we had? Lucky for him the fire came as quick as it did or he might have got pneumonia."

I reminded him that it had been fitted up pretty snugly.

"You can't make a place like that snug," he told me. "There's either a fug or you're frozen. Only one window, wasn't there? That was the one he worked at, so how could he have kept the place aired? Looks to me as if he didn't lose much time before he set it on fire—if he did."

I said it was almost a certainty that he did, and I referred him to the insurance company. They'd make no bones about talking now Wesslake was dead.

"Then what the devil was the fellow's idea?" demanded George. "He couldn't have been on the make. And what that aunt suggested to Ellice was all bunkum. He didn't try to get his wife trapped in the fire. That's right, isn't it?"

I said it was. Then his eyes were shifting towards the wood that backed the other side of the lawn—the wood through which we'd come.

"And that's where he and that cousin of his went shooting jays and magpies," he said. "And the son was there too."

I made no comment. The last thing I wanted was to go over all that story again. I did say that the gate set in the far hedge would be to the path that Camille Wesslake had taken. And what should there be just then but the crack of a gun.

"What's that?" George said.

A jay flew screaming through the wood. George was making for the side of the house to where the sound had come from. There at the back in the kitchen garden Upman was tying a dead jay to the top of the pea sticks. We met him as he came back to the house.

"A good shot, was it?" Wharton said.

"You have to be to get them with this old .22-inch," he said, and showed us the rifle. "I shoot them out of the kitchen window here. Don't make much difference though, sir, the more you shoot, the more there seem to be."

Our scratch meal was ready in a matter of minutes and there was something in the kitchen for Wharton's driver. When we had come back to the lounge, George had had a quick look at those keys he had left in the desk, and he had given what sounded to me like a disappointed grunt when he had found them undisturbed.

When I said that I thought the Upmans as honest as the day, all he had said was that one never knew.

We were both pretty hungry and it didn't take long to dispose of the bread and butter, cheese and tomatoes. George pushed the bell for Upman and said he might leave the tea-pot.

"Let me see," he said. "The police rang Mrs. Wesslake, but what about you? Did you ring her yourself?"

Upman looked a bit disconcerted. He said he'd rung her because he thought it his duty.

"And quite right too," Wharton told him. "And how did she take it?"

"She was very upset, sir. I took it upon myself to warn her, though, that she oughtn't to come down here. It wouldn't be a pretty sight, sir, if she was to try to see what's left of him."

"Very right and proper of you," Wharton said. "She's a bit of an invalid, isn't she?"

"Mrs. Wesslake, sir?" He smiled. "She never ails a thing."

Then he was remembering something. Mrs. Wesslake, he said, never had anything really serious the matter with her. She did have something wrong with her in the spring but the doctor said it was only a gastric attack.

Wharton looked at me and asked if that would be Dr. Smith.

"Smith, sir?" Upman said. "I don't know a Doctor Smith. This was Doctor Ames of Charnworth."

Wharton let that pass. There was just one other thing he wanted to know, he said. What members of the family had been at Millside since the Upmans had returned from their holiday?

"Well, there was Mrs. Drina, sir. She just came and went, so to speak. That was when everyone first began to get worried about the master."

"She just wanted to see if you could throw any light on things?"

"That's right, sir. And Mr. Deen, of course. He came down once or twice."

"And what did he come down for?"

"The same thing, sir. And he wanted some papers or other. Urgent, he said they were. Something to do with books."

"He had access to that desk?"

"Yes and no, sir. He didn't have any keys but he brought some of his own and we found one to fit."

"I see," Wharton told him, and frowned. "But just one other thing. We haven't seen the garage but I suppose Mr. Wesslake's car is there?"

Upman said it had been jacked up ever since the abolition of basic petrol. Mr. Wesslake was intending to take it out again immediately after his return.

"Which he won't do now," Wharton said, and the sigh was probably for man's mortality. "That's all then, Upman. Tell your wife I shall want to have a look at the upstairs rooms."

The door closed and he was rounding on me.

"Upset, was she? Thought you said she hadn't any use for him. In love with that cousin, or something."

I said there were still such things as crocodile tears. In any case, Camille Wesslake was entitled to her memories. There'd certainly been a time when she'd been in love with Wesslake.

George helped himself to the last of the tea and made some notes in his book. Then he was saying that I might go through that desk while he had a look at Wesslake's bed-room. He reminded me that I ought to find some of Deen's prints.

Mrs. Upman came in for the tray. George left with her and I settled to an examination of the contents of that desk. It was of the type that locks and unlocks all the drawers by a turn of the key in the lock of the flap. I had a look at the main drawers first and found them partly filled with stationery and filed copies of short stories or scenarios. Then I had a look at the small drawers and found nothing but some household receipts, gardening catalogues, a local bill or two and still more oddments of stationery. I dusted some of them for prints and all I found were some of Wesslakes. That seemed odd, so I rang for Upman.

"There must have been some accumulated correspondence here by the time Mr. Wesslake was expected back," I said. "What happened to it?"

"I expect Mr. Deen took it away to attend to it," he said. "The last time he was down he told me to re-address everything to the flat."

A minute or two later George came down. He'd found nothing of significance in Wesslake's bedroom, or in Camille's. He did say that there were some of Wesslake's clothes in the drawers and ward-robe and hot-press, and he sniffed when he said that even the pyjamas had his initials on them. He seemed mightily chagrined when I told him what I'd discovered about prints. That was something he should have spotted for himself.

"What's it mean?" he said. "He must have touched everything that's lying on the top there. He couldn't have been wearing gloves."

I said that looked like the only answer. Deen, for some reason or other, didn't want his prints found. And that meant he knew more about Wesslake's disappearance than he'd admitted to the family enquirers.

George gave his old Coliseum look—that of the lion who espies a succulent Christian.

"One way to find out," he said. "By this time tomorrow we'll have his prints. I'll just check up on that doctor's name and address and we'll be pushing off."

I asked if he was going to interview the doctor and he said he was only keeping him up his sleeve. I went to the kitchen and offered the Upmans a tip which they wouldn't take, and inside five minutes we were on the way back to town, and we were taking a slightly different route.

We did precious little talking. George was making copious notes and I was feeling as if my mental stomach was crammed with ill-digested gobbets of this and that. I supposed that George already had some pattern in his mind, but what it was I couldn't at the moment see. Not that it mattered to me. If two men ride a horse, one has to ride behind, and I that morning had been firmly on the pillion. But it struck me, and I wasn't to be far out, that before long we'd have to have, as it were, a second horse. Far too many people would have to be questioned, and George wouldn't be able to waste time by letting me be a mere adornment to even his own inimitable self.

Near London he put his book away and began giving me my orders. The vital thing was that I should go to Broad Street, complete with Bill Ellice that Wesslake dossier, and then rush it to him at the Yard. By the morning he'd have digested it, and after that we'd see. Eight o'clock would be early enough to report, which was a time that suited me. A few minutes later the car was dropping me near enough to Broad Street and heading back towards the Yard.

CHAPTER 13
OLD ACQUAINTANCE

GEORGE WAS in a reasonable state of mind that morning. He even admitted that Bill Ellice had saved us an enormous deal of work, provided everything was correct. That was the sting in the tail, though principally directed against myself and the part I'd played in Bill's researches. I said that Bill couldn't afford to make mistakes, but in the defence I didn't include myself. Not that that was to save me when the time came.

But that was something that neither of us foresaw. George said he'd digested that dossier and his reactions had been that about the Wesslakes generally there'd been a very fishy smell. He put it in terms far less polite. He did add that Alice Stonhill seemed the only respectable one among the lot, and the rest were little more than emetics, and that went also for the dead Wesslake. There was

Collinson, he virtuously said, making love to another man's wife, and that man his cousin and collaborator. There was Wesslake's son doing the same thing or worse. There was the daughter, who ought to have had her backside slapped. There was the Drina woman who had struck him as capable of anything, and the widow who'd been little more than a feather-pated fool. The whole lot seemed to him, in fact, to be a justification for Aneurin's classification under the heading of vermin.

Then he was giving me a paper and asking me to check it. It was what we knew of Wesslake's movements.

DATE	MOVEMENT	AUTHORITY
May 14th	Millside	Upmans
,, 16th	Flat	Upmans
,, 17th	Broad Street	Ellice
,, 18th	Malfroi Arms	Alice Stonhill
,, 21st	Embarked	Shipping Company
,, 22nd	Copenhagen	Hotel records
,, 26th	Martins Forlag	Secretary
,, 30th	Roskilde	Miss Chrome, etc.
June 3rd	Tisvilde	Housekeeper
,, 4th	Hillerod	Photograph
,, 6th	Leave Copenhagen	Hotel records, etc.
,, 11th	Embark	Shipping Company
,, 12th	Land	Ellice

I said it seemed to me to be absolutely correct.

"There's a further check-up with Collinson," he said. "He saw him in Copenhagen. That's one of the things I want you to get out of him. When he saw him, and why. Not that I want to tell you your business."

"I'm seeing Collinson?"

"Deen first," he said. "I've fixed for him at ten-thirty this morning. Didn't tell him your name. Said it'd be a representative of mine. Collinson was told the same thing. He's fixed for twelve o'clock."

Then he was asking what I was amused at. I said it was a kind of ironic anticipation. Both had seen me before and had accepted different views of me, and now I couldn't help wondering what their reactions would be when they saw me without the sheep's clothing.

"Ought to be interesting," he said. "You know what you have to do with Collinson, but you might also try to pump him about that decision to end his association with Wesslake over the Colin Lake books. Deen's a different proposition. Get his prints, for one thing. And find out exactly where he was on the night of the twenty-ninth of May."

It took me a moment to see what that date meant.

"You think he might have been implicated in that attack on Mrs. Wesslake at the swimming-pool?"

"I didn't say so," he told me irritatingly. "But if he wasn't, he's got to be cleared off the list, hasn't he?"

I let him have it his own way, though I certainly didn't see why Deen should have or could have been in cahoots with Ferotti.

"I'm due at that Mrs. Stonhill's place at eleven o'clock," George was going off-handedly on, and as some kind of palliative for my not going too. "The old lady's none too well again, so I was told. Wesslake's death was a shock and she isn't as young as she was."

I said it was all to the good that he should go to Ashenby alone. While I rather relished unmasking before Collinson and Frank Deen, I didn't feel quite the same about those two women.

"You'll be a sort of reserve," George told me. "We might have to put the screws on pretty soon, for all we know. By the way, the son's coming home for the funeral and so on. Staying with his mother. We'll see her later when he gets there."

There was no other news and nothing I could do except collect a Warrant Card. Just before half-past ten I was once more ringing the bell of Flat Number eight, Bridge Mansions, Westminster.

You'll have gathered that I'm the sort of person whom once to see is never to forget. No wonder then that Deen looked startled. And he didn't move back to let me come in.

"Good-morning," I said. "I think you're expecting me."

His eyes popped again as he said he thought there was some mistake. I gave him my Warrant Card, and there wasn't a shadow of doubt about his being badly scared. He couldn't even speak for a moment and it was quite involuntarily that he drew back.

"That other call of mine some weeks ago was an amazing coincidence," I said. "Don't you remember? I was looking for a Mrs. Wellington and came to this flat by mistake."

That put him a bit at his ease, though he was still dithery. He gave me back the Card he was still holding, and asked me to come in, even if I was in already. He said would I sit down and would I like a drink or something, which was merely babbling for time. I said, and I hope charmingly, that it was good of him but far too early. I was hoping not to keep him long, and, whatever he could or couldn't tell us, we should be very much in his debt. That put him much more at ease.

I accepted a cigarette and told him why I was there. Five minutes of nothing followed: what a shock things had been to him, what a comparative relief it was to know the horrible truth, and what a harassing time he had had since Wesslake's non-return.

"He actually landed on the twelfth," I said, "which may be news to you. After he boarded the train at Parkeston Quay, every trace of him was lost. You've no idea where he could have gone?"

"He didn't come here," he said. "I was here from the eleventh. I'd been on holiday, you know."

"So we've been told," I said, and let him think that over. Then he was supposing that he must have gone straight to Millside—not to the house but the woods. He must have had a brain-storm.

"I suppose it was suicide?" he said. "The papers didn't give any clue; only that his body was found in the wood."

I said it hadn't been determined yet, though what he had just told me might be helpful. But just why should Wesslake commit suicide? He hemmed and hawed and made a show of reluctance.

"I suppose everything's confidential?" he said.

I assured him it was.

"Well, it might have been the loss of the Colin Lake books," he said. "Perhaps I'd better explain."

I let him explain and there was nothing new. Wesslake the spender had been faced with the loss of a very big slice of income, and he'd taken it pretty hard. That was the gist.

"He wouldn't have been able to afford to keep you on?" I asked him.

That all depended, he said, and proceeded to give me a series of hypotheses. If Mr. Collinson had been willing to transfer the name Colin Lake to Wesslake, then the disaster wouldn't have been so great.

"Let me get this right," I said. "I thought Collinson supplied the sophistication and Wesslake the action. If Collinson dropped out, wouldn't the Colin Lake books have lost all their character?"

Deen tried to be modest. What I'd said was partly true but there was more in it than that. He himself had been a kind of general editor and he'd acquired what might be called the knack and technique of the Colin Lake books. If he'd been given the chance he thought he could have produced something that the general public wouldn't have known from the original series. But there was an alternative. Wesslake, with Deen to collaborate, could have begun writing detective novels under his own name, if Collinson had been unwilling to transfer the Colin Lake name.

"That'd be what Collinson was seeing Wesslake about in Denmark?" I suggested.

"In Denmark?"

"Yes," I said. "It's our job to find out things. We know that Collinson flew to Copenhagen on Tuesday the first of June and came back on the Thursday—"

"What's the matter?"

Never did I see a man so taken aback. His face had gone a greyish white and his hand went to his side. I thought he was having a heart attack. A moment and he was pulling himself together.

"It was a nasty shock, Mr. Travers," he said. "You're sure of your facts?"

I said we couldn't afford to make mistakes.

"Then it looks to me as if there's been some double crossing," he said. "I can't explain why—not till I've worked it out. I will tell you that I know now that Collinson had turned against Mr. Wesslake for some reason or other. It's all tied up with that refusal to go on with the Colin Lake books."

"You're not suggesting he was sufficiently hostile to him to have killed him?"

"You mean he was killed. Murdered?"

"I mean nothing of the sort," I said. "I'm putting a strictly hypothetical question strictly off the record. If Wesslake was murdered, could Collinson have murdered him?"

"That'd be ridiculous," he said.

"Well, perhaps you wouldn't mind explaining what you meant about double-crossing."

"I should have been consulted," he said. "There wasn't any written contract over the Colin Lake books. It was a gentleman's agreement, but it was distinctly understood that if any alterations were made, I was to be considered—given a percentage share in fact. Mr. Collinson was going behind my back if that was what he saw Mr. Wesslake about in Copenhagen. And not mentioning it to me since."

I said that seemed a domestic business and rather out of our line. What I'd like was the name of Wesslake's solicitors and his bank. I'd also like to have a look at the room where he usually worked. It was apparently the best room in the flat and with its handsome desk, bookshelves and filing cabinets looked just the sort of room where a man like Wesslake would find it congenial to work.

"You don't live here yourself?" I asked Deen.

He was a bachelor, he said, and had rooms a few minutes away. His landlady was an elderly widow with the name of Bond, and the address was 85 Ypres Gardens, Kennington.

"There's just one more thing," I said, "and we hope you'll take it the right way. You knew about an attack on Mrs. Wesslake when she was staying at a hotel near Winstode."

"Yes," he said. "She told me about it herself over the telephone. Some crook staying at the hotel, wasn't it?"

I said the Yard was having doubts about that. At any rate there was to be an enquiry into the alibis of everybody connected even remotely with the family. Not my doing, of course. I was just an underling.

"When was this attack?"

"Saturday the twenty-ninth of May, at about ten o'clock at night."

He frowned for a moment, then nodded to himself.

"I was in Edinburgh. Staying with a friend named Baird, at 5, Penstone Terrace. That's just off Abercromby Place."

"Just jot it down for me, will you?"

I saw him hesitate.

"Won't you want it in your note-book?" he said, and began dictating it, so I jotted it down with the other information he'd given me. And that seemed to be all, though I did ask him one last question.

"Still off the record, just what kind of man—as man—was Wesslake?"

"Generous and considerate," he said, "provided you acknowledged the fact that he was the directing brain of everything. Flamboyant and spacious, perhaps, and what you might call conceited, but plenty of charm with it. Fond of the limelight and a bit of a showman and yet—well, I was fifteen years with him and I haven't many regrets."

I gave a Whartonian chuckle and almost dug him in the ribs.

"Sounds like a character study from a book. No wonder you fellows made a name for yourselves."

I smiled a goodbye, said I didn't think we'd have to bother him again, and off I went. I took the Underground to Hampstead and found myself with time on my hands, so I had a cup of coffee and jotted down some impressions for Wharton. I noted that Deen had been shaken badly at the first sight of me. I was dead on time and so he must have known me as from the Yard, and therefore the fright must have been for that first visit I had paid when I had supposedly mistaken the flat for that of the opportune Mrs. Wellington. But that had been before the Malfroi Arms business, and therefore something had been going on then which it now scared Deen to recall. Something, in fact, had warned him that that first visit had been a fake.

There was the question too, of his hesitation to write down that Edinburgh address and so provide me with his prints. Not that I worried. I'd handed him the brand new Warrant Card from which I'd carefully wiped all prints, and my own hands had been gloved. And I'd had plenty of time to slip along to the Embankment and hand that card over to the department. In my pocket was my old Card which I would show to Collinson. Then the thought of him gave me a notion. Collinson would be expecting Ludovic Travers. Deen, I was absolutely sure, would have rung him the very moment

I left the flat. All I would have to do to verify that would be to watch Collinson's reactions at the first sight of me.

Romney Court was a snug little spot. It had once been a yard of some sort with probably a little factory. Now the building had been made into two flats with quite a pleasant prospect over someone's spacious garden. The Court was entered through an unsuspected and narrowish alley, and part of the original building had been made into twin garages. Collinson's was the bottom flat.

I guessed at once that Deen had rung him. The surprise was too dramatic, and a little heavy humour went with it. I was facetious too. One had to live, I said, and he must pardon my masquerading at the Malfroi Arms as an ordinary decent citizen.

"Come in," he said, "and tell me what it's all about. Rather nice, as a matter of fact, dealing with someone like yourself. Have a drink?"

I said regretfully that I was on duty, and sleuths on duty, as he of all people ought to know, weren't allowed to get familiar with suspects.

"Fine," he said. "But you won't mind if I have one. Cigarette?"

I took a cigarette and he poured himself a drink and nodded a good health before taking a sip.

"To tell you the truth," I said, "I don't know exactly why I'm here at all. What I imagine is that it's the thought you might throw a bit of light on this appalling business of poor Wesslake. Perhaps you might tell me, strictly off the record, just what your relationships were, business and private."

I heard just what I'd expected—that Wesslake had become very difficult to work with; hogging the credit in the Colin Lake books and becoming very swollen-headed generally. He had, in fact, become something of an egomaniac. And Collinson had become tired of the detective stuff. He didn't need the money and publicity wasn't in his line, and so he decided to drop the partnership.

"Was it about that that you saw him in Copenhagen during the P.E.N. Congress?"

His eyebrows lifted artistically.

"So you know that, do you?"

"It's our job to know a devil of a lot of things," I said. "Murder's a mighty serious business."

"Murder? You mean that Wesslake was murdered?"

"There's more than a likelihood," I said, "though that's strictly confidential. But tell me about the Copenhagen visit."

He said it was about what I'd surmised. Wesslake was desperately anxious to have the partnership continued, and he'd written to say he'd pay all expenses if Collinson would fly over and see him. What he'd offered had been a larger share of the profits, and he'd also suggested that Deen should be given a percentage share. But Collinson had been adamant. The two had parted reasonably amicably and that had been that.

"You didn't stay at his hotel," I said casually, and I could almost feel his quick look.

"No," he said. "I stayed at the Hotel d'Angleterre. That's in the Kongens Nytorv, you know. A very comfortable place where I'd stayed some years before."

I said it didn't matter. The real thing was if he could offer any suggestions as to who had killed Wesslake, and why.

But there he was at an absolute loss. Wesslake, he admitted, was the kind of man likely to make enemies, but enemies and murder weren't necessarily the same thing. "You're sure it was murder?" he said. "I might understand his committing suicide. I think he was up against it and I know his mental balance wasn't any too steady."

"You saw the newspaper reports," I said. "He was found shot through the head. But what the papers didn't add was that there wasn't any gun."

"Who found him?"

"We don't know. An anonymous letter tipped off the police."

"Then couldn't the letter-writer, who first found him, have taken the gun? It'd have been a temptation, wouldn't it?"

I said that was out of my line, so to speak, but I'd certainly pass so admirable a suggestion on to my superiors.

"If they agree, that'll alter the complexion of everything," he said, and I had to admit it. And that made a longer stay seem a bit superfluous, even if I did hang on for a few minutes longer. I said, for instance, that I'd seen Deen that morning, and I asked Collinson's opinion of him.

"A first-class man," he said. "He was paid six hundred a year and was worth every penny of it."

"And his private character, so to speak?"

"Above reproach. He isn't public school and all that, but he's a very decent chap. Just a bit apt to take himself too seriously at times, but aren't we all?"

"Well, it's a bad business," I said heavily. "How did Wesslake's wife take it?"

He shot me a quick look.

"Naturally she was pretty badly shocked. So was Mrs. Stonhill. Mrs. Stonhill, I believe, had a minor breakdown and had to be got to bed."

I clicked a sympathetic tongue as I got to my feet. These things, I said sombrely, always fell heaviest on those who were left.

"But tell me something," I said. "Strictly in confidence, of course, but wasn't that ménage rather a peculiar one? Why couldn't Wesslake have lived and worked at Burnbury, instead of mostly in town?"

"Town has a fascination for men like Wesslake," he said, and then smiled ruefully. "It has for me, so I oughtn't to speak."

"That goes for me as well," I said. "But were husband and wife on good terms? I only ask that because it seemed to me at the Malfroi Arms that she was remarkably shy about even mentioning him. Wouldn't a wife rather like to talk about a famous husband?"

He frowned, and he wasn't looking at me.

"Strictly between ourselves I think she did very well to live with him as long as she did. He could be a highly exasperating person."

"She wasn't exactly off the top shelf, was she? Mind you, I think she was very nice, and I liked her."

"Who the hell cares about the top shelf!" His voice had risen, then he was shaking his head. "Sorry, I shouldn't have said that, but the least suspicion of snobbery always makes me see red."

"Me too," I said, "I'm the one to apologise."

I held out my hand and began offering thanks. He asked me if I had a car. When I said I was going back by Tube he said he'd walk to the station with me. He was due for a bit of fresh air.

It was no distance at all and when he turned back he was saying that I wasn't to hesitate to call on him for any possible help. And would I let him know the reactions to his suicide theory. And, of course, I must give Bernice his very kindest regards.

I went on down and then nipped back again. Only by luck did I escape disaster, for he was still watching at the entrance. I marked time and soon he was moving away.

A quick peep showed him well down the street but I let him get out of sight before I left my shelter. Then I took a back street and came out near enough to that place where I'd had coffee. It was the rush hour but I tipped a waitress and she did the best she could. It wasn't a window seat but by craning a bit I could just see the entrance to Romney Court.

It was just before a quarter past one that I saw Deen go hurrying by. He disappeared into Romney Court, and I could give myself a pat on the back. Something, as I had guessed, was pretty rotten, and it might even be in the state of Denmark. All that Deen chatter about double-crossing was sheer humbug. Weeks had gone by since Collinson's trip to Copenhagen, and I wasn't believing that Deen and he hadn't discussed business at all. Nor did I, strange as it might sound, think Collinson capable of that petty kind of double-crossing. Capable of murder in some extraordinary crisis— yes, for who's to say what can happen in a sudden brainstorm. And Wesslake's treatment of his wife might have brought on that brainstorm. That Collinson was in love with her, there was no doubt, for in spite of the strong hold he had had over himself, he had not been able to keep back that resentful outburst when I had decried Camille's origins.

As for Deen, that he and Collinson were working together there seemed no shadow of doubt. It was possible that Deen might even be doing a spot of blackmailing, and if so, he knew who Wesslake's murderer was. And Collinson had been both apt and anxious in trying to make Wesslake's death one of suicide. And Collinson had made another slip, when he had taken me at my face value and hadn't asked to see my Warrant Card.

I finished what was on my plate and hastily made my way back to the Yard. What I discovered there ought to have been staggering, but somehow it wasn't, and I wondered if Wharton would feel the same. But the whole morning was now bringing to a head a kind of accumulated restlessness and I steadied myself by dictating a long report. Just before I'd finished it, Wharton turned up, and he wasn't looking any too cheerful.

Nothing much had happened at the Briars, except that he'd acquired a bit more of the Wesslake background.

"A pretty woman, that Mrs. Wesslake," he told me. "Rather the helpless kind, though."

"What about Alice Stonhill?"

"She was in bed and I couldn't see her. She ought to be up in a day or two, though; then we might drop in again."

"So you didn't learn anything?" I said.

"I wouldn't say that," he told me, and kept whatever it was to himself. George is niggardly like that. He's like an elephant crossing a swamp. One foot doesn't grope forward till the other three are dead plumb sure.

"I've had a good morning," I said, "and I think you'll say so when you read these reports."

"What about Deen's alibi for the night of the twenty-ninth of May?" he was firing at me and making his own guess.

I gave him the Edinburgh address where Deen had been staying, and reminded him of a postcard I'd seen addressed by him from there to Collinson.

"I'll see it's checked at once," he said.

"Wait a minute," I said, as he went towards the buzzer. "There's something else first. Deen's prints."

His eyes popped a bit.

"He's got a record?"

I passed him the report so that he could read it for himself. What it said was that the prints were those of a Frederick Dowland, sentenced in 1931 to a term of eighteen months for embezzlement.

<h1 style="text-align:center">CHAPTER 14
THE LION MISSES</h1>

WHARTON SENT down for further information and then was grabbing those reports of mine. They didn't take too long to read, but it seemed to me that long before he'd finished the excitement had petered out.

"Why shouldn't all that yarn of his be genuine?" he wanted to know.

"You didn't see him, George," I said. "The man was in a dither about something, and I'll swear it wasn't altogether to do with Collinson, or that record of his. It absolutely hit him clean in the wind when he learned that Collinson had seen Wesslake in Copenhagen."

Wharton began stoking his pipe and his forehead was furrowed.

"This writing business isn't in my line," he said. "You explain it again."

I did so, and I added something else that seemed to stand out a mile.

"So you see, George, that if Deen could manage to dispose of Wesslake, he'd be sitting pretty himself. I don't know who Wesslake's heir is, or executor, but it wouldn't take much persuading from Deen to convince them that he was perfectly capable of carrying on the Peter Arden and Colin Lake names by himself. In other words, the estate would have a valuable property. He as good as said so to Bill Ellice."

"Then why was he such a fool?" Wharton fired at me. "If that was his murder motive, why'd he broadcast it?"

"Sheer egoism, probably," I said, and then the buzzer went and George was taking down details of Deen's conviction.

It was at Newcastle that Deen, then Frederick Dowland, had been sentenced for fraud. He had been manager of a large book and stationery store, owned by Northern Libraries Limited, and, as they say, had got the firm's money mixed up with his own. The frauds, which had begun in a small way, had gone on for about three years, and at the end, with Dowland's desperate efforts to recoup his losses, had snowballed to quite a fairish amount—well over a thousand pounds.

"Something's worrying me, George," I said. "When I first clapped eyes on Deen I had an idea I'd seen him before. When I saw him today the idea wasn't nearly so strong. To tell the truth I didn't think of it at all."

"You couldn't have seen him at his trial," George said, and waved away my blathering with an impatient hand. "The thing is, what are we going to do?"

Everything was awkward, as he said, and solely because it was impossible to determine the date of Wesslake's murder. To check up the movements of a suspect under those conditions was a hopeless task. Both Deen and Collinson were bachelors, which meant no domestic check. Each was a free man, so to speak, and could do what he liked with his time. If either stated that he'd done this or that or had been here or there, we had no means of disproving it.

"I wonder," George said, and pursed his lips. "Do you think a bluff might work?"

"If it didn't, it might scare him into making a false step," I said.

"I'll have him here," George said, and gave himself a nod of the head. "You see if that Edinburgh check has come through."

Out he went and I was asking about that alibi request we'd made to Edinburgh. It had just come through. Hector Baird, with whom Deen had said he had stayed, had confirmed that Deen had been in Edinburgh at the time stated. Baird, I was told, was a reporter on a local Communist paper.

George came back and on his heels came a pot of tea. Deen, he said, had been located at his rooms where there was a telephone, and he had agreed to come to the Yard straightaway. That left us about a quarter of an hour, with George planning his moves and drinking his tea at the same time. Deen turned up five minutes sooner than we'd expected him.

Usually the Old Master is at his absolute best when examining a suspect. That moustache, the hunched, careworn shoulders and the antiquated spectacles combine to give him a forlorn and fatherly air, that has been the undoing of many a trustful witness. The room, too, looked a peaceful, humdrum sort of place, with the tea-tray still there as evidence of its homeliness. Even the unobtrusive stenographer had camouflaged himself by pretending to be filing documents, and George was careful to get Deen seated with the stenographer at his back.

Deen himself was surprising me, for he didn't look like a man who had anything to fear. Neither in his speech nor his movements was there nervousness or a trace of perturbation. He even gave a dry smile when Wharton thanked him for coming.

Then George made play with moving certain papers on his desk and taking his time in putting on his antiquated spectacles. He peered at Deen over their tops and in his voice was an infinite sympathy. There was something, he said, that he wished to make utterly clear. When a man was convicted, the sentence wiped the slate clean. Provided he went straight, that man had nothing to fear from the law. All the same wasn't it rather a pity that Deen had not seen fit to take the law—in the person of Mr. Travers—into his confidence?

"Aren't you wanting it both ways, sir?" Deen asked him quietly. "You know all about me. I knew you'd know that when Mr. Travers tried to get my fingerprints this morning. There's no point in denying that I did what I did, but if you say it makes no difference to the law, then why do you bring it up?"

"Because we like to start with a clean sheet and on a straight footing," Wharton told him speciously. "What I said was that if a man went straight, the law wasn't interested in him. I still think you weren't quite straight when you withheld that information. You, in your particular profession, must have known it would have been received with the most implicit confidence."

"May I show you something?" Deen asked him.

"Why not?" George said, and bestowed the peering look on me. Deen took a paper from his wallet. Wharton read it and passed it to me.

"I take it, it means that every penny was paid back," I said. "Every penny," Deen told us. "I answered Mr. Wesslake's advertisement under my present name and I was paid eight pounds a week. Mr. Wesslake was more than satisfied with my work and gave me subsequent rises, but I scraped and saved and in five years I paid back every penny, as you see. And there's something else, gentlemen, I think you ought to know. I took the original money to send my wife to Switzerland. The doctor said it was her only chance, and then I had to gamble to try to get it back. Then my wife died and I gave myself up. That's why my sentence was light. All those facts can be proved. I can give you the doctor's name and that of the Swiss sanatorium." Wharton let out a sigh as he gave back that receipt.

"God forbid that I should sit in judgment on any man," he said, and then was leaning forward across the desk. "But there *is* one important thing. You told Mr. Wesslake all this?"

Deen moistened his lips.

"No, sir; I didn't. That was where I was wrong."

Wharton stared. He shifted the look of surprise to me. "But why not? If we—usually supposed to be cold-blooded officials—accept your story, why not Mr. Wesslake?"

Deen's hand rose, and fell. It was the same old story. He had intended to, and then, as his position became more and more secure, he had kept putting it off. Most of his life had been spent up north, and he had no relatives, and the passing of years had made confession seem less and less necessary.

Wharton sighed heavily.

"A pity. But there—who am I to judge? But tell me something. What would have happened if Mr. Wesslake had found out?"

"I don't know," Deen said, and then his lip drooped. "I think he'd have pretended to be shocked and virtuous—I mean if it had been quite recently. But he wouldn't have done anything drastic. I say it myself but I'd become indispensable." He shook his head and frowned as if to look back. "All the same I'd never have felt comfortable. It would have given him a sort of hold over me. And he could become unbearable when he had the upper hand, or thought he had. You can take the remark how you like, but he was a man eaten up with conceit."

Wharton grunted. He took the spectacles slowly off and leaned forward again.

"You realise, of course, the dangerous position in which all this might have put you?"

Deen's look was suddenly wary.

"We're reasonable men," Wharton was going on, "but there are some who aren't. Some might even have had the idea that Mr. Wesslake discovered this secret of yours, and was threatening—shall we say?—to broadcast it. That might have meant ruin for you."

Deen hadn't seen the implications.

"But he didn't," he said. "If he had, then I'd have known it. It was the sort of thing he'd never have kept to himself."

"That may be so," Wharton told him. "But let's say it was as I said. Mightn't those same uncharitable people have made all that a motive for murder?"

Deen shot him a look. His tongue went nervously across his lips again. A moment, and his shoulders were straightening.

"If you think I killed him, then all you have to do is to charge me. I've told you the truth. I didn't kill him—if he *was* killed. I had no reason to kill him. I'd every reason to wish him alive."

Injured innocence was hardly the term for Wharton's look. Mr. Deen mustn't make hypotheses into facts, he told him sadly. All the same, there was just one thing he must do, and that was to insist that Deen stayed in town. Not, of course, because of anything so ridiculous as a charge, but merely as an important witness and a source of information. For instance, Mr. Deen could tell us . . .

It was another half-hour before Deen left and Wharton had squeezed him dry about Wesslake as author, employer and man. He'd also contrived to bring in Collinson, of whom Deen now spoke in terms of respect. Collinson, it appeared, was quite prepared to present Deen with the Colin Lake goodwill, provided he was sure the standard of those books would be fully kept up. Deen even volunteered the information that he'd gone post-haste and furiously angry to Collinson that very afternoon, and had discovered that Collinson had had no intention whatever of doing any double-crossing.

So Deen was at last allowed to go. Wharton's look was that other Coliseum one—that of the lion who's missed his first snap at the plump Christian.

"He's a damn crafty chap," he told me. "He and Collinson have got everything worked out."

"But he told the truth about his private affairs."

"A sprat to catch a mackerel." He gave me a glare and a sniff. "Not that it'll save Collinson. He's the man we've got to concentrate on. Wesslake's wife, that's who he was after. And I'll wager that's why he flew to Copenhagen. Tried to get Wesslake to give her a divorce, and Wesslake wouldn't."

I didn't argue, even if it was on the tip of my tongue to say that a divorce was the very thing that Wesslake wanted. And then George was glancing up at the clock and giving a start of surprise. He'd fixed an appointment with Nelda Hawden and her husband and I'd just have time to make it. Hawden and his wife were playing the suburban halls, and he and his wife were living at the Claverhouse Hotel in Cowper Street.

"What's the idea?" I said. "What am I supposed to elicit? General information, or what?"

George tried a kind of bluster but his heart wasn't in the act. Hadn't Wesslake and his then wife objected to the marriage? Mightn't Moroni have removed Wesslake? Hadn't the marriage been far too hurried, and with Nelda giving a false declaration of age? And even if Moroni and his wife hadn't been concerned with Wesslake's death, didn't we have to clear them off the suspect list in any case?

I mildly agreed. George rang down for a police car, but even then I was five minutes late.

The newly married couple had a small suite—bedroom, bathroom and sitting-room. Nelda was curled up on a chesterfield smoking a cigarette, and her eyes simply bulged when I walked in. Hawden had opened the door for me, and to me he also had been a bit of a surprise. I'd expected the dapper type with the usual streak of moustache, but found a tall fellow who didn't look a day over thirty, and had an earnest, student-like air. His voice was positively cultured.

"Why, Mr. Travers!"

Nelda flushed and got hurriedly off the chesterfield. Hawden was looking puzzled. I did the explaining.

"Well, sit down, sir," Hawden said. "My wife told me about you but the last thing we expected was to see you here."

"Have some tea," Nelda said, and out had to come the old joke about hob-nobbing with suspects. Hawden seemed to take it a bit seriously. I did some more explaining about red-tape and routine. In any case, I said, I didn't expect to be there more than a very few minutes. And I was thinking that marriage seemed to be agreeing with Nelda. She was almost plump, and she was looking far prettier with half her old amount of make-up.

"Your father's death must have come as a shock," I said, and there wasn't much conviction in her voice when she said it was. I switched to the waggish again.

"A pity you young people didn't somehow contrive to get his consent beforehand. But there, people in love are always in too much of a hurry."

Once more Hawden chose to take me far too seriously, and I was glad afterwards that he did.

"We did all we could," he said, "but what people won't realise is that we've got the right to live our own lives."

"But his blessing—not to say his money—might surely have been useful?"

"His money!" Nelda said, and sniffed.

"We didn't want his money or anything else," her husband was cutting in. "I can make all the money we want, Mr. Travers, and more."

Then he began telling me something which, after my first summing-up of him, I had no reason to disbelieve. He had always had a passion for music, and his father—a Midland manufacturer—hadn't discouraged him. Hawden had in fact studied at the Royal College of Music with the idea of becoming a composer, and then he had realised that that would be a slow and uphill job. A chance hit with a bit of light music had given him new ideas. Now he was running his own combination and doing his own arrangements and finding it a paying game. He'd no false pride, as he told me, and while he still might have a few furtive ambitions, he had no regrets. He liked the work and his father was proud of his publicity. It was his mother, now dead, who'd been the high-brow member of his family.

I asked if he'd had any personal encounter with Nelda's father.

"Tell him, darling," she said, and viciously enough, not that her husband was to need any urging to vent his grievances.

He had seen Wesslake only once, he said, and that was when he made a scene in a Paliceum dressing-room. He had been high-handed in the extreme and even offensive. Hawden claimed to have been more than reasonable but Wesslake wouldn't listen to sense. The fact that Hawden was a dance-band leader was sufficient damnation.

I gave sympathetic nods and grunts. Nelda was so pleased that she asked if I wouldn't change my mind about tea, so I damned the regulations. And over that tea there was the chance to talk about a whole lot of people and things. For Camille both the Hawdens had, unreasonably and illogically, nothing but contempt. Nelda liked Collinson enormously, but with Deen she'd had few contacts. Towards her mother her attitude was pitying, and David she was now regarding as something of what is known as a scream.

"Tell me something," I said. "You remember that Sunday morning after that robbery at the Malfroi Arms? You had an early swim, didn't you?"

"Did I?" she said, and was trying to think back.

"You did, because I remember I saw you. At the time it made me wonder something. I expect you'll laugh when I tell you what it was."

What it had made me wonder, I said, was if she'd had the idea that since the attacker had been disturbed, he'd thrown Camille's jewellery into the pool, and she'd therefore been trying to recover it from the bottom. She only laughed.

"I wish I had. It'd have been lovely to have made her cough up something as a reward. Mother used to keep me very short, you know."

I asked about the funeral. It was to be at Burnbury, she said, but only David was going, unless Camille chose to go. She gave a little pout of contempt at that but she didn't look at me, and I guessed she was remembering that scene in the wood when we'd taken that walk.

"What about your aunt—Mrs. Stonhill," I said. "How is she, these days?"

There was almost the first really pleasurable smile as she told me she was now very well indeed. But perhaps I didn't know that she'd been seriously ill soon after she'd left the Malfroi Arms.

"She rang us up just before you arrived," she said. "It was nice to hear her, wasn't it, darling?"

Hawden said it was and added that he liked her enormously. She was what he described as a sensible woman, which meant that she'd condoned the marriage and, if not too profusely on the side of the couple, was at least a long way from hostile.

That was about all. I gave the Hawdens my belated good wishes, accepted some complimentary tickets, and left. When I got back to the Yard, Wharton was there. I thought he'd been there all the time but he hadn't. He'd fixed up a hurried appointment with Wesslake's solicitors and had just learned the contents of the will. It was a brand new one, drawn up about a fortnight before he had left for Denmark and its contents had come as a big surprise to George. They surprised me too. I'd have guessed that everything would be left to Drina or the children, but it wasn't. We didn't yet know how much there was to leave, but whatever it was, it had been left to Camille, who was described as "my dear wife". But everything was in trust for the two children. If Camille remarried, she lost nothing. She would still have the use of the estate, though at her death it would revert. The bank were the sole executors. Collinson, by the way, got a hundred pounds as a gesture of appreciation and respect, and the Upmans a hundred pounds each. Confidence was expressed in Deen as well able to handle the literary interests, and he was also left a hundred pounds.

"Either we've been told a whole lot of lies," George said, "or that will's a remarkable change-about. Everything to his dear wife, eh? What was the idea?"

I said—and how luckily right I was to be!—that if we knew that we might know who'd killed him. That brought the snort it seemed to merit and he was asking what had happened at the Claverhouse Hotel. I told him that in my opinion we could wipe the Hawdens off the slate, and when he had heard everything he was minded to agree. Then I told him about Alice Stonhill and how she had rung up the hotel that very afternoon. He didn't quite see the point.

"The telephone in her house is in the hall," I said, "and there isn't an extension in the bedroom. I know because I was in there. In other words, Alice Stonhill was supposedly far too ill to see you this morning, even for a minute, and yet she was well enough to come downstairs soon after you'd gone and to ring up the Hawdens. And just for a bit of friendly chit-chat—or so I gathered."

George thought I was making a mountain of a molehill. A lot of people, let alone an old lady of eighty, would do a lot to avoid seeing the police. I said maybe he was right, and asked what next, and he said we might as well call it a day. In the morning he was running down to Burnbury for the inquest, and he was arranging for a local house-to-house call in case some chance observer had seen a car parked suspiciously near the wood where Wesslake's body had been found.

My next day's assignment was to go to Merridale to interview Drina and David, and later that evening he would ring me about the appointment time. When he did ring it was to say that the appointment was for eleven o'clock, and a car would pick me up at my flat.

I was up at my usual time, and that left me well over an hour after breakfast before the arrival of the car. Just as I was settling down to the newspaper, Wharton rang me up. He was just off to Burnbury.

"I was looking through those notes of yours last night," he said, "and that Wesslake diary in Denmark. You have a look at it yourself and see if something doesn't strike you as wrong."

"Tell me yourself," I said.

"Well, according to the Malfroi Arms chit-chat, he was supposed to be staying on in Denmark after the Congress so as to look up relatives. But he didn't. You work it out."

I said I would and with that he rang off. And I was telling myself that George wasn't any too sure of his facts or else he'd have made that call a reprimand instead of a reminder.

And then the complacency went. George had spotted something not quite right. Wesslake had definitely said he was taking a week's holiday *after* the Congress in order to look up relatives. But he had looked them up before it had ended—if there'd been a *them* at all. What he'd done was to visit the Jensen home at Roskilde on the Sunday before the Congress opened, and his uncle—Mogens Jensen—at Tisvilde while the Congress was sitting. And since Mogens Jensen had no children, what other relatives were there to visit, unless they were exceedingly distant cousins from the grandmother's side? And surely one would never regard such remote connections as relatives?

That was what Wharton had spotted, and then I was realising that he might have spotted something else—that in effect, Wesslake had been giving himself a kind of alibi. Drina knew well enough that the only real relative—Mogens Jensen—was living at Tisvilde, in Zealand, and yet she too seemed to have accepted the story about looking up relatives. But, if my memory wasn't playing tricks, Miss Chrome had told Bill Ellice that Wesslake was intending to spend that extra week exploring Fynen and Jutland. Had Wesslake then changed his mind, or altered his original intentions? And if so, why?

It was all very confusing but intriguing nevertheless, and I was making up my mind to speak to Drina about it. Perhaps I'd see Miss Chrome, and with that I got to my feet and made for the telephone. Enquiries gave me her number and in a few moments I was hearing her voice. It was a brisk, attractive voice; the voice of a woman of culture and charm. I said I represented the Insurance Company in the matter of the late Mr. Peter Wesslake.

"What a dreadful shock it was to me!" she said. "Such a charming man too. And the very last thing you'd have thought he'd have done."

I agreed. And I said I might have some interesting news for her.

"Do tell me now!" she said.

I playfully said it would keep. Besides, it was too confidential for the telephone.

CHAPTER 15
DAZZLE OF TRUTH

DRINA FARMAN'S was a beautiful house: early Georgian with fine large windows and a superb porch. It lay back from the road as one entered Merridale village from the London side. As our car went along the short drive, I could see that everything shrieked money, from tended lawns and flower-beds to swing garden seats and coloured umbrellas beneath a huge copper beech. I was also noticing something else—the Daimler standing just beyond the porch.

David Wesslake came out as my car drew up. In his far from customary suit of solemn black he looked vastly different from when I had seen him last, and there was nothing of the supercilious in his manner.

"Hallo, sir," he said, and even gave me a smile. "We didn't know till Jim Collinson sprang the news, that you were in the detective line."

I said I was and I wasn't, so to speak, and he caught me running a quick eye over those sober garments of his.

"I'm due at the funeral tomorrow," he told me, "and I thought I'd stay over-night in town. I'm rigged up like this to save carting a huge bag about."

I said I needn't detain him unless there was something he'd like to tell me himself. He said he couldn't think of anything. Why his father should have taken his life he didn't know.

I didn't disillusion him, and I was thinking too that only a fool would take David Wesslake for a patricide. And I was wondering if those garments of his and the haste to be going might mean he was meeting Camille in town. And thinking of Camille reminded me of that scene in the wood.

"Just one little thing you might possibly tell me," I said and took his arm and gently led him away from the house. "Naturally I'll regard anything you happen to know as most confidential. I only ask you because I know you were just a bit friendly with Camille."

His face flared and I knew that Nelda hadn't been able to resist a cattish revelation about what she and I had seen on a certain afternoon. But I didn't let my knowledge fluster David Wesslake. I let the vague hint of blackmail sink in and then put my question.

"What I'd like to know is this," I said, "and I repeat that it's most confidential from both our sides. It's about that attack on Camille at the swimming-pool that night. I'm dead sure in my own mind that she didn't go to that pool by chance. Can you tell me why she went?"

He moistened his lips and was saying perhaps he could. But it would make him out an awful liar.

"What's a lie or two between friends?" I said. "But suppose I try to spare your blushes by telling you. You slipped a note into her hand that night during the dance, didn't you?"

"You saw me?" he said, and stared.

"You answer the question," I said.

"Well, as a matter of fact, I did. But afterwards I didn't want to get her name mixed up with mine, so I said I'd seen her by chance. Afterwards I got her to keep quiet about the note."

"And everything else you told the police was perfectly true?"

"Everything," he said. "I'll swear to it. I didn't know whether she'd come or not, and that's why I stood out there watching, and I didn't follow her at once in case we should be seen together."

"Forget it," I said. "It just clears something up, that's all. Now you can get on to town, and I'll have a word with your mother."

We went back to the house and into a lavishly furnished drawing-room of the old-fashioned kind. Drina came in as if she'd seen us and had been waiting. David did some quick talking, gave her a peck of a kiss, waved me a goodbye, and left. I began uttering condolences, and they were received with what I might call a majestic patience.

"Jim Collinson tells me the police have some ridiculous idea about murder," she said. "But do sit down. We're having coffee, by the way. I remembered your coffee at the Malfroi Arms."

I said it was very nice of her to have taken all that trouble, and as to the question of murder—well, I was afraid there wasn't the slightest doubt. Mr. Wesslake had very definitely not killed himself.

"Then it must have been one of those dreadful hold-up cases we read so much about," she said, and then happily the coffee came in. The tray, carried by an ancient maid, was early Georgian and the coffee set Queen Anne, and the sight of them made me wish for a moment that I could be a hold-up man too. Drina herself was looking highly expensive that morning, and I couldn't help thinking what a handsome lass she must have been when Wesslake married her. Even now, if she could get rid of a certain astringency, most men would give her a second look.

We skated round a lot of very thin ice, and it was only when I was holding my lighter for her cigarette that I ventured on my first real approach.

"Now that David's gone," I said, "I'd like to ask you at least one very confidential question. It's a question between friends, if you'll allow me to put it that way, and it's this. You and your ex-husband were always on friendly terms?"

"At first, no," she said, and with a snap. "Then, of course, he knew what a fool he'd made of himself, and he wanted to come back to me."

"I know," I said, and I knew something else. Brains were not her strong point, and even a brainy woman can often be flattered. That's why I said it was bound to happen. Marriage in a mad moment of haste and then an even hastier repentance. Anyone in his senses, I said, and was trying to give her an admiring look, could have foreseen what would happen.

"But tell me something else, and still in strict confidence. By the way, may I call you Drina? It seems rather stilted to call you anything else."

The astringency was going and she was even simpering. What she needed was a man in her life, though I didn't think that at the moment she had more than the remotest designs on myself. A minute or two and I was able to ask her if Wesslake had written to her from Denmark, and she was admitting that he had.

"We'd always kept in touch with each other, you know. Besides, when there are children . . ."

We were like two bugs in a rug. She even fetched the two letters, though she didn't let me handle them. But she made no bones about answering my question. Wesslake had told her about his visit to Roskilde.

"When did he go there?" I said, and more for the sake of conversation than anything else.

The diamonds flashed as she turned the pages over.

"On the twenty-ninth," she said. "The letter's dated the thirtieth, and the postmark's the thirtieth. Let me see now. That was a Sunday, and I got in on the Wednesday. I remember thinking how quick it had been."

"Don't think me too inquisitive," I said, "but are you sure it was a Saturday when he was at Roskilde?"

"But of course," she said, and read me the passage.

> I never did like Saturdays, so yesterday I paid a duty visit to Roskilde to look up the old family home. There wasn't quite the thrill I'd thought . . .

"But you don't want to hear the rest," she said, and then was giving me a curious look. "But why were you so anxious to know?"

I explained that Camille had applied to the police and that they had followed up Wesslake's movements in Denmark and I'd been of the impression, now erroneous, that the Roskilde visit had been on a Sunday. Not that it mattered in the least.

But after that I was anxious to be gone but it took a further ten minutes before I could slip gracefully away.

She walked with me to the car and gave me the most pressing invitation to come again. And she didn't mention Bernice.

There was no need to return through London. What we did was to make for Hatfield and then by Ware towards Braintree. At Braintree there was nicely time for lunch. The morning, in fact, had been detection in high life and I ought to have been feeling on top of the world. As it was I was doing a bit of worrying. George had expected me to provide him with the reason why Wesslake had changed his Danish plans about that final week of holiday. I'd also been supposed to induce Drina to participate in an orgy of scandal, and thereby let fall some possible clue. Above all I should have brought in Collinson, and I hadn't. I'd done practically nothing that I'd been told and I'd got away from Merridale as if it were infected. And all because of a discrepancy between what Wesslake had written in a letter and what I'd proved for myself at Roskilde.

Maybe I was tracking down a mirage and there'd be the devil of a lot of explaining to do to George if Miss Chrome could furnish some feasible explanation. And if not, then maybe I'd think of something on the way back to town. Perhaps I could switch the responsibility somehow to George, or perhaps he might have discovered something for himself at Burnbury.

But I didn't let it spoil my lunch and I was feeling happier when we set off on the last seven miles to Sedford. There we did some enquiring and ran The Retreat to earth in a side lane we'd already passed.

Phoebe Chrome was at the front gate, for we were dead on time. I'd made the driver take off cap and tunic so that she wouldn't spot us for the police, and we drew up a good few precautionary yards away, and then he drove on to reverse when Phoebe and I were making for the cottage. And a delightful cottage it was. It was wrong, as I told her, for her to have so many lovely things that ought by rights to be in my flat.

"You'll have coffee?" she said, and I regretfully said I'd had it at Braintree. All the time I'd been—in a Whartonian phrase—running my rule over her. Her hair was greying and she looked about sixty. Vivacious was just the word for her, and there was nothing of the kittenish or coy.

Of course she was on to me at once about that secret at which I'd hinted. I told her the truth.

"I knew it," she said. "I knew a man like Mr. Wesslake could never possibly do anything so dreadful as taking his own life. When do you think it happened? As soon as he got back to England? Why I say that is because he told me he was due at once in America."

"He never got there," I said. "This is highly confidential, by the way, but we insurance people are naturally anxious to know just why he didn't go. To tell you the truth, we've been tracing his every movement from the day he left England to go to Denmark."

"I'd no idea you did things like that," she said. "It makes one wonder about one's own insurance."

I explained that that had been done before we knew it wasn't suicide. Had it been suicide it would have affected the insurance payment. It might even have invalidated everything. But, as I said, we didn't want to talk about that. How had she herself enjoyed her trip to Denmark?

"It was perfectly lovely," she said, "and the Danes treated us absolutely royally. We went everywhere and saw everything."

"But what about the Congress? I suppose you and Mr. Wesslake aired your views?"

She laughed at that. She had spoken once, but only with great trepidation. As for Mr. Wesslake, he'd been very lazy indeed. He'd attended the barest minimum of sessions and had spent most of his time exploring Copenhagen.

"How'd you come to meet him?"

"We happened to be staying at the same hotel," she said. "We were the only English people there, so naturally we made each other's acquaintance. I was absolutely thrilled to be in the company of so famous an author. I know his books aren't high-brow, but then I'm not altogether high-brow myself."

"And you'd like to have his royalties."

"Heavens, yes!" she said, and laughed again. Then her face straightened. "But he was very modest about himself. You simply couldn't get him to take the part in Congress he ought to have taken."

Curiouser and curiouser, I thought.

"But going back to your trips in Denmark," I said, "I needn't ask you if you went to a favourite spot of mine—Roskilde."

"But of course I did," she said. "Actually I went there with Mr. Wesslake. His grandfather used to live there, you know. A very famous painter and author."

"What day did you go?" I said. "There's a dear little museum there, you know, and I only mention it because it's closed on . . . let me see now, what day is it? I think it's Saturday."

"It was a Sunday when we went," she said. "But we didn't go to any museum. I didn't even know there was one."

And for a very good reason, I could have told her, for I hadn't a notion if one was there at all.

"It was a lovely day," she was going on. "I landed on the Saturday and it rained all the afternoon. It was raining on the Sunday morning too, and then it cleared up and the sun came out and it was lovely."

That rang a distant bell. What that bell was telling me I didn't know, unless it was that Wesslake had changed his plans because of the Saturday's rain. And yet how could he?

"Mr. Wesslake ought to have been thrilled," I said. "Did he speak the language at all?"

"Just a few phrases," she said. "He said he'd forgotten practically all of it. I didn't know a word, of course, but one could manage very well. Most people seemed to understand English."

I was wondering just what it was that I wanted to know, and I couldn't for the life of me think. So I merely kept the conversation going.

"It must have been a thrill for a man of Danish ancestry to go back to his mother's country after all those years," I said. "I met him myself once, by the way, and I thought how like his mother he must have looked. That blond hair of his made him look like a Dane."

"Blond?" she said, and frowned. "I shouldn't have called it blond. Not the sort of yellowish, Danish blond. I'd have called it white. Like my own will be in a very few years' time, I regret to say. Or is that vanity?"

The bell was ringing again. I made some vacuous remark about vanity and shot back to Wesslake.

"Some years since I saw him," I said, "and even then I didn't actually speak to him. How old was he, by the way?"

"I didn't hear him say," she said. "I should think in the early fifties. But he was a most attractive companion. What I'd call the perfect listener."

And there, believe it or not, the visit ended, or at least the part of it that concerned Peter Wesslake. She showed me over the cottage and we walked round the little garden, but when she begged me to stay for an early cup of tea, I had to discover that I'd already stayed too long and that I'd be late for my next appointment. I wouldn't let her come the few yards down the lane to the car but said goodbye at the gate. And I had to promise that I'd most certainly come again, and in a purely private capacity. And, to be honest, I would have liked to stay for that cup of tea for she was a charming soul. I knew something else too that I hadn't quite appreciated before—just why Wesslake had found her such excellent company.

"To the Yard, sir, or your flat?" the driver asked me as we came well into London and I'm prepared to bet any reasonable sum of money that you'd never guess where it was that I told him to go. Back to Sedford? To Ashenby and Alice Stonhill? Back to Merridale and Drina Farman? To the Malfroi Arms? On to Burnbury in case Wharton hadn't left? To Hampstead and Collinson? To Kennington and Deen?

I went to none of them but where I did go you'll learn in a minute. I told the driver to get on as quickly as he could, for it was nearer five o'clock than four. By the time I'd done what I wanted to do and had the vital information, it was well after five o'clock and we went on to the Yard. Wharton was not yet in but was on his way. I had tea brought in and set about a marshalling of the facts, and I had everything in hand when George at last appeared.

"Had a tiring day?" I said, and poured him a cup of the still-warm tea.

"A bit solicitous, aren't you?" he was telling me suspiciously.

"Grateful's the word," I said.

"Grateful? Grateful for what?"

I was treating myself to one of George's conjuring tricks. He likes to produce things out of a hat and receive the plaudits of myself as onlooker.

"Grateful for that tip you gave me this morning, George. The one about the discrepancy in Wesslake's movements."

"You're on to something?"

"More than that," I told him soberly. "I'm even open to bet that inside twenty-four hours we'll have this Case cracked."

He shot me a look from under his shaggy eyebrows.

"Well, what're you waiting for? Let's hear it."

"The whole gist is this," I said. "Wesslake wasn't in Denmark at all during the first fortnight he was supposed to be there. *It was Deen who was there, deputising for him.*"

His lips pursed out till that moustache of his was like an awning for his chin.

"You mean Deen was giving him an alibi?"

"That's it," I said. "An alibi for that attack on Camille Wesslake at the swimming-pool. By rights she ought to have been found drowned."

"You mean that Wesslake was Ferotti?"

"That's all it *can* mean," I said. "But wait till you hear what happened this morning and how I arrived at it."

It all sprang, I said, from that discrepancy between Wesslake's announced intentions and what he actually did. I'd intended to verify the intentions through Drina Farman, but she'd let fall a remark that had led to something far more profitable.

"I went to Copenhagen, George, as you know, and I proved that Wesslake was at Roskilde on Sunday, May the thirtieth. Drina produced a letter from Wesslake, written on the thirtieth and posted on the thirtieth, which said he'd been to Roskilde the previous day, and he expressly mentioned that it was a Saturday. Now I ask you, how could he write a letter on the Sunday and say he'd been somewhere on the Saturday, when he'd really been there on the day he was writing the letter. It doesn't make sense. *Unless the letter was written beforehand.* But even that doesn't quite explain why he put May the thirtieth at the head.

"So I decided to see Miss Chrome and there I struck oil practically at once. She confirmed that it was on that Sunday that she and Wesslake visited Roskilde, but she also let fall that the Saturday afternoon had been very wet. It was wet also on the Sunday morning, and then cleared up. I don't know if that gives you ideas, but it seemed to me to be connected somehow with that Drina Farman letter. Just how I couldn't see—till she began telling me about Wesslake.

"And what a Wesslake! Unassuming, hating the lime-light and a good listener. The Wesslake of all those reports of yours, George, reminds one of Chesterton's appraisal of Dickens—thumping a big drum at the head of the procession and wearing a sunflower in his buttonhole. Then when she said his hair wasn't blond at all, but white, I really saw things. That's why I hurried back from Sedford and made for the Passport Department of the Foreign Office. I had to use my Warrant Card but I learned that a new passport had been issued to Peter Wesslake because his had been destroyed in a fire. Now we know why he set fire to that summer-house. He arranged it so that he couldn't lose money over it, and the loss of the summer-house wasn't comparable with the loss, say, of the house. It's something like Lamb's Chinaman who worked out that it wasn't necessary to set a sty on fire every time he wanted to roast pork. But the Foreign Office are damnably strict, as you know. They won't issue a new passport unless they're dead sure and after the most stringent enquiries what's become of the old. Well, the fire was good enough evidence and a new passport was issued—and it had Wesslake's photograph only—not his and his wife's.

"So there you are, George," I said. "I reckon you can work the rest out for yourself."

"You carry on," he told me.

"Well, one or two other things are explained," I said. "You remember I told you that when I first saw Deen I had the idea that I'd seen him somewhere before. I now know why. It was because I went to him with my head full of ideas about Wesslake whom I'd just seen in Ellice's office. I'd just seen a rather unusual head of blond hair, and when Deen opened the door to me, I saw a head of white hair. And Deen's just the size and build of Wesslake. At any rate you know what passport photographs are—usually cheap and just a bit like and no more. Or Wesslake, for all we know, may have induced Deen to have Deen's photograph on that new passport. Deen will tell us the truth about that. Personally I don't think it was necessary. Blond hair photographs like white. I saw a photograph of Deen taken from above at a place called Hillerod, and I never questioned it for a minute. I took him for Wesslake."

I asked if he still wanted me to go on working things out, and he did. I told him we now knew a lot more about things that had rather puzzled me and Ellice.

"This was a long planned scheme," I said, "and it started when Wesslake learnt about the P.E.N. Congress at Copenhagen. He joined the P.E.N. because of the scheme and for no other reason. And I think there's some light thrown on those two supposed murder attempts. They haven't been enquired into because Wesslake is dead. I suppose you didn't see that doctor, by the way, when you were down there today?"

"I did," he said. "I think I know what you're working up to, and I think it fits in. You know what doctors are. The Hippocratic oath and all that, and you can't get a thing out of them about a patient. I shouldn't myself if I hadn't pointed out that Wesslake was dead, and then he loosened up a bit. He confirmed that the Camille woman's had been a very severe gastric attack and possibly induced by some drug, but definitely not by poison. Then he let out something else—that Wesslake had seen him privately and hinted that Collinson had been the cause. Asked the doctor never to breathe a word. Collinson's family on the mother's side were liable to insanity, and Wesslake was going to keep a careful watch over him in future, and a whole lot of bilge like that."

"There we are, then," I said. "The devil of it is we can't go into it now. Undoubtedly Collinson must have been in a position to put the drug in, but we can't prove it. And the same with that shooting business. Wesslake must have contrived it to throw considerable suspicion on Collinson—but again we can't prove it. But Collinson was his fall-boy, as they say. He knew Collinson was in love with Camille. But to get back to the scheme.

"Deen was induced to go to Copenhagen and it was announced that he was taking a bus-tour holiday and so that nobody could get into touch with him and prove where he was. We can make Deen tell us how that Edinburgh postcard and alibi were wangled. But the Upmans were cleared out too and I rather think that Wesslake made the house his hide-out till the beard had grown. That would be doped with the usual sulphide preparation which would turn it a greyish black, and so would the hair. I think he also had a hair-cut and got the barber to shave a tonsure as well. He probably also injected a wax preparation under the bridge of his nose, but I wouldn't swear to that. The dark glasses concealed his blue eyes and there was a disguise that no one on earth could have seen through. The weekend at the Malfroi Arms was fixed up, and I haven't the faintest doubt that he went there with the fixed intention this time of really killing his wife, only he intended to do it so as to put suspicion on Collinson. How I don't know. Perhaps we shan't ever know. All the same I think he'd have given evidence against Collinson and harked back to those two abortive attempts. All that, by the way, explains the new will he made just before he left for Denmark. How could a man who left everything to his dear wife be suspected of her death? Or that's how he argued."

"An egomaniac," George said, and grunted. "Like that typewriter business in the fire. Who's to suspect the great Peter Wesslake!"

"There's something else we'll have to work out," I said. "He even had the nerve to try to kill Alice Stonhill after he'd just missed killing his wife. Why, I don't know exactly, but we'll probably find out, unless he was hoping in some way to pin that on to Collinson too. But there—I agree with you that the man was an egomaniac. Eaten up with conceit as everybody agrees."

"What about the two passports?" George said. "How do they come in exactly?"

"Just how they *did* come in," I said. "He used one of them, after he'd bolted from the Malfroi Arms, to go to Denmark from Dover and Ostend and on by train to Copenhagen. That's a recognised route. And that's the way he came home. He didn't make contact with Deen or take his place because Deen was already established at the hotel and the Congress as Wesslake. Why Deen didn't take any part in the Congress is easily explained, by the way. Someone might have been there who happened to know Wesslake—the real Wesslake. I don't think it was very likely. Wesslake's type of pal wouldn't be the kind who'd belong to the P.E.N."

"And when he got back to England?"

"We don't know," I said, "but I believe Collinson killed him. But to go back just a bit. There's a crook who operates rather on the fake Ferotti's lines, and it wouldn't have been hard for Wesslake to have consulted the files of the *Police Gazette*. Not that it matters. What does matter is that Collinson, although he never for a second had the vaguest suspicion who Ferotti might be, did recognise that that third attempt on Camille's life was a sequence, and he came to the conclusion that Ferotti simply had to be Wesslake. That's why Collinson flew to Denmark.

"As to what Wesslake did when he left the Malfroi Arms that early morning, I'd say he went back to Burnbury. But he had to have a hidey-hole somewhere. He had to bleach his hair to the blond again and let the hair grow, or else there might have been suspicion over the passport. He also had to get rid of that subcutaneous wax, though how the devil he'd do that I don't know. Then he'd have to arrange his passage from Dover."

George had been padding round the room. Now he came back to his desk, and he was frowning away and scowling to himself.

"You were right," he told me. "This Case is due for cracking. The question is, which is the best way to set about it?"

"I'd have both Deen and Collinson watched from now on," I said. "Collusion must be going on. Collinson knew Deen was being Wesslake in Copenhagen and Deen knows that he knew. They've got some new plans of campaign worked out. And maybe a whole new set of alibis. On the whole, though, I'm inclined to think we'd do best to get at Deen first. Stagger him with what we know, and even charge him with creating a public mischief. That'll be enough to scare him into telling what he knows. You agree?"

George merely gave that same old Coliseum smile.

CHAPTER 16
CONFESSION

IN A MATTER of minutes everything was fixed up. Deen happened to be in again and Wharton asked him if he'd be so good as to help us once more.

"We're very grateful to you," Wharton told him unctuously. "I'll send a car to fetch you, by the way . . . You'd rather come by bus? Well, please yourself, but don't say I didn't offer. In about a quarter of an hour then." If Deen did leave the Yard he would be picked up and kept under observation from then on. But two men were already on the way to Romney Court, and the car would be kept handy in case Collinson should decide to do a bolt. For Deen would almost certainly be ringing him and telling him of that new visit to the Yard, and both the conspirators would be doing some pretty quick and anxious thinking. Not that it mattered who bolted, as George said. Neither could remain at liberty for more than a few days, though even that might give us a bit of trouble.

But we were both a bit anxious whether or not Deen would turn up. That coming by bus had sounded suspicious, but we needn't have worried. Deen did turn up, and this time he was looking just a bit anxious. And the room didn't look nearly so home-like. Even the stenographer made no pretence of being other than he was.

"Sit down," Wharton said abruptly. "This is an official visit, by the way. I'm asking you if you're prepared to make a statement."

"About what, sir?"

"Everything," Wharton told him curtly, and was raising a minatory finger. "The truth this time. No lies and false alibis. The truth, or before you can say Jack Robinson, I'll have you under arrest."

"Under arrest?"

"Don't spar for time," Wharton snapped at him. "You understand English, don't you? Or do you think I'm bluffing?"

Deen shuffled on the chair.

"Let's hear it," Wharton said. "Tell us why you went to Denmark."

Deen shot a look at him and moistened his lips.

"I didn't do anything wrong," he said. "I just went to Denmark as Mr. Wesslake asked me to. I admit I was wrong about that Edinburgh alibi."

"He admits he was wrong," Wharton told me sneeringly. "Just wrong, mind you. Only a little thing like perjury. And conniving at murder."

"You've got me wrong," Deen protested. "I didn't mean that, sir."

"He didn't mean it." Wharton told me with an assumption of patience. "I wonder what he did mean. I wonder if he'd be so good as to start from the beginning."

Deen started.

"It was like this, sir. Mr. Wesslake sprang it on me one day early in the year. He said he had a lady friend and had the chance of a holiday with her, and naturally he didn't want his wife or anyone to suspect. Then he told me what he'd planned about the P.E.N. Congress at Copenhagen and put it up to me that I might go there in his place. He was very plausible, sir, and I fell for it. He also was strange in his manner. There was a kind of threat behind it, and I had the idea he'd discovered about that slip of mine."

"But you were flattered all the same," I said.

"I admit it," he said, "but I had a right to go, in a way. The credit for a good bit of his work ought to have been mine, but I own now I was wrong. I admit I rather liked the idea of being someone at last, even in Denmark, and so I agreed. All I had to do was to be him, except that I wasn't to take any part in the Congress itself once I'd reported. He also gave me a list of things I had to do and some letters and postcards I had to post on certain days. This was just before I left, of course, and we'd discussed what I could do to make an alibi for myself. Then I remembered Hector Baird. He'd been present at that trial of mine and had told me afterwards that I'd been badly treated and he'd do what he could for me, so I went to Edinburgh to see him on the Wednesday after I was supposed to start on my holiday. I told him it'd be as good as my job was worth if my boss—I didn't say he was Mr. Wesslake—was to find out I was attending a Communist conference in France, and he fell for it. That's why he sent off a post-card for me and promised to swear to an alibi."

"Very clever," Wharton told him grimly. "And what next?"

"Well, I went to Denmark, using Mr. Wesslake's passport. I did everything he'd told me to do and I came back on the Saturday as arranged. Then when he didn't turn up himself, I got into touch with his family. Not too quickly, of course. I thought something had happened between him and his lady friend and he hadn't been able to get back as soon as he'd thought."

And that, he said, was all. Wharton leaned forward and his lip was drooping.

"Oh no. Not by any means. Tell us what happened—no lies mind you—when you discovered that Mr. Collinson was aware of the fact that you were masquerading in Copenhagen as Wesslake."

"Well, I admit I wasn't quite truthful about that," Deen told him. "But I wasn't anxious about myself. I didn't want to let Mr. Wesslake down."

"Not after he was dead! What do you think we are? Fools?"

"There might have been family trouble. And when a man's dead you don't throw dirt on his grave. You'll admit that, sir."

"You're doing the admitting," Wharton told him sneeringly.

"Well, I saw Mr. Collinson and I did tell him. I told him all I've just told you. He agreed that there oughtn't to be a scandal, and I promised to keep my mouth shut. I was wrong, of course, in thinking that you wouldn't be able to find out."

"How much did he pay you? And don't put on that virtuous look. I'm not such a fool that I can't smell a liar a mile off."

"He didn't pay me anything," Deen said with an attempt at dignity. "All he promised was that he'd do what he could in the matter of the Colin Lake books. But it'd be up to me."

"If that isn't bribery, then my name's Robinson. And that's all you've got to tell us?"

Deen said it was. I cut in with a question.

"Perhaps Mr. Deen would like to know just what it was that gave him away. He didn't go to Roskilde on a certain Saturday as arranged because it was raining cats and dogs. Isn't that so?"

Deen admitted that it was but I didn't tell him any more. Wharton was coming in with something startling.

"I suppose you know, Deen, that you've had an uncommonly lucky escape? Wesslake wasn't with any lady. He was planning a murder and you were his alibi. You know what that means?"

Deen didn't get it, but the one word had given a new alarm.

"If you were his alibi," Wharton went on, "then it wasn't safe for you to be left alive. If someone hadn't killed him first, he'd most certainly have killed *you*. That was part of his scheme. You'd have been done away with, and if he really did know about that slip, as you called it, he'd only to say he'd taxed you with it and you'd bolted. He could have said he'd found you a thief or any kind of a rogue he liked. You wouldn't have been able to disprove it. You'd have been comfortably underground somewhere, or lying in that wood at Burnbury and a gun in your hand."

Deen was shocked, there wasn't a doubt about that. As for his story, we questioned him about Denmark and heaven knows what, and couldn't find a flaw. Then Wharton cursed several kinds of hell out of him for the lies he'd told, but that didn't get us any further either.

"I could still get you put away," Wharton told him at last, "but I'm not going to. Kindness of heart has always been my ruin. That's why I'm telling you—telling, not asking—to stay in those rooms of yours. No funeral for you tomorrow. No nothing. You stay there till I tell you otherwise, and heaven help you if you try any tricks. That understood?"

Deen said it was, and got up with a look that said he was only too glad to go.

"No hurry," Wharton told him. "There'll be a statement to read and sign. When that's all done, we'll see."

Deen left at last, and at nearer nine o'clock than eight George and I were both pretty tired and hungry and we agreed to call it a day. But the latest report had come in from Romney Court. Collinson had come out and had posted a letter and then gone back.

Deen had almost certainly rung him as soon as he got to his rooms, but that letter might have been anything. It didn't necessarily have to do with the Case.

"We'll let him have a good night's rest," Wharton told me grimly, "then the first thing in the morning we'll have him here. I'll work out our lines of approach."

"There's one thing we can rely on now," I said. "It only dawned on me after you told Deen what'd have happened if Wesslake hadn't been killed first. As soon as Wesslake landed at Dover he must have intended to go hotfoot for Deen. Deen had to be killed at once. Therefore—or so it seems to me—someone must have intercepted Wesslake before he could return to town."

"I know," George said. "And who but Collinson? He'd work out that Wesslake would have to come back the Dover-Ostend way. And Dover isn't all that tremendous distance from Burnbury."

That was that. I left George there and went home, and I was asleep that night as soon as my head hit the pillow.

I was sound asleep at half-past seven when the telephone went. The bell was even part of my dreams and Bernice had to rouse me.

It was Wharton at the end of the line.

"Get here just before nine o'clock," he said. "I didn't like to disturb you last night but Collinson rang up very late and asked for an interview this morning. Said he thought he had some information that might interest us."

It was well before nine o'clock when I entered George's room. That I was excited and intrigued stands to reason but I didn't know that I was to be in for one of the big surprises of my life. Wharton wasn't anticipating anything but more lies, but we didn't have time for much surmise. Collinson, due at nine, turned up early, and it was still short of the hour when he was ushered into the room.

"Sorry to disturb you at this unearthly hour, gentlemen," he said as he eyes roved around.

"As far as we're concerned, we've half finished a day's work," George told him jocularly. "But take a seat, Mr. Collinson. Tell us what it's all about."

Collinson took his time. I hadn't quite realised till that moment what a good-looking chap he was. Maybe it was the way he was diffidently smiling.

"As a matter of fact," he said, "I've come here to give myself up!"

Wharton stared. I asked for what.

"For manslaughter," he said. *I was the one who killed Peter Wesslake.*

It was a moment or two before Wharton spoke.

"You realise what you're telling us?"

"Oh, yes."

"And you wish to make a statement?"

"Why not? I shall have to make one sooner or later."

Wharton grunted. Even though the initial surprise had gone, there was still something that worried him about Collinson's manner. It was too assured; too matter of fact and unconcerned.

Wharton waved a hand at the stenographer.

"Very well, Mr. Collinson; let's hear what you want to tell us."

Collinson actually gave a little smile of thanks. He wanted to know if he was to start at the very beginning.

"It's up to you," Wharton said.

"Well, the beginning's usually a good place to start," Collinson told him dryly. "I don't know if you know about Wesslake and the two attempts he made on his wife's life—or so I think."

"Assume we know nothing," Wharton told him.

So we heard about those two murder attempts and for me there was a certain gratification, for Collinson was trying to prove that Wesslake had made deliberate plans for casting suspicions on himself. That was new to us in so far as the evidence was concerned. In that matter of the shot in the woods, Wesslake had said that since he hadn't fired at that particular time, then Collinson must have been the one. That talk about a stranger in the woods had been a kind of after-thought and palliative. As for the gastric attack, Collinson said he could prove that Wesslake had taken over the tray. Then he had called to Collinson, "Hand these round, will you, Jim?" That of course, put Collinson in the position of being able to slip the dope into Camille's glass.

From all that it was only too logical to assume that that attack on Camille at the swimming-pool had been somehow engineered by Wesslake. Then Collinson had seen Ferotti behaving suspiciously but never for a moment had he suspected that Ferotti was Wesslake in disguise.

"He was a cunning devil," he said, "and I ought to have known. When I did begin to have pretty strong suspicions, it was too late."

"One moment," Wharton said, "I suggest that you give us any information you may happen to have about that other attack—the one on Mrs. Stonhill."

"Sorry," Collinson said. "I should have mentioned that. What I think is that he was venting his spite on her. He'd failed in that attempt on his wife, and he took it out on Mrs. Stonhill. She'd as good as told him that if she had her way, Mrs. Wesslake would never come back to him. He wanted a divorce, you know, and Mrs. Stonhill was opposed to it. She had very great influence over Mrs. Wesslake."

"Thank you," Wharton said. "Perhaps now you'll go on."

"Well, you see what the problem was," Collinson said. "If Wesslake was Ferotti, then he couldn't be in Denmark. So on that Sunday morning I went to town and arranged to fly to Denmark. When I got to Copenhagen I discovered the truth."

He gave a quiet little smile and he might have been talking to himself.

"It was rather funny, really, if it hadn't been so damnably serious. I was like someone in one of my detective stories: false moustache and dark glasses and all that. Then as soon as I spotted Deen, I came back and tried to run Wesslake to earth. He wasn't at the flat and he wasn't at Burnbury, or if he was, he had the house barricaded, so to speak, and as far as I was concerned, there was nobody there. I kept on trying but it was no good and I decided that he'd really gone to Denmark with a false passport. That meant he'd be coming back some other way, or so I thought. I didn't think he'd risk using the route that Deen had taken and it seemed to me that he'd take the Ostend-Dover route. I didn't feel either too sure or too happy about it, but I had to take a chance.

"What I did was to go to Dover a day before he'd announced his intention of coming back, and meet the incoming boats. He didn't come on the twelfth so I went again on the thirteenth, and that's when I spotted him. I ought to tell you, by the way, that he must have had a false passport because I made enquiries and he didn't travel under his own name. At any rate I spotted him, as I said. I watched him board the train and I did my disguise act in the lavatory and got in the far end of the train. When we got to Victoria I nipped out and gave a porter a good tip to hold a taxi. Then I followed Wesslake. He had only one bag and was carrying it himself. I managed to barge into him.

"'Good Lord, Peter!' I said. 'What're you doing here?'"

"He said he'd come home by a different route for a change of scenery and I said I'd been seeing someone off. I also said I had a taxi and would give him a lift. While he was putting his bag in, I slipped a chit to the driver about going to Hampstead. When we started off I began chatting away so as to divert his attention and he was spinning me a yarn about what had happened at the Congress. Then, of course, he did spot that we weren't going Westminster way, and I told him I had to drop in at Romney Court first and then I'd take him back. There wasn't anything he could do about it by then but I could see he was damnably suspicious. I kept on asking him questions about his experiences and I gave him all the family news and finally we got to Hampstead. I told the driver not to wait, and I told Wesslake I had to take out my own car as I was dining with some people in Bromley.

"We went in and I suggested a sherry. While I was getting it, he must have opened his bag, as you'll see in a minute. At any rate he took the glass and I had one too and then I began telling him things. I didn't get at all angry. I just spoke in a normal voice as if it were an ordinary friendly conversation, and he listened with his eyes screwed up as he always does. I told him all I knew and finally I reached for the telephone and said I was calling the police. That's when he whipped the gun out."

He paused there. His head went forward and he was rubbing his eyes as if they were tired. A moment, and he was giving that dry little smile again.

"If I were writing a book I could tell you so much better. But it all happened so damnably quickly.

"'You're not going to ring the police!' he said. 'You're never going to ring anybody.'"

"He began moving towards me, the gun in his hand. It was what they call a vicious-looking automatic, and I don't mind telling you I was stiff with fright. How I did what I did I don't know, but I happened to have my hand down at my side—like this—-and in a flash I hurled the cushion at him and dived forward. He let off a shot that missed—you can see the mark in the wall of the flat—and then I had him by the wrist. We fought like a couple of cats. I was bigger but he was shorter and more compact and—well, then the gun went off again. I'd got his hand twisted round and the bullet must have gone into his brain. He just collapsed. There he was on the floor."

There was a longish pause before he went on.

"It took me a minute or two to come round. Luckily there wasn't anyone at home in the upper flat, or perhaps it was unluckily. If there had been anyone there I'd have had to tell them what had happened and then call the police. As it was I decided on something else. I didn't want any scandal for one thing. I don't expect you to understand that, but that's how it was. What I actually did was to get rid of his bag and things, and get his body into my car. I left certain things in his pockets, and there's something you might be interested to know about them. I noticed he had a different wallet and an unmarked handkerchief. His own handkerchiefs were always beautiful linen ones with a monogram, but this one and the wallet were obviously ones he'd bought specially in his character of Ferotti. Not that that matters particularly. I had his body in the car, as I said, and well after dark I took him to Burnbury. I drove very carefully because naturally I didn't want to be stopped for any reason by the police. When I finally got to Burnbury the moon was up and I went round by the lane and dumped his body behind a holly clump in the wood, and I left the gun by his hand with his prints on it to give the impression of suicide. I did all that because I knew I could produce excellent reasons for his committing suicide, and it seemed to me that the wood near his own house would be the best place. I also left a piece of paper with a message scribbled on it in pencil—I knew his writing well enough—to say he'd decided to end it all. But you'll know what I said. I expect you found it."

"Maybe," Wharton told him. "But carry on."

"Well, that's about all there is. When there wasn't a hue and cry, so to speak, about his body being found, I didn't worry. I knew that sooner or later he must be found, if it was only when the wood was cut again. Then when Deen came to me—Mr. Travers had told him about my going to Denmark—I heard all he had to say and told him for his own sake to keep his mouth shut. I said Wesslake had been telling the truth about a lady friend, and he'd probably gone off with her altogether. We'd know in good time, but in the meanwhile his policy was to know nothing. Then when you discovered all that Denmark business, I knew it was time for me to come forward. I just couldn't make trouble for that poor devil, Deen. He hadn't a thing to do with it at all. He was just Wesslake's tool. If he told lies to you, it was at my instigation, and I'm prepared to take every bit of the blame."

He let out a breath and straightened himself in his chair.

"And that's all?" Wharton asked him.

"That's all I am prepared to say."

Wharton got to his feet.

"It's my duty to impress on you the seriousness of what you've been telling us."

I had been scribbling a hasty note, and now I handed it to Wharton. He pursed his lips as he read it, then laid it on the desk.

"I repeat. You realise the seriousness of what you've been telling us?"

"I do," Collinson told him soberly.

"And you know what my duty now is?"

Collinson nodded and slowly rose from his chair.

It was over an hour later when George and I were in that room again, and the first thing he did was to pick up that note of mine and nod to himself as he frowned at it.

"Something fishy, you think?"

"It's purely a hunch," I said, "I feel it in my very bones that there's something wrong. There was how sure of himself he was. I know a man of his breeding and upbringing would face any kind of music calmly—"

"Why shouldn't he?" George said, and curled his lip. "What's he got to fear? You heard what he said after I'd cautioned him. Wesslake was a maniac who'd really killed himself, and even if he hadn't, then we ought to be grateful to Collinson for having saved the expenses of a hanging. A trial'd be a farce. We can't prove or disprove his statement. His counsel would have him out of court in an hour."

"Everything was too pat," I said. "And what about that suicide note. That wasn't found."

"The rain'd have rotted it long ago. If not, the gales would have blown it away. And, according to his story, he was right about that gun. Whoever wrote that anonymous letter helped himself to it."

"I know," I said. "But I'd have been prepared to swear that Collinson himself wrote that letter."

"Why?"

"Look, George," I said patiently. "Collinson wants to marry Wesslake's widow. How could he if Wesslake wasn't known to be dead? It might be years before that wood was cut. Do you tell me that Collinson was prepared to wait all that time? Not a bit of it. After a suitable interval Wesslake's body just had to be found."

"Mightn't anybody go into that wood?"

"If it was to relieve nature, there's wasn't any need to go half as far. Boys wouldn't go bird-nesting because there wasn't nearly enough undergrowth. Poachers wouldn't go because you and I didn't see a single rabbit burrow in it."

"Yes," George said, and frowned. "But somehow I thought he was telling the truth. I don't mind telling you that I liked him, and hadn't been prepared to."

"Let's call him a professional story-teller," I said, "rather than a novelist. All that talk about what he could have done if he'd been writing a book was just bunkum. That story of his had logic and sequence. His pauses and his gestures were perfect too."

"But if he was telling lies, how could he have known about the nature of the bullet wound, and that wallet and handkerchief? Tell me that."

"Upman could have told him all that."

His finger went to the buzzer. Five minutes later he was speaking to Upman. He warned him of the seriousness of repeating to a living soul what was going to be said, and then he put the question. Upman swore that Collinson had never questioned him about the wound or the wallet or the handkerchief.

"That's that, then," George told me.

"So far, so genuine," I said, "but I still hold the story was too pat. Tell me this. Wasn't it too great a stroke of luck that Wesslake should return by Dover? Couldn't he have flown back? And wouldn't a man like Wesslake who knew London like the back of his hand have been suspicious at once when Collinson didn't *tell* the driver where to go? And when the taxi headed away from Westminster? And why should Wesslake have had a gun in his bag at all? He'd come straight from Denmark, and what did he want a gun for there? As for that bullet mark we're supposed to find at Romney Court, Collinson could have made it at any time. Then there's the—"

"All right, all right!" George told me impatiently. "You think something's wrong. Suppose you tell me what I'm supposed to do about it?"

"One thing you can't do," I said, "because Collinson's queered the pitch. I mean we can't check up on Wesslake's return by Ostend-Dover because Collinson says he had a false passport. In other words, he knows we shouldn't find that Wesslake *did* return that way. Though why Wesslake should use a false passport after firing his summer-house to get a genuine second one, beats me altogether."

"I know, I know," George told me. "I can put two and two together as well as most people. But you still haven't told me what to do about it."

"It's for you to decide," I said, "but I'll do this. This is definitely a case where you can urge that Collinson oughtn't to be brought before a public court. Have him brought before a Magistrate this afternoon, and then remanded. Bail must be absolutely refused. That will give us the chance to do a whole lot more testing."

"I don't think I'm so senile that I can't manage that," George told me, and straightened his shoulders. "But what particular testing do you propose?"

I said that was a hurdle we could jump when the time came, but one thing to do was to find the taxi-driver.

"Do something for me, George," was what I finally said. "I'll get right away from here and go over my notes again and do some thinking back. If I do find anything I'll let you know at once. If I don't—well, we can decide on what else we're going to do."

George reluctantly agreed. He even added that he might do something of the same sort of thing himself.

CHAPTER 17
THE HAPPY WARRIOR

I RANG Bernice and said I mightn't be in till late. It was a grand August morning and I made my way to St. James's Park and sat in the shade of a tree and began to think. My thoughts at first were all disjointed, with little odd events coming back to me—Deen having told Miss Chrome that he was going at once to America, and so ensuring that she'd never write to or look up the real Wesslake; Collinson's trip to town on that Sunday morning and why it had taken him so long to fix up a plane that he hadn't come back till one in the morning. There were a dozen other things, and they got me nowhere. The Park, I decided, was too distracting, so I went round to my club and lunched there, and then entrenched myself in the deserted reading-room. And I tried the approach I ought to have tried from the beginning, and I mean that I began at my first entry into the Case in Bill Ellice's office, and I slowly relived each relevant day till I should come at last to the story I had just heard from Collinson.

Through my mind there went things in which I still saw no new significance—things perhaps that you have spotted as vital a longish time ago—and I read a significance into things which I afterwards knew were mere trifles, for that's always how it goes in a job like mine. I spent another hour with Alice Stonhill in Ellice's office, and maybe I chuckled at so vividly remembering her. I tried a new appraisal of Wesslake when he was at Broad Street, too, and I was of the opinion that Collinson had exaggerated when he had called him a maniac. An egomaniac—yes, and with that kind of cunning that has in it the overweening conceit that makes mistakes. I went to the Malfroi Arms and lived those eleven days again. I saw and I spoke with Nelda and David and Drina and Camille, and I smiled again at the remembrance of Alice Stonhill and her birthday. There was the dance; the attack on Camille and the intruder in Alice Stonhill's room. And then my hands went suddenly to my glasses. *Something was wrong.* Something was out of character—or wasn't it?

For a few moments I concentrated, then made a note to come back to it if anything else emerged. I let the Case peter out and then came to Drina in Bill Ellice's office. The Case petered out again and then Wesslake's body was found, and I want to Burnbury with Wharton. I went over my calls on Deen and Collinson and then I realised there was something that I'd left out. Long before Wesslake's body was found I paid a supposed courtesy call at The Briars. Alice Stonhill had been very ill but I had seen her. I had talked with Camille. . . .

Then I remembered something else: something Camille had told me at the time. Alice Stonhill had been delirious and she had been muttering something. I looked at my notes and found I had written down the very words. *Peter knows. They shan't do it (to her).*

That was what she said she had heard, though admitting that the words had been only a faint muttering that she'd only just been able to make out. And there in my notes was what I'd thought at the time—that Alice Stonhill had connected that attack at the swimming-pool with Peter Wesslake. *Peter knows*. He had known about it and somehow engineered it.

I stretched out my legs, closed my eyes and began desperately to think. I said those words over and over again, muttering them as monotonously as Alice Stonhill must have done. And I thought that Camille had made a definite mistake. There had to be some sort of logic about those phrases. What Alice had said was that Peter knew and that *he*—not *they*—couldn't do that to Camille. I muttered *he* and I muttered *they*, and I told myself that I was right. In those scarcely heard words Camille had made a mistake. Not that it seemed to matter a great deal. *Peter knows* was enough to show that Alice Stonhill had guessed—as Collinson had later guessed—that Wesslake had been responsible for that attack at the pool. *Peter knows*, I kept saying to myself, and then, in a moment of less concentration, I got even those two words muddled. And that was when I shot up in my chair. If anyone had come into that room he would have thought I was mad. Then I smiled sheepishly and sat down again and began polishing my glasses. I went back to the Malfroi Arms. I went further back—to Bill Ellice's office. Then I was moistening my lips as I got to my feet.

The time was a quarter to four, and I wondered if Collinson had been remanded and if Wharton was back. Then I decided to ring him on chance and he wasn't there, but they said he ought to be in at any time. I took a bus that dropped me at Westminster, and walked to the Yard from there. Wharton had just come in.

Believe it or not, it was only half-past five when our car drew up just short of the Briars, which shows we had moved pretty fast. And we had to, for we wanted the business over before Camille might return from the funeral. We hadn't even warned Alice Stonhill that we were coming, and there was the chance that we mightn't find her in. But we did. We approached cautiously along the grass verge to where the cottage hedge began, and there she was sitting in a comfortable chair under the tree, and wearing her glasses and busy on what I guessed was her embroidery. She didn't see us till we were through the gate and stepping across the lawn. Then she got to her feet and put her embroidery aside, and her old eyes were shrewdly on us both as we came near.

Wharton took off his hat and gave a smile and a bow. He always boasted that no one could handle women like himself.

"I believe it's Mrs. Stonhill. I'm Superintendent Wharton. I saw your niece-in-law here quite recently and she told me you were indisposed. I do hope you're better."

"Quite better," she told him, and her eyes shifted to me. I couldn't smile. Somehow it would have been too great an hypocrisy. I gave a little bow and I saw already that her hands were shaking.

"Mr. Travers I believe you know," Wharton told her. "But do sit down, Mrs. Stonhill. Perhaps you'll allow us to sit down too."

He made no bones about helping us to a couple of wicker chairs. Alice Stonhill's eyes were on me again and there was something she was trying to ask me. Then she picked up the embroidery as Wharton and I sat down, and the fingers that held the needle were still shaking.

"How's Camille?" I asked her.

"Very well," she said. "Very distressed, of course, at what has happened. But there; youth is very resilient."

"And so is age," I said. "You're looking almost as well as ever I saw you."

She smiled quietly at that.

"Mr. Travers is a flatterer," she told Wharton. "But you were asking about Camille. She's at the funeral, of course. Then she's staying on at Burnbury for the night."

"You mean you're going to be here alone?"

"And why not?" she asked me with a touch of her old spirit. "Who should be interested in an old woman like me?"

"Age is a very relative thing," Wharton said sententiously. "I wouldn't call you old. All I wish is that if I get to your years, I may look half as young."

"You see where I've learned what you call flattery," I told her. "But you'll be wondering why we've come. Or do you know?"

"I'll put this embroidery away," she said. "So distracting, don't you think, when you want to talk."

A wicker table was at her elbow and she laid the embroidery down beside her handbag. She smiled at us as if to say that was that.

"Now what were we talking about?"

There was a delicious artlessness about it, and somehow in the quietness of that little country garden it didn't seem of all that moment even if it were artifice instead.

"Mr. Travers was asking you a question," Wharton reminded her. "Do you know why we're here?"

"Yes," she said, and gave a little frown. "Jim—Mr. Collinson—wrote to me last night and I had his letter this morning."

"You know what he admitted having done?"

"But I told you!" she said. "I had his letter this morning."

"He's under arrest," he told her. "Remanded in custody. You know what that means, Mrs. Stonhill?"

"I think so." There was just a touch of asperity. "I'm not altogether uninformed, you know."

"Then you know what's likely to happen to him?"

"Happen to him?" The head went aside and the shrewd old eyes were peering. "Nothing can happen to him. He was merely defending himself."

"Where's his evidence?" Wharton asked her. "At his trial there'll be only his word. And some mighty damaging information may be brought against him."

There she was, light as thistledown and something that George could have lifted with a hand, but drawing herself up once more with the dignity of a six-foot duchess. Even George instinctively quailed at the look she gave him.

"James Collinson? You're daring to insinuate that James Collinson could have been *guilty* of anything?"

Wharton gave me a look, then let out a breath. Much as we hated doing it, the screws would have to be put on.

"Listen, Mrs. Stonhill," he told her patiently. "At the moment we're talking confidentially. There's nothing concealed and there's no trap. We're men of honour and we're behaving as such. But you're a material witness, and after we've had our little confidential chat it's more than likely that we shall have to ask you to accompany us to Scotland Yard. All we're asking of you is that you should tell us all you know about the death of Peter Wesslake. Where he was killed, and how and when."

"But Mr. Collinson has already told you!"

Wharton made a gesture of despair. Another moment he'd be telling her what we knew about Collinson and Camille, and suddenly I knew I didn't want that kind of pressure.

"Mrs. Stonhill," I said. "Will you answer just one simple question. Collinson says Wesslake tried to kill him at Romney Court on the evening of June the thirteenth, and there was a struggle in which Wesslake got killed. Will you here and now swear on the Bible that you have no reason whatever for believing that to be untrue?"

The glasses were still on, and she took them off and slowly wiped them. She put them in their case and the case in the bag.

"I object to swearing," she said. "I always have objected. Besides, I don't see how I'm in any way concerned. All I can tell you is what an utter blackguard Peter Wesslake was. In my judgment he deserved everything he got. If James had shot him in cold blood it wouldn't have been more than he deserved."

"This is hopeless," Wharton told her. "You force me to be blunt. You're prevaricating and you're playing for time. Mr. Travers asked you a simple question and you shuffled out of it."

He drew back rather like a boy who has ventured to touch the tiger's tail, but all she was doing was to give a puzzled look.

"I don't understand," she told me. "Perhaps it is something to do with my memory. Ever since my late illness I've found it playing queer tricks. My husband was the same before he died."

Wharton's eyes narrowed. He recognised the new line of defence.

"Well, we're sorry to hear about your memory, Mrs. Stonhill, and perhaps you'll allow Mr. Travers to refresh it. Would you mind listening carefully while he tells you just how and when and where Wesslake was killed?"

Now there wasn't the suspicion of a tremor. All along she had known what was coming but she had gained her time. She could even give that puzzled look again.

"But this is extraordinary," she said. "Of course I'll listen to Mr. Travers."

"Let's go back to the Malfroi Arms then, Mrs. Stonhill," I began. "I'm going to tell you what happened there. All I tell you may not be exactly right but that's something you'll have to excuse. Details don't matter if the main facts are right.

"So there we are, all back at the Malfroi Arms again, and on May the twenty-ninth, and your eightieth birthday. You were feeling easy enough in your mind. Those two attempts that Wesslake had made on his wife's life—perhaps you'll allow me to call her Camille—had failed, and Wesslake, the man responsible, was in Denmark and would be there for a further fortnight. Camille was now under your immediate protection and you hadn't any doubts of your ability to protect her. Do you remember saying that to someone? I heard you say it myself, quite by chance, in the office of a Private Detective Agency. You didn't want the protection of the police for Camille, you said. You could protect her yourself. And you were proposing to do so. But we'll let that pass.

"We go back to your birthday. Something spoiled it—that attack on Camille at the swimming-pool. Wesslake took her jewellery to give an impression of theft, and you and Collinson accepted the affair—at least at first—for the theft with violence which it was meant to appear to be."

"No, no!" she said. "You must be surer of your facts. He tried to kill her. And he would have killed her if he hadn't been disturbed."

"It's irrelevant," I told her, "except in so far as it was what you afterwards guessed. All the same, even when you were upstairs with me outside Camille's room, you must have been wondering about that attack. Knowing it couldn't have been made by Wesslake and all the same fearing that it had. But you came down later and joined me in the dance room. You were rather quiet and still a bit puzzled. I think you were asking yourself if in any conceivable way Wesslake could still be in the hotel and possibly about to make another attack.

"Then you saw something. It was just after that noisy business with the intoxicated man. You gave a start.

"*My God, no!*' That was what you said. I asked if anything was the matter. You were still highly perturbed, but you said you'd been worrying about Camille. Then you got up quickly and left the room and you wouldn't let me accompany you. You were so *distraite* that you were almost rude to me when I suggested it. And what you had seen had made you so upset that you had to support yourself by the banisters when you went up the stairs. You can't deny those facts, Mrs. Stonhill. They were noted by me at the time. What I'm asking then, is if you'd now care to tell us what it was that you saw. What it was that so disturbed you—"

"But I've told you," she said, and her little hands fluttered a gesture of helplessness.

"Then I must tell *you*," I said. "What you saw in that dance room was a man fingering his nose—like this. That was a trick of Wesslake's when he was thinking, and in his character of Ferotti it was the one thing he forgot. Collinson knew it and everyone who knew him knew it. Collinson tried to put us off the scent about it. He said Wesslake's trick when thinking was wrinkling up his eyes. But it wasn't. I repeat: it was fingering his nose—like this. Isn't that what you saw, Mrs. Stonhill?"

The blow was temporary and no more.

"I believe he did have such a little nervous trick," she said. "But do go on."

"I'll tell you how we know it," I said. "You inadvertently gave it away. You hurried away from the Malfroi Arms partly because you didn't want to be questioned by the police, and partly because the place was to have dreadful associations. When you got back here, all that business was still heavily on your mind—it had to be. Then at once you went down with pneumonia. You were delirious for a time. All those events at the Malfroi Arms were running through your disordered brain. One high-light, if I may call it so, kept monotonously forcing itself. Over and over again you kept muttering something to yourself. Do you know what it was? It was this. 'Peter's nose! He shan't do that to her. Peter's nose! He shan't do that to her.' That's what you told us, Mrs. Stonhill."

That shook her again, but only for a moment.

"But that's foolish of you," she said, and even appealed to Wharton. "If I was delirious, of course I might be thinking of him!"

"As you wish," I told her. "But believe me, there's far more to come. You went upstairs to tell Collinson what you'd seen, but he wasn't there. I think he was outside getting some air, because of that attack on Camille—you're well aware, of course, that they're in love with each other—was a pretty big shock to him too. But, as I said, he wasn't there. So you decided to act for yourself. You fetched that little automatic you were keeping for the protection of Camille—it was probably one your husband had bought some time in France—

and you went to that room in the annexe. You hid yourself behind the bed or the wardrobe and waited till Wesslake came in. Probably when he did come in he didn't trouble to go on being Ferotti and he gave himself away still more. Then suddenly you appeared, and your finger was on the trigger of that gun.

"I repeat that what happened we don't actually know, but Collinson will tell us. He'll have to, in order to save you. Just another quixotism, if you like, or piece of chivalry. But that you shot Wesslake is certain. I think he tried to bluff that he was Ferotti, and when he didn't succeed, he came towards you. That was what was in Collinson's mind when he made that false confession of his. He came towards you. He was smiling. He was cocksure you wouldn't shoot. *Can't you see him, Mrs. Stonhill? He's getting nearer and he's still smiling. Then, just when he's almost on you, the gun goes off!*"

"I didn't mean to shoot—"

There was a gasp, and a look of horror at the realisation of what she had said. Her head sank. All the defences were down. The slip of a moment had made her plans no more than a tawdry devastation. Then miraculously she was recovering herself again. Her hand went out to her bag. Wharton's hand closed over it.

"I'll take that bag, Mrs. Stonhill."

For a moment she looked puzzled. Then she actually smiled, even if the smile was wan.

"It's not that," she said. "What is it they're supposed to have? Poison of some sort in a phial, like that dreadful Göring. But it isn't that. It's just my handkerchief that I want."

Wharton didn't even look inside. He removed his hand, and she dabbed her lips—not her eyes—with the dainty little handkerchief. I caught its perfume; a fragrance like lavender.

"I'm so sorry," she told us.

"Nothing to be alarmed about," Wharton told her, and not very much to the purpose.

"Alarmed?" she said. "But I'm not alarmed. I've never been afraid in my life. Why should I be alarmed now? Relieved, perhaps, and even sorry—but not alarmed. But I was interrupting Mr. Travers's story. Do please go on."

"There's nothing much else to say," I told her. "You threw the gun into the bathing pool and then you found Collinson and told him what you'd done. He took over. Everything would be in his hands, he said, and you were not to worry. All you had to do was carry out certain instructions. One was to open the bottom window of your room so that he could climb up the wistaria and give the impression of a burglary. The other was that you should alarm the hotel in the early hours because a man was in your room. But, of course, there never was a man. He was to be the same man who'd attacked Camille and robbed her, but I hadn't the sense to see that at the time. There were two things that stared at me, and yet I didn't see them. Your teeth are still excellent, Mrs. Stonhill, but not all of them are your own. You have one plate if not two, and that night you, a woman in a state of terror, shrieking in the hotel corridor, had had the presence of mind to slip in the plates. The glass of water that had held them was still on your bedside table. And, of course, the last thing you'd have done was to shriek or get into a panic. That's not flattery; it's a sober fact. You've got the pluck of a tigress. To come to that, I think that even if a tigress had come through your bedroom window you'd not have lost your presence of mind."

She smiled as she shook her head.

"We'll pass over that fainting fit of yours," I went on, "and come to what happened in the morning. Collinson retrieved that gun at dawn. He'd lugged Wesslake's body somehow to his car and with it stowed in the commodious back he drove to Romney Court on the Sunday morning and he didn't return till long after midnight. What he had to do was to work on Wesslake's head—bleach the hair and shave off the beard and so on, and get him another suit of clothes. When Ferotti was Wesslake again he took him to the woods where he was ultimately found, and, as Collinson had hoped, with just that amount of decomposition to destroy the possibility of determining the date of the death, and also to conceal the loss of the back hair which Wesslake had had shaved to resemble a tonsure. But there was just one other thing. He had to write an anonymous letter to the police about the body. Once it had been there long enough to disguise the fact that the bullet hadn't been fired from point-blank range—so that it might look like suicide, for instance—he wanted it found. He couldn't marry Camille so long as Wesslake might be still alive."

I said that was all that mattered, and Wharton was asking if she wished to make any comment.

"I don't think so," she said, and was trying hard to be matter-of-fact. "You wish me now to go with you to Scotland Yard?"

"It's my duty to take you there," Wharton told her. "Everything has to be official."

"Shall I need to pack a bag? Or do they supply you with everything where it is I'm going to?"

Wharton had to smile.

"No need to pack a bag. We'll probably be bringing you back here again tonight. All you need do is—well, just what you'd do if it was an ordinary journey. But no tricks in the house, mind you. You give us your word that you'll get ready and be down at once?"

"Of course I give it," she told him. "You've both been very nice to me, and considerate."

She picked up the bag and the embroidery and we watched her to the house. She went almost jauntily, head high and her steps dainty and quick.

"She's a grand old lady," Wharton told me. "You said she was and I didn't believe you."

"She's a fighter," I said. "A happy warrior, that's what she is, George. But what'll happen to her exactly?"

He snorted.

"What *can* happen to her? Put her in the dock on half-a-dozen charges and she'd be loose inside an hour. She was telling us the truth, wasn't she?"

I said she certainly hadn't told us much except that slip, but there wasn't a doubt but what her statement would be truth. George grunted and began filling his pipe. He seemed ashamed of what might be construed as sentimental weakness.

"Not that she's going to get away with it all," he told me belligerently, and that was all he said, for Alice Stonhill was already at the door. She stood for a moment in the porch, buttoning her gloves. She even opened her little handbag and took a last look at herself in the mirror. Then she locked the door behind her and at the same time Wharton's car drew up at the gate. Plucky as they make them, I was telling myself. But not for herself. It was for Camille and maybe also for the decencies that in her own young days had been commonplaces that she had been and still was fighting.

"So sorry to have kept you waiting." She was smiling at Wharton.

He waved her on and she bowed and smiled again as if she were going with friends for an evening ride in their car. And it seemed natural that she should go on ahead, for I was having the furtive feeling that the triumph was far from ours.

Wharton nipped forward and held open the gate. Then he opened the door of the car.

"No handcuffs?" she said, and smiled at her own sally.

"No handcuffs," Wharton told her gravely, but I think there must have been a twinkle in his eye. And he did sit with her in the back while I went to the front with the driver.

"It's a grand evening," I heard him telling her, and then the car moved on.

THE END